M

O'Marie, Carol Anne

Advent of dying

K692 14.95

DATE DUE

ADVENT OF DYING

ADVENT OF DYING

Sister
Carol Anne O'Marie

DELACORTE PRESS/NEW YORK

Published by
Delacorte Press
1 Dag Hammarskjold Plaza
New York, N.Y. 10017

Grateful acknowledgment is made for permission to reprint an excerpt
from the following:

First four lines of "I Have It on Good Authority"
From VERSES FROM 1929 ON by Ogden Nash
Copyright 1935 by Ogden Nash. First appeared in *The New York
American*
Reprinted by permission of Little, Brown and Company.

Manufactured in the United States of America

First printing

Library of Congress Cataloging in Publication Data

O'Marie, Sister Carol Anne.
  Advent of dying.

  I. Title.
PS3565.M347A64   1986   813'.54
ISBN 0-385-29506-5
Library of Congress Catalog Card Number: 86-4536

To my parents,
John and Carrie O'Marie,
my aunts and uncles,
Sis and Mick Mangan
and
Hal and Dosie Garden,
who first taught me to love and laugh
and
try anything twice!

ADVENT OF DYING

NOVEMBER 30—FEAST OF ST. ANDREW

It was Friday afternoon. Everything about Sister Mary Helen felt like a Friday afternoon. She checked the large wall clock. It groaned a low electric groan, then the big black hand jerked downward to four-thirty. Four-thirty, at last! Long winter shadows dimmed her small inner office. Slowly, the old nun pushed away from her desk. Stretching, she stared out the narrow window.

An early dusk darkened the gray sky. The rasp of the foghorns warned her that a low fog was already billowing in through the Golden Gate. Soon it would blot out the Presidio, then roll up the hill and shroud Mount St. Francis College for Women. Her mind's eye could see the gray blanket closing over Anza Street. Ugh!

Turning back to her desk, Mary Helen began to straighten up the papers scattered across its glass-covered top. She blew away a pile of eraser crumbs. Whoever did away with the old rolltops should be shot, she fumed, rearranging the piles.

Methodically, she flipped the calendar over to December. Adjusting her bifocals, she frowned. It didn't seem possible. Sunday would be December 2, the first Sunday of Advent. She had been in the alumnae office for over a year and the year before that was when she had been sent to the college to retire. Mary Helen smiled. Retire indeed! Where had the two years gone? she wondered. "Time is flying, never to return," good old Virgil had observed fifty years before Christ. In Latin, of course, Mary Helen presumed, but his observation was certainly just as true in any language.

"What are you doing tonight, Sister?" Suzanne Barnes's low voice startled her. The young woman was hanging about just inside the doorway. Her straight black hair fell in limp clumps over her narrow shoulders. A bit of color flushed her plain flat face.

"Nothing much. Why?" Mary Helen perked up, hoping she didn't sound too tired. If Suzanne had a suggestion for the evening, she hated to squelch it. Poor girl seemed to have so few. And, to Mary Helen's way of thinking, there was no reason for it. Suzanne was bright and efficient, and there was something so good about her, you couldn't help but love her.

"Did you have something in mind?" Mary Helen coaxed. She still felt a little guilty about cutting the girl off earlier in the week.

"Are you happy in the convent?" Suzanne had asked her out of the blue.

The question had annoyed Mary Helen. "Would I have stayed fifty odd years if I were unhappy?" is what she wanted to say. Instead, she had mouthed some platitude.

Suzanne had hesitated a moment, as if she were going to confide something. Then she turned without a word and left Mary Helen wondering what it was all about. Maybe this was what she had been leading up to.

"If you're not busy, maybe you'd like to go with me to the Sea Wench." Suzanne dropped her voice to a whisper.

Shoving her glasses up the bridge of her nose, Mary Helen studied the young woman's face. Suzanne's watery blue eyes sparkled. At least Mary Helen imagined she caught a sparkle before the lids closed over them and Suzanne looked away.

"I'll pick you up about seven," Suzanne said, then

added nervously, "If you'd like, you can bring a couple of the other nuns. Tonight's my first night. I'll be singing." With a quick, frightened pull, she closed the glass door of the inner office behind her, leaving Mary Helen gaping.

"Well, I'll be switched," she muttered aloud, listening to Suzanne's quick footsteps leave the outer office, then scurry down the stone corridor. Imagine thin, shy little Suzanne singing! It all goes to prove you just never can tell the book by its cover. And if anyone should know that, old girl, you should, Mary Helen reminded herself. Why, for years you've been camouflaging the most spine-tingling mystery stories in your pious plastic prayer book cover.

Chuckling, Mary Helen flipped off the light and left the alumnae office. Gingerly she pattered down the darkening hall toward Sister Anne's campus ministry office. The whole basement floor of the college was deserted. Nothing like a Friday afternoon to clear the entire area. She neared Anne's door. The sweet smell of sandalwood incense permeating the corridor told her that the young nun was still there.

"Come in," a soft voice answered her rap. Cautiously, Mary Helen pushed open the wooden door. She was not surprised to see Sister Anne, eyes closed, pretzeled into her lotus position. A thin curl of smoke from the incense pot circled the young nun's black curly head. A small green yoga pillow jutted out from below her faded blue jeans.

Anne opened one eye. "Hi," she said. "Just relaxing. It's been some week." She sighed. "What's up?"

"What's the Sea Wench and do you want to go?" Mary Helen wasted no time on preliminaries.

Anne's hazel eyes shot open. They looked very wide behind her purple-framed glasses. "It's a bar in Ghirardelli Square," she said, "and the question, more importantly, I think, is, Do you want to go?"

Again Mary Helen shoved her bifocals up the bridge of her nose. "A bar?" she asked, trying not to sound too surprised. "Why, Suzanne told me she was singing there tonight."

Anne closed her eyes again, dropped her head forward, and slowly began to roll it counterclockwise. "She probably has a job waiting tables," Anne explained. "All the waiters and waitresses sing there. Part of the charm of the place."

"You've been?"

"Yep." Anne did not explain. She just continued to circle her head.

Mary Helen chose to let sleeping dogs lie.

"Still want to go?" Anne asked.

Want to go? She was dead set to go and get a glimpse of Suzanne's other side. At my age, I should be a little prudent and circumspect, she reminded herself. On the other hand, what's the advantage of being my age if you can't throw a little caution to the wind?

"Yep," she answered, pulling Anne's door closed. "Meet you at the front door of the convent at seven."

"Okay." She heard Anne's muffled voice call through the wooden door.

Deliberately, Mary Helen set out to find her old friend Sister Eileen. By now, Eileen should just about be closing up the Hanna Memorial Library. Even the most diligent scholars usually didn't stay in the library past five on a Friday night. Mary Helen trudged up the stairs from the basement floor where she and Anne shared office space with the athletic department, the communication center, the development office, and all the other departments that came into vogue after the massive stone college had been built in the early thirties. The offices were renovated basement storage space, but like making a silk purse out of a sow's ear, no amount of interior decorating had been able to hide the fact that they were still in the basement. The concrete staircase leading to the ground floor was narrow and dark. Someone had hung a tapestry on the wall to add a touch of class, Mary Helen supposed. Unfortunately, in her opinion, the dark heavy cloth had merely added a touch of bleakness to the musty stairwell.

A loud moan from the foghorns echoed through the deserted stone building. Pulling open the door to the first floor, Mary Helen marveled at how a place could be so alive and vibrant one moment and so dead and dismal the next.

A web of shadows had begun to knit across the arched ceiling of the long parquet hallway. Standing in the deserted hall, she couldn't help thinking of Thomas Moore. "I feel like one Who treads alone some banquet hall deserted, Whose lights are fled, Whose garlands dead, And all but he departed," the old bard had said. She knew his meaning was far more profound, but this afternoon, standing here, she had never understood his simile better. Mary Helen was glad to spot Eileen at the far end, looking for all the world like a plump ball of navy blue, fumbling with a heavy ring of keys. She watched her friend bend forward, insert one of the keys into the lock, then give it a firm twist. Finally, Eileen tugged at the beveled glass door. All was secure.

"Yoo-whoo." Mary Helen's voice rang down the corridor.

Eileen whirled around. An easy smile lit her round wrinkled face. "I was just about to go looking for you," she said with just a slight lilt of a brogue. "How about a nice walk before supper?" She moved quickly down the hall toward her friend. Eileen must have had a bad week, too, Mary Helen reckoned, since walking was one of her favorite panaceas. Cleaning was the other. Mary Helen was glad she'd chosen walking.

"I've a better idea," she said, relieved at how easily the

subject was going to be introduced. "How about going to the Sea Wench with Anne and me tonight?"

Eileen's bushy gray eyebrows arched. "The Sea Wench?" she asked incredulously. "Glory be to God, why?"

Maybe it wasn't going to be so easy. Eileen obviously knew what the Sea Wench was. "Because Suzanne is going to sing there tonight and I'd like to support her," Mary Helen said. *Support* was one of the "now" words Anne always used. It seemed to fit in perfectly.

"Our Suzanne? Singing?" This time Eileen's voice really registered surprise.

"It does seem a bit out of character," Mary Helen agreed. The two old nuns ducked out a side entrance of the empty college building and made their way across the campus. The wet fog had all but swallowed the hill.

Eileen lifted the collar of her navy blue Aran sweater to cover her ears. Wishing she had worn hers, Mary Helen shivered and pulled her blue wool jacket tightly around her. Someone had told her a suit jacket always looked professional.

Who cares how professional you look if you're frozen to death? she wondered, starting down the curved driveway toward the convent, which she could never get used to calling the Sisters' Residence. Although it was only a little before five o'clock, slits of light shone from many of the small windows in the stone building.

"You know, Mary Helen." Eileen's words came out in little white clouds of breath. "One could expect to find Suzanne singing in a church choir someplace, but a public bar?" Wide-eyed, Eileen stared at Mary Helen.

"Did you even know she could sing?"

"No. I've told you before, I never even met the girl until you hired her. You do remember that?"

Mary Helen remembered it, much as she hated to admit it. The incident was one she would never forget.

It had happened shortly after she had helped Inspector Kate Murphy solve the Homicide on Holy Hill murder case. Sister Rose, the Superior of her order, had called for an appointment.

"Mary Helen," the Superior had begun kindly but firmly, "when I sent you here a year ago to retire and do a little research, I had no idea it would lead to finding half a dozen bodies."

Fair enough, Mary Helen had conceded. Who could have foreseen the murder of the head of Mount St. Francis's history department or exactly where the investigation would lead?

"Maybe the history department was a poor choice on my part." Mary Helen did not disagree. Let her squirm a bit; however, she knew squirming was not what Sister Rose did best. She waited silently for the other shoe to drop.

"And since you've become somewhat famous in The City . . ."

Mary Helen was glad she hadn't used the word notorious, although the Chronicle had hinted at that when they reported her part in solving the case.

"And since you are acquainted with at least one alumna . . ."

Here comes the bottom line. Mary Helen braced herself.

"Kate Murphy. And a very prominent alum at that. Why, the council and I thought it would be a wonderful thing if you would consent to be the alumnae moderator for Mount St. Francis."

"You do realize I'm not an alumna?" Mary Helen had asked, knowing full well the Superior did.

"Yes, of course."

"Nor have I ever taught here."

"I realize that too."

"Those are disadvantages, you know," she had said.

Sister Rose smiled. "But you have a special knack for turning disadvantages into advantages," she said, then launched into the hackneyed proverb about "keeping your eye upon the doughnut and not upon the hole."

Spare me, O Lord, Mary Helen thought, opening her mouth to comment.

"Besides," the Superior rushed on before the old nun had a chance, "the alumnae moderator just quit to get married and Sister Cecilia is desperate." Mary Helen had noticed Cecilia at the breakfast table that very morning. The woman did look haggard, but Mary Helen figured Cecilia was the college president and it did tend to get very lonely at the top. "Please, Mary Helen." Sister Rose was nearly pleading.

"As long as you put it that way, Sister," Mary Helen had said, "I'll give it a whirl."

What the Superior had neglected to mention was that not only had the alumnae moderator resigned but so had the entire staff, which consisted of one secretary. It had taken Mary Helen less than half a day in her new job to realize that a secretary was essential.

She smiled now, remembering how desperate she had been a year ago when she'd suddenly thought of Eileen. If anyone will know where I can enlist an alum to be my secretary, good old Eileen will. Eileen had been at the college for as long as anyone could remember. Anyone, that is, except Mary Helen. Her memory of Eileen went way back. The two had been in the novitiate together. That was where they had become such fast friends and pinochle partners. Mary Helen rarely brought it up, however, since neither of them wanted to admit it was over fifty years ago. Well, you are, after all, only as old as you feel, she had reasoned, rushing down the corridor toward the Hanna Memorial. She met Eileen coming the other way with a thin, black-haired young woman in tow.

"Eileen," she had blurted out, completely ignoring the young woman. "I'm desperate for a secretary. Do you know of any alum that might want the job?"

"Isn't this a coincidence." Eileen smiled warmly toward the silent young woman on her left. "Why, Suzanne Barnes here was just inquiring about a position in the library, but we have a full staff."

Quickly Mary Helen had scrutinized the young woman. Plain but pleasant-looking. About thirty, she calculated. Good, we won't have a flock of boys from the University of San Francisco hanging around the office. Shoulders dropped a bit, probably shy. Mary Helen had studied her eyes. After fifty years of classroom teaching, she considered herself an expert on eyes. The girl's were pale blue and timid, but clear and candid nonetheless, with a certain depth, a little toughness. Good. Probably the type of woman that wears well. I'll take her, Mary Helen thought.

"Coincidence, nothing, it's an act of God," she had said aloud, whisking the startled Suzanne downstairs to her cramped office. She noticed Eileen sputtering and she had wondered why. Halfway through the interview she knew.

"Why didn't you tell me you just met the girl?" she had asked Eileen when she arrived in the Sisters' dining room for lunch.

"For the love of all that's good and holy, who had the chance?" Eileen's gray eyes snapped.

"And that she wasn't even an alumna?"

Eileen set her lips tight and completely ignored the second question. "You do remember saying the whole meeting was an act of God?" she asked instead.

Mary Helen remembered, of course, although she was reluctant to admit it. "Well, I hope it doesn't turn out to be an act of stupidity," she muttered.

Eileen had had the decency to take another bite of her tuna salad and for a few moments say nothing. "We've an old saying at home, you know, and I think a very true one," she had said finally. "It is an ill wind turns none to good." Quickly, she took another bite of tuna fish.

Mary Helen had stared at her friend in amazement. Eileen had an old saying from home to fit every occasion, though she'd left Ireland over fifty years ago. Sometimes Mary Helen suspected she made them up just to fit the circumstances.

All that had happened over a year ago now, and Mary Helen had to admit that Suzanne had worked out well. Very well indeed. In fact, Mary Helen had come to rely on the young woman.

Suzanne was the perfect secretary: efficient, reliable, eager to please. But, something about Suzanne worried Mary Helen. The girl was a little too eager to please. She wished Suzanne could relax, lose a bit of her uneasiness. Mary Helen had tried everything she could think of. Once she even started calling her "Suzie" to see if that would loosen her up, but it didn't seem to fit. Somehow, Suzanne was just not the nickname type.

Hard as she tried, Mary Helen could never quite make Suzanne—what did Sister Anne call it?—"hang loose." And what's more, she could never really tell exactly what was going on behind those watery blue eyes.

If she were perfectly honest with herself, Mary Helen would have to admit that was what bothered her the most about Suzanne. She could not figure the girl out.

Once, right after she hired her, Mary Helen had thought that Suzanne was on the verge of telling her a bit about herself. Maybe she had been too eager to listen, a little too attentive. Whatever, Suzanne had stopped abruptly, almost midsentence, coughed convincingly, and left the room to get some water. Mary Helen had attributed it to shyness. Lately she was beginning to wonder if maybe Suzanne wasn't so much timid as she was just plain guarded. A guarded person. That might be the perfect description of her. And what, she wondered, was Suzanne guarding?

"She never talks about her family or where she's from," Mary Helen had confided to Eileen several weeks before.

Eileen shrugged. "Well, old dear, do you?" she asked.

"Well, no," Mary Helen had had to admit, "but she's young. She never even mentions what she does on the weekends. And if she gets a personal call in the office, which is seldom, she answers in monosyllables."

"I would, too, if I thought you were listening."

Mary Helen did not dignify that remark with a reply. She just played her trump card. "And she has a nun's watch," she said, shoving her glasses up the bridge of her nose and staring smugly at her friend.

"A nun's watch! How in the name of God do you know it's a nun's watch?"

"I can just tell. It has that large round face, a second hand. It's plain, almost masculine. Bought strictly for use, not for style."

"And don't all the nurses wear the same kind?"

"Yes, but why would a nurse take a secretary's job at the salary we pay when she could get a good position right down the street at St. Mary's Hospital?"

"So, are you telling me you think she's a nun in disguise?"

"No, an ex."

"I'd say you had better stop reading those mystery books," Eileen had said, shaking her head. Deliberately she pointed to her temple. "If you ask me, old dear, you're getting a bit soft up here. The poor girl minds her own business. She won't let you pry into her private life, for which I don't blame her, and she wears a plain watch and straightaway you have her an ex-nun."

"Not right away," Mary Helen had said, hoping she didn't sound too defensive. There were several other "nunny" things she'd noticed about Suzanne during the year. Not the kinds of things you could put your finger on and say, "See," but the kinds of things you just feel; a certain innocence and a kind of "otherworldliness" that novitiates inspire.

Well, at least after tonight she'd know a little bit more about the private life of her secretary. Maybe find out if her suspicions were correct. Mary Helen could hardly wait.

Right after dinner, Sister Mary Helen rushed to the convent building, then up to her second-floor bedroom. Tonight's spaghetti coupled with the sourdough French bread had made one large starchy lump in her stomach.

"Why do we always have spaghetti on Friday night?" she had asked Eileen while they were still at the dinner table.

"My guess would be to use up the end-of-the-week leftovers?" Mary Helen wasn't sure if that was a statement of fact or a question. Eileen had never quite lost that Irish way of making a statement sound like a question. Over the years, the habit had probably saved her many an argument.

"End-of-the-week leftovers? What did they do around here before we could eat meat on Friday?"

"If I remember correctly, we always had spaghetti on Thursdays." Eileen had let a shower of golden crumbs fall around her plate.

Popping a Rolaid into her mouth, Mary Helen scanned her small closet, looking for an appropriate Sea Wench outfit. Unable to decide exactly what one wears to a singing bar, she closed the closet door and eyed herself in the mirror.

The navy blue suit I have on looks just fine, she thought, spitting on her thumb, then rubbing a small spot off the sleeve of her jacket. She smoothed the back of her straight skirt, assuring herself that the sitting lines wouldn't even show if the place was at all dim. She did decide to change from her white tailored blouse into the powder blue one with a bit of lace around the collar. More festive!

When she put the jacket back on, she studied the narrow silver cross on the lapel. Should she leave it on or take it off? Off, she looked like a conservative tourist. On, she looked like a "with it" old nun. She decided, without a moment's hesitation, to leave it on.

Quickly she snatched her latest mystery from her nightstand. Shoving it into her faithful plastic prayer book cover, she dropped the paperback into her pocketbook and clutched the handles. Mary Helen had tried an over-the-shoulder bag, but she could never manage to keep the blasted thing on, much less over, her shoulder. She patted the rectangular bulge the paperback made, and smiled. Some women never went anywhere without their gloves. She never went anywhere without her book.

Although some considered it a fetish, she considered it an extremely constructive habit. Not only had this practice enabled her to devour hundreds of mysteries, it had saved her untold hours of impatience. In fact, it was getting so she actually enjoyed waiting in doctors' offices, dentists' offices, airports, for repairmen—all those places and times people are forced to wait.

Grabbing her heavy coat, Mary Helen hurried down to the front parlor. She was the first to arrive. She checked her watch. Fifteen minutes early. She was delighted. Sinking into an overstuffed chair, she opened her book, flipped back the ribbon marker, and began to read.

This Advent she had decided on a very painful sacrifice. She was going to give up mysteries for the duration. She had resolved to do some spiritual reading instead. Therefore, she was determined—hell-bent might have been a more accurate term—to finish this one before Sunday.

Mary Helen was just settling into the last half of a chapter when the front door of the convent burst open. Sister Therese bustled in, muttering under her breath.

Nervously Therese threw the double bolt across the door. Yanking against the handle, she made sure it was securely locked, then muttered some more. Since the murders had taken place on the hill, Therese had become the self-appointed doorkeeper. If Michael the Archangel had enlisted Therese in his army, Mary Helen often thought, his troubles would have been minimal. She could see Raphael's painting: Michael vanquishing Lucifer with Therese leering over his shoulder, muttering and checking the Pearly Gates. Another rattle from the doorway brought her back to reality.

"Don't bother, Therese," Mary Helen called from the parlor. "I'm going out."

Therese jumped and gasped.

"You scared the very heart out of me," she said, laying her arthritic hand against her collarbone. "What on earth are you doing sitting all alone in the parlor?" Therese rolled her eyes toward Mary Helen.

Without waiting for an answer, her high-pitched voice tumbled on. "Praying, I see. And well you might. Anyone your age going out in San Francisco on a Friday night should be praying." This time Therese rolled her dark eyes heavenward.

Mary Helen bristled, yet she held her peace. She didn't

feel even a twinge of guilt about letting Therese think she was praying.

"I just let her think it," Mary Helen had told Eileen the first time Therese had misinterpreted the plastic cover. "She's really much happier that way." And so am I, she added, but only to herself.

"That's a very lame excuse," Eileen had said, but it was all the excuse Mary Helen needed.

"I don't know what The City is coming to." Therese had barely stopped for breath. "A body isn't safe anyplace anymore. As well you know!" she said, rolling her eyes back toward Mary Helen. Mary Helen could feel her blood pressure start to rise. Gratefully, she heard Anne and Eileen hurrying down the hallway toward the parlor.

"Why, I just read about a seventy-year-old woman right down here on Clement Street . . ."

The soft chimes of the front doorbell interrupted Therese.

Saved by the bell! Mary Helen pushed herself up from the parlor chair, opened the heavy door, and smiled out at Suzanne. Suzanne was radiant, or at least as radiant as Suzanne could be. Her cheeks were flushed and that little bit of color brought out the clear blue of her eyes. The front locks of her long dark hair had been swept upward. The height made her plain flat face look longer. Someone had arranged a topknot of blue silk flowers that matched her eyes perfectly.

"You look lovely," Mary Helen said.

"Thank you." Suzanne blushed. Then, like a flasher, she threw open her long tan trench coat to reveal her costume.

The black velvet bodice fit tightly and was cut low. A narrow crimson lace trim did little to cover her ample bosom. She looked for all the world like a wench right out of an eighteenth-century English pub, except that the red crinoline skirt stopped abruptly just below a pair of black velvet panties. Her long legs were covered with spiderweb black stockings. Not even her black shoes were sensible. The heels were much too high.

"How do you like it?" Suzanne asked.

"Amazing" was the only word Mary Helen could think of to say.

"Why, Suzanne, dear, you look so—so—sophisticated." Eileen had saved the day. "And I just love your hair that way. It is ever so becoming." Mary Helen smiled, relieved. Good old Eileen! You could always count on her for chit-chat.

"My friend Mimi fixed it. She lives in my apartment building." Suzanne steered the trio down the convent steps toward her car.

Imagine Suzanne having a friend called "Mimi"!

"And speaking of Mimi," the young woman continued, "she'll be there tonight and I've asked her to take you home after the first show. I don't get off until after two and I was sure you wouldn't want to stay that long." Her voice trailed off.

By two A.M. I'd be snoring out loud, Mary Helen wanted to remark, but she simply smiled and climbed into the backseat of Suzanne's car. The car was a faded blue, flat-looking Buick, probably a '69. The fenders and heavy doors bore several battle scars. Driving in Suzanne's car always made Mary Helen feel like a low-rider. All it needed was a pair of angora dice hanging from the rearview mirror.

Yet the old Buick managed to get you where you were going. Somehow, to Mary Helen, the old car matched Suzanne perfectly. Worn, yet eager to please, efficient, and, above all, reliable.

Leaving the college, they turned right on Turk, right again on Parker, and finally right onto Geary. The boulevard was ablaze with lights. Already groups of people, huddling together to ward off the cold, had begun to queue up in front of the small restaurants lining both sides of the street.

Mary Helen marveled that one could choose to eat the food of Mexico or Morocco, France or China, Thailand or Pakistan by simply crossing Geary Street.

"It seems like the middle of the night," Anne remarked when they emerged from the Masonic Street tunnel. She pointed to the brightly lit buildings of downtown that lay before them.

"It's just after seven," Suzanne assured her, stopping for a red light in front of St. Mary's Cathedral. All the lights of the huge concrete structure were on, illuminating the brilliant stained glass in the spire.

When the cathedral was first built, some wag had called it St. Mary Maytag. Studying its gyrator-shaped dome, Mary Helen could understand why.

Suzanne's Buick wiggled around Starr King Way and on to Franklin Street. Here and there, Christmas lights shone from windows in the apartment buildings lining the hilly street. As they rode along, Mary Helen admired the stately Victorians sandwiched in between the tall buildings.

"One of these days we must take that tour." Eileen nudged her as they drove past the gray and white Haas–Lilienthal mansion. The old Queen Anne Victorian was set back on a small patch of perfectly manicured lawn.

Franklin Street dead-ended at Fort Mason. With a few clever turns Suzanne was fortunate enough to find a parking place on Van Ness right across from Aquatic Park, a short walk from Ghirardelli.

"You've brought me luck so far," Suzanne remarked as she curbed the Buick's wide wheels. "Hope it lasts."

"I'm sure you'll do just beautifully," Eileen gushed, "and we must be sure to make a special wish. This is the first time you and I have been to the Sea Wench." She smiled over at Mary Helen, who tried not to look too amazed.

"I thought you were entitled to a special wish the first time you visited a church!" Anne took the words right out of Mary Helen's mouth.

"That's three wishes for a church," Eileen corrected. "So I would suspect that at a bar we should get one," she explained with a bit of logic that eluded everyone.

Still shaking her head, Mary Helen stepped out of the Buick and carefully checked her door handle to make sure it was locked. She pulled in a deep breath. The sharp crisp prickle of salt air stung her face and made her eyes water.

Halos of fog formed around the old-fashioned street-lights lining the lip of the bay that curved into the shoreline. Below her she could hear the surf lapping against the narrow beach of hard sand.

In the distance the beacon from an invisible lighthouse shot across the sky.

The four women started along the footpath toward the Maritime Museum. Atop it, the flags waved in the flood-lights. Across the street, the large Ghirardelli sign and the famous clock tower were sparkling with tiny golden lights. The dense fog swirling in from the Golden Gate could not dim the arcade shops, brightly decorated for Christmas.

Holding tightly to the banister, Mary Helen made her way carefully up the brick stairs to the courtyard. She paused for breath by the large water fountain. Even the brass mermaids in the bubbling fountain looked chilly. Tiny white lights strung through willowy trees and over banisters gave the courtyard a fairyland appearance.

Mary Helen stopped for a moment to admire the Kite Shop, Corn Poppers, Inc., and the Fine Crystal Shop. Whoever had refurbished the old brick candy factory had done a lovely job, she thought, cautiously ascending the wide, moisture-laden steps to the second floor of the Chocolate Building.

Suzanne stopped in front of a thick wooden door with an ornate brass handle. "This is it," she said, motioning toward the door. "Mimi will meet you inside. I go around to the back." With that she hurried down the walkway and turned a corner.

The three nuns stood for a moment in the foyer, waiting for their eyes to adjust to the dark. "How will we know Mimi?" Mary Helen asked. The question was needless.

"Hi, I'm Mimi," a pert little voice piped in the dark. They turned to find a petite young woman holding three menus. Mimi was dressed much the same as Suzanne—tight bodice, minimal lace covering very little of her small but full bosom. Her costume, however, had puffy sleeves and a long, straight crimson satin skirt. To Mary Helen the girl looked for all the world like a small blond Snow White.

Apparently Mimi was the hostess. Her short curls bouncing, she threaded her way among the round wooden tables and led the nuns to a small table in the corner. Smiling, she plunked down the menus.

"I'm so glad to meet you." Her pug nose crinkled. "Suzanne has talked so much about you."

Mary Helen looked up, unable to believe that Suzanne talked much about anything. Her eyes met Mimi's. Maybe it was the flickering candle on the table. She blinked and looked again. She tried not to stare. Sure enough, Mimi had one brown eye and one blue one.

The girl pushed her short bangs aside, leaned over the table, and whispered, "Order anything you like. Drinks are on the house. My shift is over at ten. I'll take you home."

A tall, hairy-looking man planted a sound slap on Mimi's small firm bottom. Quickly she straightened up. "Come on, babe," he growled without even looking at her.

"Shake it! You got customers." The man moved away toward the back of the room.

Mimi winked her brown eye. "Mr. Rosenberg, the boss," she whispered. "Enjoy!" she said aloud, moving back toward the front door.

Before any of them could comment, a tall, thin waitress appeared to take their orders. Mary Helen studied the menu. Blackbeard's Revenge and A Long John Silver left her cold. Impatiently the waitress tapped her pencil on her pad. "Beer," Mary Helen ordered. "To settle my stomach," she added, feeling she had to justify her choice. The waitress glanced up, but said nothing. Both Eileen and Anne ordered white wine. How sensible and ladylike! Mary Helen wished she had waited. Oh, well, Fools rush in where angels fear to tread, she conceded, and there is no fool like an . . . Before she could finish her thought, the house lights dimmed, although she wouldn't have thought that possible. Several baby spotlights illuminated a small patch of raised wooden floor that served as a stage.

A group of bright young waiters and waitresses began a medley of Broadway hits. Mary Helen glanced over at her companions. Both Eileen and Anne seemed absorbed in the show. And from the expressions on their faces, both seemed to be enjoying it.

Mary Helen took a sip of ice-cold beer and gazed around the Sea Wench. The room was nautical to the nines. A fierce-looking figurehead of a noble maiden complete with large nose and lace ruff loomed over the bar. Three-cornered pirate hats hung on weathered brown walls above crossed swords and mysterious maps. Here and there, the carved faces of one-eyed buccaneers leered down at the customers. Open treasure chests bulged with goodies. Mary Helen would have fully expected to pay in pieces of eight had not the tote bags, cameras, and walking shoes given away the fact that the Sea Wench was full of tourists. An occasional distinguished-looking older man held hands with a svelte, glamorously dressed younger woman. Businessmen and their secretaries, she figured, wondering for a moment what these men told their wives.

Adjusting her bifocals, Mary Helen watched Rosenberg swagger around the room. A cigarette drooped from the corner of his narrow mouth. Here and there he paused long enough to fondle a black velvet bodice or pat a black velvet bottom.

The nerve of the fellow! Mary Helen thought, wondering for a moment just what else he did. Mary Helen had to resist her schoolmarm urge to tell the fellow to keep his hands to himself. She half wished one of the young waitresses would turn around and give Mr. Boss a good swift kick.

Suddenly she felt Eileen nudge her. "Suzanne," she said in a stage whisper. Mary Helen slid forward on her chair.

Suzanne appeared on the wooden platform, wreathed in lights and without her glasses. For a moment she blinked uncertainly at the audience. Mary Helen stiffened. Between the spotlights and no glasses she was sure the poor girl couldn't see a thing.

For heaven's sake, stay in the middle, she wanted to whisper aloud, so you won't fall off! Realizing this would be terribly out of order, she simply crossed her fingers instead. The orchestra began a short introduction. Suzanne gripped the microphone. Mary Helen gripped the edge of the table. Suzanne opened her mouth. Mary Helen held her breath. Then, softly, a little hesitantly, Suzanne sang the first few notes of a plaintive melody from a Broadway show.

Mary Helen began to relax during the next few bars when Suzanne's voice gained volume and certainty. She watched, delighted, as midverse the girl removed her tight grip from the mike and began to gesture, ever so slightly, toward the audience. The gesture wasn't much, but even a slight gesture was better than no gesture at all, she assured herself. She slid back in her chair. She felt a little swell of pride when Suzanne hit the crescendo in a rich, full voice. The girl seemed to be at ease, and what was more, she seemed to be genuinely feeling the mournful lyrics.

Pleased, Mary Helen glanced around the darkened room to see how the audience was taking to Suzanne. As far as she could tell, the audience was appreciative.

Two or three young fellows, she noticed, moved up in their straight-backed chairs and were quite attentive. Good! In the flickering candlelight she tried to study their profiles, but couldn't make out anything very clearly. One light-haired fellow at a table several over from them looked about Suzanne's age. What she could see of his profile seemed handsome enough. Perfect. Maybe he'd be smitten. Love at first sight. How romantic! Just then Mary Helen noticed the young man was already with a girl. Too bad! She scanned the rest of the "moved-up" fellows, but they were really very difficult to appraise in the dimness. Frustrated, her eyes went back to the stage.

As she smiled and sang a final chorus Suzanne's eyes swept the audience. Good, smile some more, Mary Helen urged silently, even if you can't see who you're smiling at! Maybe someone out there will introduce himself afterward. Something might develop and about time too. Imagine, poor Suzanne. Thirty years old and no boyfriends, at least not any that Mary Helen knew about.

During the last few bars of the song Mary Helen noticed Suzanne visibly stiffen again. What in the world happened? she wondered, watching a tense expression return to the young woman's face.

The music ended and the audience began to clap.

"Bravo, bravo." One young man on the other side of the room rose and began to clap enthusiastically.

Smile, smile, Mary Helen willed. But Suzanne turned away quickly and left the stage.

Oh, blast it, Mary Helen thought as the house lights came up ever so slightly. Won't that girl ever learn to flirt? Mary Helen stopped. She could not believe she had thought that. Why, she was behaving like a pure . . . a pure . . . she could hardly bring herself to admit it, even to herself . . . like a pure chauvinist! Or would it be sexist? Whichever, she was glad Sister Anne couldn't read her mind.

The waiters and waitresses resumed their duties. Mary Helen waited for Suzanne to come by the table so she could congratulate her and encourage her to smile more. Whatever the motive, performers should smile, she assured herself. But Suzanne didn't come.

"Wasn't she just wonderful?" Eileen asked no one in particular.

Anne and Mary Helen both nodded in agreement.

"Where do you suppose she went?" Mary Helen asked.

"Over there, with the boss." Anne pointed across the room.

In all that dimness and candlelight it was difficult to see exactly what was going on. Suzanne seemed to be talking rather heatedly to Mr. Rosenberg, who was nodding his head.

I wonder what on earth that was all about, Mary Helen thought, watching Rosenberg move away and start to circle the room.

"Can I get you anything else?" Mary Helen was forced to turn back and look at the waitress. "No, thank you," she answered quickly, and just as quickly turned away from the waitress and back to watching Rosenberg, who had stopped several tables over. He was leaning forward saying something to the couple at the table. The fellow rose abruptly and headed toward the exit.

"Wait for me, Cluey," his girl friend called after him. At least that was what Mary Helen thought she called him. Or was it "Cooy"? It was hard to distinguish above the noise of the crowd.

Standing up, the girl, Mary Helen noticed, looked about sixteen. At least from this distance she looked sixteen. Underage. Could that be what Suzanne was telling Mr. Rosenberg? How did Suzanne notice the couple, if indeed she had? Odd, Mary Helen thought, and what an odd name the fellow had. "Cooy," or was it "Cluey"? Who would name a child Clue? Only a mystery reader, she thought, which brought her mind scurrying back to the whodunit in her pocketbook.

She hoped she'd get home early enough to read a few chapters tonight. She checked her watch. It was ten o'clock already. She couldn't believe it!

Just then Mimi came by. "Are you ready to go home?" she asked in a lively bright voice. The three nuns smiled, gathered up their coats from the backs of their chairs. Mary Helen scanned the room once more for Suzanne, but she didn't see her. She'd call her tomorrow to congratulate her on a wonderful performance.

Mary Helen took what she suspected was her last look around the Sea Wench, made her wish, and dutifully followed Mimi to her parked Honda.

Quickly Mary Helen slipped into her flannel nightgown. Sitting on the edge of her bed, she wound her alarm clock. Tonight had been truly amazing. Timid Suzanne in her wench costume, belting out the blues to a captivated audience. "Belting out the blues" was a bit overdrawn for Suzanne's performance, but it was probably as close to "belting" as the girl would ever come. Who could have ever imagined? As much as she hated to admit it, maybe her impressions of Suzanne were wrong. Perhaps the young woman's uneasiness was, indeed, a need for privacy. And that "whipped dog" look. Had she misjudged it? Was Suzanne really just guarded? Even those watery blue eyes: Mary Helen had always noted a hint of toughness in them. Perhaps toughness was the wrong word. Crazily, "unconquerable soul" came to her mind. How did the rest of it go? That was the dickens about getting old. Some days she could only remember parts of things. Some days she couldn't remember who wrote them and some days even why. She was reluctant to admit the same thing had happened when she was young! "In the fell clutch of circumstances, I have not winced or cried aloud; Under the bludgeoning of chance, My head is bloody, but unbowed."

"Bloody but unbowed." That fit Suzanne and her Buick to a tee! Perhaps she should encourage her secretary to pursue her career, branch out, and, as chauvinistic as it seemed, find a gentleman friend. She would urge the girl to make something exciting and interesting of her life. She'd point out her rapport with the audience, how radiant the plain young woman had appeared.

On the other hand, perhaps she should mind her own business, read a little, then try to get some sleep.

Mary Helen climbed into bed, fluffed her pillow, and switched on her electric blanket. Leaning over, she felt on the nightstand for her book. Gone! She remembered she had taken it with her. She rifled her purse. Not there! It must have fallen out in Suzanne's car or Mimi's. Good excuse. Better than a phone call. She'd go over to the apartment first thing in the morning, talk to the young woman, and reclaim her mystery.

SATURDAY—DECEMBER 1

Mary Helen awoke with a tingle of excitement. She fumbled for her glasses, then checked the clock on her bedstand.

Seven o'clock. Perfect! She had plenty of time to shower, dress, and say her morning office. The office was always private on Saturday mornings, in case any of the nuns wanted to sleep in late. Then she would walk down to St. Ignatius Church for the eight o'clock Mass. Father Adams always said the eight, thank God. He prided himself on being able to get from the opening antiphon to the final blessing with homily included in twenty-five minutes flat!

After Mass, she would grab a quick piece of toast and a cup of coffee in the Sisters' dining room and be off to Suzanne's apartment.

Mentally she calculated her time schedule. She should arrive at Suzanne's in the neighborhood of nine o'clock, maybe a few minutes before. Nine o'clock was a bit early to call on someone who had left work at two A.M., she realized. For a moment she felt a slight twinge of guilt, but only for a moment, when she considered why she wanted to visit Suzanne. Rather than being annoyed, Mary Helen assured herself, the young woman would be grateful. And, heaven knows, one might as well strike while the iron was hot.

Furthermore, the fact that she had inadvertently left her mystery, the one she wanted to finish by tomorrow, in either Mimi's Honda or Suzanne's Buick—now, that must be more than a coincidence. It was a sign, probably a sign from God, that she should visit Suzanne first thing this morning. "Right, Lord?" she prayed.

As she moved slowly toward the window to check the weather, Mary Helen was thankful once again that God seldom answers back.

Warily she turned up a corner of the short drape. To her amazement the morning was clear, not a hint of fog. Another good omen, she concluded happily. Good grief, old girl, you are beginning to sound like Eileen, she admonished herself. Everything is getting to be a sign or an omen. She shrugged. After fifty years of friendship, maybe that was inevitable.

When she had finished her breakfast, Mary Helen stopped by the deserted personnel office long enough to locate Suzanne's emergency file and jot down her address.

Back at the convent, she signed out the brown Nova on the car calendar. She wrote her initials and *8:30–10:00* in the square. Deliberately, she avoided writing where she was going. No sense having to explain her destination to Therese. Sister Therese, Mary Helen suspected, considered reading the car calendar her sacred duty, second only to spiritual reading. She had often wondered where Therese would rank mystery reading!

Slowly, Mary Helen eased the Nova down the steep college driveway. She couldn't resist the temptation to stop halfway down the hill to admire The City. San Francisco was having one of those crisp sunny days that it jealously hides from the summer tourists, then proudly presents to the natives when most of the country is buried in snow.

Mary Helen closed her eyes, took a deep breath, and felt genuinely happy to be alive. At seventy plus, she thought, conscientiously avoiding remembering exactly what the plus equaled, you have to make every day count. Yes, indeed, it was a glorious morning. "The morning air is all awash with angels."

The impatient tooting of a car horn behind her snapped her back to reality. Obviously, the morning was awash with more than angels. In her rearview mirror, she caught Sister Therese's face. One look at the raised eyebrows and pursed lips told her it was time to move.

Before deciding which way to turn on Turk Street, Mary Helen checked her watch. Eight forty-five. Early. Good, she thought, turning left. She'd take the roundabout way, along the Pan-Handle, through Golden Gate Park, then up to California Street and Suzanne's apartment. Roundabout was right, almost a circle, but the park had its own special magic on a sun-filled day and Mary Helen enjoyed being part of it. She was delighted to see Sister Therese's indicator signal right.

Even this early on a Saturday morning, the Pan Handle was crowded with long-haired men and women looking for all the world like middle-aged hippies, dressed in dark karate pajamas and completely ignoring one another. Each was intent on tai chi and not a one was an Oriental.

Entering Golden Gate Park, she passed McLaren Lodge set back on a lush carpet of lawn. Good old McLaren had been responsible for turning miles of sand dunes into this gorgeous park.

Already roller skaters had begun to congregate on the pedestrian pathways, equipped with helmets, kneepads, elbow guards, and radios. In a few hundred years archaeologists would wonder whether these people had been going in for combat or out for recreation. And you wouldn't blame them, Mary Helen mused, for she had often wondered about it herself.

Leisurely, the old nun drove past the Conservatory of

Flowers. With Victorian smugness, the milk-white glass building—thirty-three tons of glass in all, if she remembered correctly—overlooked two rectangular flower beds. One had recently been replanted in the form of a white dove holding the olive branch of peace.

Turning right, Mary Helen took Eighth Avenue out of the park and followed it up to California. Along the way she noticed several Christmas tree lots already going up. They looked strangely out of place in the brilliant sunshine. Why, even Arizona, where she had been born and raised, could muster up a bit of snow at Christmastime. After making a left on California Street, she drove several blocks before slowing down and beginning to check house numbers. She had never been to Suzanne's apartment. In fact, she had not known exactly where the young woman lived until she had looked up the address in the emergency file. Well, this was an emergency, she thought, justifying the little qualm she had about using the file instead of calling ahead. And, the strangest thing: Suzanne had only her own address on the card, no next of kin, no friend to notify. Somehow, it didn't seem likely that efficient Suzanne would slip up on something as important as that, but she had discovered several unlikely things about Suzanne lately.

The old nun dismissed the thought the moment she spotted a parking place in front of a two-story building bearing the correct number. Suzanne's apartment building was a squat structure, two lots wide, squeezed in between a green stucco flat and a peaked-roofed, diamond-shingled Victorian. The slanted bay windows of each apartment bulged out from the second floor like so many dumplings set atop the lower floor of garages. Mary Helen peeked through the French glass front door into a drab carpeted lobby. MANAGER was tacked on the door of the only apartment on that floor. Beside it a narrow staircase led up.

Mary Helen ran her index finger along the row of metal mailboxes lining the entryway, looking for Suzanne's. Quickly, she located *Suzanne Barnes, Apartment 204.* The box to the right of it read *Mimi Heagerty/Lee Slater, Apartment 206.* Why, Mimi lived right next door to Suzanne. For a moment, Mary Helen speculated whether Mimi's roommate was a girl Lee or a boy Lee. But only for a moment. Her biggest concern right now was whether to ring Suzanne's bell and announce herself, or to ring the manager's, get into the building, and surprise her secretary.

The problem was solved when a slight young bearded fellow in a jogging suit coming out of the apartment building held the door open for her.

"Want in, Sister?" He smiled politely and didn't seem a bit reluctant to let Mary Helen into the building.

Looking like a nun! What a great disguise for a serious-minded crook, Mary Helen thought, smiling politely and nodding her thanks toward the young man.

The inside of the apartment building smelled musty; not dirty or unkept, but a respectable, old-fashioned musty—the kind that comes from years of resisting damp fog and being occupied by generations of young people just starting out in life. There was something solid and unpretentious about the old building. Mary Helen mounted the narrow staircase to the second floor. Pausing to catch her breath, she silently thanked God that Suzanne's building only had two floors, not six.

Narrow windows at each end of the second-floor hallway captured enough light to reveal the numbers painted on the wooden doors.

Sister Mary Helen hesitated before Apartment 204 and frowned. The door was slightly ajar. Now, that was odd. In this day and age it was hardly safe to leave your door unlocked, let alone ajar. Good grief, she was beginning to sound like Therese!

Putting her ear to the open crack, she listened. No sound of movement came from inside. Poor Suzanne was probably still in bed. But then—why wasn't the door shut? She knocked. Nothing. She knocked a little harder. No answer. The third time she could hear her hollow knock echo through the silent apartment. Still no one answered.

Mary Helen felt a little wave of uneasiness. Don't overreact, she cautioned herself. Perhaps Suzanne had just stepped out for a moment. She couldn't have gone too far, since she'd left the front door open. What a shame to have come all this way and to miss her! She'd just wait.

Mary Helen peered into the small apartment. The front room was dark. All the drapes were drawn. Obviously the girl must have just rolled out of bed. A door on the far side of the room was pushed back. Maybe Suzanne was still asleep. But in that case why on earth was the front door ajar? For heaven's sake, calm down. Nothing is wrong, she assured herself, stepping into the darkened room. Midway across the living room, she stopped. What if someone was in the apartment? Someone besides Suzanne, that is. Why, she'd seen that happen dozens of times on TV. What would she do if someone jumped out at her? Nonsense, she thought, stopping to listen just in case. But the apartment was still. No sound but emptiness. Of course she was alone! And in the quiet she heard all those noises you never notice unless you are alone: the flush of plumbing in a distant apartment; the swish of the traffic on California Street; and closer, a steady tick, tick, tick. Was there a clock in the living room? She looked around. No. Could Suzanne have left her big nun's watch on an end table? Again she looked around, but she could see no watch. Still, the tick, tick, ticking went on. Or was it a tick? Perhaps it was a drip. The staccato drip, drip, drip, like a leaking faucet. That was it!

Mary Helen tiptoed across the rest of the room, trying to quiet the loud bumping of her own heart. If Suzanne was asleep, she certainly didn't want to startle her. Silently, she peeked into the bedroom.

Even in the dim light she could tell that the small room was in a shambles. A wadded bedspread prevented her from pushing the door completely open. Across the room an end table was overturned. Bits of broken glass from the bedside lamp were splattered across the floor. Pictures hung askew. Someone had apparently fallen with force against the dresser, cracking the mirror and toppling perfume and cosmetic bottles. Perfume from an overturned bottle was what she had heard dripping. Dripping on a piece of porcelain from a small ornate figurine that had shattered in the fall. Blood was everywhere.

Across the rumpled bed, Suzanne lay on her back, motionless, her costume torn, her net stockings shredded. Her long black hair fanned out like a halo framing her bruised face. The blue silk flowers were crumpled. Mary Helen stared in horror. The handle of a silver letter opener protruded from a deep slash in Suzanne's blood-soaked breast. The watery blue eyes were forever fixed with terror. The last thing they had looked upon was the face of a murderer.

The murderer! Could he still be here? The thought catapulted in on her. For a moment she was paralyzed with fear. Slowly she forced herself to look around the room. No one. Legs trembling, she walked across to a small closed door at the far end of the bedroom. The bathroom, no doubt. Bracing herself, she swallowed hard and threw the door open. Closing her eyes tightly, she waited. Nothing happened. No one jumped out. She opened her eyes and looked around. Empty. She took a deep breath. Tightening her teeth, she walked across the small room, grabbed the plastic shower curtain and yanked it open. No one.

Pulling in two or three deep breaths, she turned and left the bathroom. Resolutely she headed toward the only other closed door in the small apartment, the closet. Mary Helen could feel the muscles in her back and shoulders tense as she clutched the door handle. Summoning up all the courage she could find at the moment, she slowly turned the knob. Then, with a quick jerk, she pulled open the door. She braced herself for the worst. Nothing happened. No one.

The old nun steadied herself against the doorjamb and closed her eyes in relief. None of the murders she had read about in her mysteries, nor the ones she had seen on TV, or even the two murder victims she had discovered a year ago at the college, had prepared her for this. A sudden weakness washed over her. She could hear her own heart roaring in her ears.

Crazily Dylan Thomas's poem came to her mind. "Do not go gentle into that good night . . . Rage, rage against the dying of the light."

Poor eager-to-please Suzanne had indeed raged against the dying of her light. Who could have done such a heinous thing to gentle Suzanne? Mary Helen forced herself to open her eyes and move across the room to the limp body. Silent tears skirted the old nun's wrinkled cheeks.

Bending over, she felt for the young woman's pulse in the hope that perhaps . . . But before she touched the twisted limb, she knew. Her dear, reliable Suzanne was dead —murdered.

Squaring her shoulders, Mary Helen wiped her face with her linen handkerchief. She adjusted her bifocals, swallowed hard, and forced herself to slow her breathing. She stood above the body, her whole being filled with emotion— grief, horror, fear, shock. But underneath it all she felt swirls of outrage. Who would dare to end a young life so savagely? It didn't take her a moment to decide exactly who could put this outrage right. Determinedly, she returned to the living room, found the phone, and, holding the receiver in her linen-lined hand, dialed her friend Kate Murphy.

The phone rang on Jack's side of the bed. Still half asleep, Kate snuggled against her husband's warm bare body. Once again she marveled at how she fit just right into all his nooks and crannies. She'd like to stay that way—warm and cozy—forever.

"Hello." She heard Jack answer the persistent ring. He amazed her. Even half asleep, he was pleasant.

"Just a moment, Sister," he said. "She's right here."

Covering the receiver with his hand, he nudged Kate.

"Sister Mary Helen," he whispered. "The old gal sounds upset."

Inwardly, Kate groaned. Unsealing her eyes, she glanced at the clock. Nine-twenty! What in the world could Sister Mary Helen want at nine-twenty on a Saturday morning? Warm slips of sunshine fell across the old brass bed.

Kate struggled up on her elbows, ran her fingers through her short red hair, and took the phone.

"Hello, Sister." She tried not to sound too groggy. "What's up? . . . A murder? Who?" Sitting up in bed, she grabbed Jack's hand. "Where are you?" Already she had swung her legs out of bed and her bare feet were searching for her slippers.

Behind her she heard Jack curse softly. "God damn, no wonder she sounded upset."

"Stay put. Don't touch anything. Yes, you can call a priest. I guess you've already touched the phone. . . . With a hankie? Good for you! Then, call the police, report a homicide. I'll contact Gallagher. We'll be right over.

"Are you all right?" she added, more like an afterthought. Kate smiled at the old nun's reassurance. "See you in a few minutes," she said, then sat for a moment on the edge of the bed with the dead receiver in her hand.

"I can't believe this." Jack scratched his curly black hair. "Two, no, three bodies in two years. That's got to be a record. Is she okay?"

Kate nodded her head. Reaching over Jack, she hung up the phone. Bending down, she kissed him gently on the lips. "Not the way we planned to spend our Saturday is it, pal?" she whispered in his ear.

Kate could feel her husband's strong hands drawing her to him, caressing her shoulder, back, then her hips.

"I had something a little more productive in mind," he murmured, ready to kiss her again.

Resolutely, Kate pulled away. She could hear Jack groan as she headed for the bathroom to splash cold water on her round, freckled face.

Woodenly, Sister Mary Helen replaced the receiver. What had Kate said? "Call the police." And yes, she'd better call a priest. The least poor Suzanne deserved was the last rites or whatever they were calling them these days. Like a pilot on automatic, she dialed the numbers. In the silence of the room her words sounded so businesslike, so sane. She could hear herself giving details like a person in a dream. Maybe she was having one of Shakespeare's "miserable nights . . . so full of ugly sights and ghastly dreams." If that were the case, she wished with all her heart she would wake up.

The final click in the receiver brought the awful reality

swirling in on her. Suzanne lay in the next room, dead, a thin letter opener protruding from her breast. The small room began to move toward Sister Mary Helen, closing in. A cold sweat washed her whole body. A ringing began in her ears.

Glory be to God, Mary Helen thought, I'm going to faint. But I never faint. Unsteadily she moved across the darkened room. Mimi's! She'd go next door to Mimi's. It was early to awaken her, but surely murder superseded politeness.

Tingling, Mary Helen pressed the bell to Mimi's apartment. The sound echoed through the silent rooms. She pressed again, then leaned against the doorjamb. From inside she heard the thump of someone stirring; finally, the slap of bare feet across the floor. Cautiously, Mimi cracked open the door. Her blue-brown eyes registered shock.

"Sister!" She threw the door open wide. "You look awful! Come in, sit down. What's wrong?" Clad only in an extra-long cotton T-shirt, Mimi ushered the old nun into a soft beanbag chair, then disappeared.

Sinking into the chair's soft roundness, Mary Helen wondered how she'd ever be able to get up again. For the moment, however, she didn't care. Quickly Mimi returned with a glass.

"Sip slowly," she cautioned, handing the old nun a tall, clear glass of water. "Do you want something stronger?" she asked, kneeling beside the beanbag.

Mary Helen was just about to answer yes when the bedroom door swung open.

"Who the hell was that?" a masculine voice asked. Startled, both Mary Helen and Mimi looked toward the door. A tall, lean, bearded young man, a Turkish towel wrapped loosely around his waist, filled the space.

"That's Lee, my roommate," Mimi muttered, hardly acknowledging his presence.

Without a word the young man grabbed for his towel. Tightening it, he ducked back into the bedroom. So the Lee on Mimi's mailbox was a masculine Lee. That was one question answered.

"What's wrong?" Mimi asked again, her round face puckered with concern.

Slowly Mary Helen sipped the water. She dreaded saying the words as if, somehow, not talking about it could make the horror go away.

"It's Suzanne," she said finally. "She's dead."

Mimi's face blanched. She sank back on her heels, reeling as if from an invisible blow.

"How?" she asked. The tears brimming in her eyes began to run down her face.

"Murdered," Mary Helen answered boldly. There was no easy way to break such shocking news.

Just then the young man reappeared, dressed in tight-fitting jeans and a powder blue polo shirt with somebody's logo on the breast pocket. Mary Helen looked up. The blue in the young fellow's shirt brought out the cold blue in his eyes. Mary Helen watched as those eyes moved from Mimi to her, then back again. No expression crossed his narrow face. Rather dispassionate, she thought, somewhat piqued, considering we are both sitting on the floor, obviously upset. No, maybe dispassionate was not the correct word. Perhaps, Lee Slater's look was more . . . more . . . clinical.

"What's the matter?" he asked. Frowning, he pulled on the pointed tip of his scraggly blond beard.

"It's Suzanne." Mimi answered him in a flat, frozen voice. "She's been murdered."

She turned to look at her roommate.

Lee's face remained fixed. If Mary Helen hadn't really

been looking closely, she would never have even noticed his jaw tighten or the slight color-change in his cheeks. "Stony-faced" would describe this fellow perfectly.

But it was those steely eyes of his that really bothered her. They were so detached, so scientific—as if he were a mere observer of life. Under other circumstances she would be curious as to what made this fellow tick.

Before she could give Lee Slater any more thought, the hallway outside was filled with the sound of heavy footsteps. The patrolmen had arrived. Mary Helen knew that soon the whole army of policemen would follow. Suzanne's apartment would be full of men shooting pictures, dusting for finger-prints, asking questions and more questions. Mary Helen would have to pull herself together. After all, after a certain age, everyone expects you to act composed.

"I better get up," Mary Helen said sticking her hand out to Mimi for help. Impulsively, the girl threw her arms around Mary Helen's neck. The two sat there sharing a beanbag chair, hugging.

A sick, empty feeling circled Mary Helen's heart, then spread through her body. She realized with sudden clarity just how much she had really cared for Suzanne and how very much she would miss her.

Inspectors Kate Murphy and Dennis Gallagher were among the first to arrive at Suzanne's apartment. Kate could tell that her partner had dressed in a hurry. Nothing matched. Mrs. G must still be in bed.

Dennis, his short cigar butt shoved into the corner of his wide mouth, fumbled in his pockets for a match.

"What a hellava mess," he muttered to Kate as they surveyed Suzanne's bedroom. He finally lit his cigar, shutting one eye against the smoke. "And that nun again? What's her name? Mary Helen? Wouldn't you know she'd be involved!"

Kate giggled. After thirty years in the Homicide Detail nothing much threw Dennis Gallagher, but dealing with Sister Mary Helen surely did. Kate couldn't help enjoying his discomfort.

"Aw, Denny," she teased, "think of how lucky we are to have the good Sister on our team again."

"For crissake, Kate." Gallagher ran his hand over his bald pate. "Why the hell can't she stay in the cloister where she belongs?"

Kate ignored his question. "I wonder where the old girl is now," she said aloud.

"Only God Himself knows," her partner muttered, following Kate out of the apartment.

Hearing a familiar voice calling her name, Sister Mary Helen stepped into the hallway, but not before Mimi had helped her out of the chair and insisted she splash cold water on her face. Setting her shoulders, Mary Helen deftly wiped the last trace of tears from her glasses. No use making things harder on Kate by looking as if she had fallen apart. Poor girl would soon have enough troubles.

Kate gave the old nun a warm hug. She must have noticed my red eyes, Mary Helen thought, but at least she has the good taste not to mention it. That was one of the many things Mary Helen liked about Kate: her unfailing good taste.

The two women stood for a moment, smiling at one another. Marriage seems to be agreeing with Kate, Mary Helen thought. Her freckled face looked relaxed and happy and there was a deep peace in her blue eyes. Mary Helen was glad. When she had first met Kate, over a year ago now, she and Jack Bassetti had been living together out in the Richmond District in the house that had belonged to Kate's parents. They certainly loved each other. That was obvious to anyone with eyes to see. Yet, for some reason, they had hesitated to get married.

Mary Helen was never quite sure why. Then, out of the blue, or so it seemed out of the blue to almost everyone, they had decided to. Mary Helen was delighted. Jack was such a nice boy. And wouldn't they have beautiful children!

Mary Helen noticed that old teddy bear of a Gallagher standing behind his partner. He was beginning to shuffle the pages of his notebook as if he were nervous.

"Tell us what happened, Sister," Kate urged, her voice gentle.

Reluctantly, Mary Helen allowed her mind to be dragged back to the horrible reality of the scene in Suzanne's bedroom. Her mouth felt dry and parched as she managed to describe her relationship to the young woman, their evening at the Sea Wench, her visit to the apartment, and her discovery of the ravaged body.

As she spoke she felt as if the jaws of a vise were closing around her forehead. She shivered with a sudden chill.

"Are you all right, Sister?" Kate asked. Gallagher's broad hands shot forward and grabbed her by the elbows. Mary Helen nodded. She didn't trust herself to speak.

"Can you get yourself home?" Again she nodded. "Why don't you go, then?" Kate said. "I'll call you later if we need you for anything."

Silently Gallagher led the old nun down the stairs and helped her into her car.

"Are you sure you're okay?" he asked before closing the door. She nodded.

"Be careful," he called gruffly, and watched her pull away from the curb.

The ride home was mechanical. The sun still shone, The City still glistened. But instead of raising her spirits, as it had when she started out for Suzanne's, the day's brilliance just made Sister Mary Helen angry. How could the day be so bright, so cheerful, when Suzanne lay brutalized in her bedroom. The whole world seemed out of whack.

Parking the Nova, she slid from behind the wheel. Quietly she let herself into the convent, returned the car keys to the hook beside the calendar, and went up the side stairs to Eileen's bedroom.

The small room smelled of Lemon Pledge. Eileen stood in the middle of it, high-dusting her dustless bedroom. Her wrinkled face was flushed with exhaustion.

"Well, hello," she said, savagely attacking a corner of the ceiling. "It simply can't be lunchtime already?"

Everything was so normal, even Eileen, that Mary Helen wanted to shout.

"My Lord, Mary Helen, you look right like something the cat dragged in." Eileen lowered the dust mop. "What on earth is wrong?"

"It's Suzanne. Poor Suzanne." Mary Helen grabbed the headboard of Eileen's bed for support. "I found her dead. Murdered."

The flush drained from Eileen's face. "Dead?" she asked incredulously. "How could that be?"

As succinctly as she could, Mary Helen related the details. Eileen's soft round face wrinkled with sympathy.

"Glory be to God, you poor old dear," she cooed. That was all the sympathy Mary Helen needed. Her brave but shaky dam burst right in the center of Eileen's immaculate bedroom.

Her friend led her down the narrow hallway to her own bed. Almost the last thing Mary Helen remembered before falling into a dreamless sleep was Eileen insisting she finish the second glass of brandy.

"But I'll be drunk," Mary Helen protested weakly.

"As the Irish say, 'May as well be drunk as the way you are,' " Eileen consoled her.

Up the Irish was Mary Helen's last thought as darkness covered her aching mind.

At suppertime Eileen arrived carrying a small, carefully arranged tray. Anne followed close on her heels with a cup of camomile tea.

"Are you feeling any stronger?" Eileen asked, sitting on the edge of her bed. Her voice betrayed a hidden meaning that her old friend recognized instantly.

"Why?" Mary Helen asked. "Did you tell the nuns about Suzanne?"

"I didn't need to go to the bother. Channel Four, the noon news, did the dirty work for me. Everything, that is, but mention the girl's name. Something about next of kin being notified. But that little detail didn't put Therese off for one moment and especially, as you might imagine, not when the newscaster mentioned you'd found the body."

Groaning, Mary Helen fell back against the pillow.

"Think positively," Anne interjected. Folding her long legs, she sank into a lotus position on the floor beside Mary Helen's bed. "You could have had to tell the nuns about it yourself. This way, Millie Chang broke the news for you. And Millie Chang doesn't have to watch Therese's face while she tells her."

"Furthermore, old dear," Eileen said, picking up the thought, "if you stay in bed till tomorrow morning, the evening news and the eleven o'clock will give them every gory detail."

Mary Helen laughed in spite of her throbbing head.

"It's very good to hear you laugh." Eileen patted her hand, smiling.

I wish it felt as good as it sounds, Mary Helen wanted to say, but she just smiled back instead.

"And by the way, if you are feeling up to it, Kate Murphy called. She wants you to ring her back as soon as you are able. It is important, I think."

Kate answered the phone on Mary Helen's first ring. The young woman sounded relieved to hear her voice.

"We have a problem, Sister," she announced with no preliminaries.

Mary Helen was glad to hear the *we*. This was certainly one murder investigation in which she wanted to be involved.

"What's our problem?" Mary Helen hoped the *our* wasn't too pointed.

"When we searched the victim's apartment." Mary Helen flinched. She hated to think of poor Suzanne as "the victim."

"Funniest thing," Kate continued. "We couldn't find anything that gave a clue to next of kin. No address book, old letters, cards, nothing. We don't know who to notify. Then it dawned on me. You must have something in your personnel file—like an emergency card."

A sinking feeling hit Mary Helen's stomach. She almost hated to break the news to Kate. "You know, Kate," she said, "it is a funny thing. This morning I looked in her emergency file and—"

"And what?" Kate interrupted, a wary tone in her voice.

"No one was listed."

A long pause followed her statement. Mary Helen visualized Kate thinking, twisting that one piece of red hair tightly around her index finger.

"Looks like we do," Mary Helen said, finally. "Have a problem, that is."

FIRST SUNDAY OF ADVENT

The front page of Sunday morning's *Chronicle* was full of Suzanne. Some alert reporter had picked up the incident on the police blotter, noticed the victim, discovered Sister Mary Helen's name, and bingo, a seventy-two-point headline!

Mary Helen and Eileen were in the small coffee room off the kitchen with the library copy of the morning paper. Purposely they had avoided the Sisters' dining room. Mary Helen had not felt up to discussing the tragedy with her morning toast, nor was she in any mood to cope with Therese's accusing stares.

"Murder Stalks Holy Hill," Eileen read aloud.

Mary Helen took a long, piping-hot swallow of coffee. "At least they didn't put 'again,' " she said, hoping to sound optimistic. From the look on Eileen's face she knew she had sounded more like a seventy-year-old Pollyanna. Ugh!

Systematically, Eileen counted off the head. Looking up, she grimaced. "They didn't say 'again,' " she stated flatly, "simply because all those letters would not fit."

"Thank God for small favors," the two nuns pronounced in unison. Eileen reached over and hooked Mary Helen's baby finger.

"What goes up the chimney?" she asked.

"Smoke," Mary Helen answered, feeling a little childish sitting across from Eileen, their fingers hooked.

"Your wish and my wish, may never be broke."

Mary Helen had gone through this silly ritual with her friend hundreds of times; every time they said the same thing at the same time, as a matter of fact. And the longer they knew each other, Mary Helen noticed, the more often this happened.

This morning she was not in the mood for Eileen's superstitions either, but she was not taking any chances. In view of yesterday's tragedy, she needed all the unbroken wishes she could wish.

"Shall I read the article aloud?" Eileen asked.

"Spare me," Mary Helen said, frowning at her friend. She hated having newspaper articles read to her, even small bits. Why, she could barely stand to have her horoscope read aloud. If anyone knew that, Eileen did. Besides, she had discovered the body. She already knew more about the scene of the crime than she wanted to.

"I was just trying to be polite." Eileen ignored her frown.

While Eileen scanned the article, Mary Helen enjoyed the quiet. She knew it wouldn't last. But for the moment she would just sit and sip and contemplate the view of the campus garden from the coffee room.

Outside, the December morning was a bleak gray. Not the thick, mysterious gray of a low drizzly fog that would burn off and, magician-like, disappear into the bay. That, at least, had a little pizzazz. This morning was cold and wet and just plain blah. It matched Mary Helen's mood.

Even the lush winter green of the manicured lawn bordered with deep red cyclamen failed to cheer or comfort her.

The indisputable fact was that Suzanne was dead. Father Adams had offered this morning's Mass in the chapel for her. He had even slowed down. Anne had led the singing. The homily was low-key and genuine.

"We are all somehow responsible for violence in the world," Father Adams had said, "insofar as we are violent. . . ."

Mary Helen's mind had wandered. She felt violent, plenty violent, toward the person who had murdered Suzanne. Maybe *shocked* was a better word. Shocked and helpless and sad; very, very sad.

"You do not know when the appointed time will come." She heard the priest's sonorous voice quote Mark's gospel. How appropriate for Suzanne. She certainly had not known when her time would come. And yet, how inappropriate. That was today's gospel, the gospel for the First Sunday of Advent. Advent marked the four weeks of waiting for Christmas. Today's liturgy should be filled with the joyful anticipation of a birth, the birth of the Christ Child. This child would come into the world bearing peace and joy and love. Yet today a pall of death and violence and fear permeated the college chapel instead.

At Communion, Anne had chosen a gentle hymn from the St. Louis Jesuits' Advent–Christmas album. One based on the ancient prophecy of Micah. Softly she strummed her guitar and the group joined in.

"A time will come for singing when all your tears are shed, when sorrow's chains are broken, and broken hearts will mend . . ." Mary Helen felt the goose bumps rise on her arms.

". . . when men lay down their armor, and hammer their swords into plows . . ." Behind her, she had heard Therese sniffling. Several of the nuns quietly blew their noses. Mary Helen had barely managed to stay dry-eyed herself.

"Where are you, old girl?" Eileen's hand on her arm brought her back to the small coffee room.

"Just thinking about Suzanne. And this morning's Mass . . . What Father Adams said about violence and unexpected death. It seems so wrong, so out of whack, that today we should all be mourning violent death when the whole

world is waiting for peace and joy and anticipating birth—"
Mary Helen stopped abruptly, not trusting herself to go on.

Eileen nodded sympathetically.

"The world today is sick to its thin blood," Mary Helen
quoted as soon as she was sure her voice would not quiver.
"And we should do something about it," she said, feeling a
sudden rise of anger. She set her mouth, conscious of two
determined dimples forming on either side of it.

Both of Eileen's gray eyebrows shot up. She blinked.
"Glory be to God, don't you be getting any ideas!" Her
brogue thickened a bit. It always did when she was excited.
Mary Helen thought she was overreacting a mite. "Besides, I
thought you told me you were giving up reading those murder mysteries for Advent." Eileen pointed an accusing finger.

"I do not intend to read a murder mystery," Mary
Helen began resolutely. She got no farther.

"Lord, help us. Getting involved in a real one is—is"—
Eileen stammered for the right word—"ridiculous!" She finished her sentence. Mary Helen knew that wasn't the word
she wanted. But Eileen was at a loss, which didn't happen
often. Good.

Now was the perfect time to drive home her point. At
the moment she wasn't too sure what she'd do or how she'd
do it, but do it she would. Somehow or another, she would
help Kate Murphy find Suzanne's murderer. It was the least
she could do for the sweet, plain, efficient young woman who
had served her so well.

"Shouldn't I be concerned?" she began quietly, knowing full well that the best defense was a good offense. "Don't
you think it's our duty to be concerned?" The volume of her
voice rose a bit. Quickly she continued before Eileen had a
chance to answer. "Don't you want the police to find Suzanne's murderer?" Her voice became still louder.

Dramatically, Mary Helen rose from the kitchen chair and put her coffee mug down on the Formica-topped table. "Don't you want to live the message of the Scripture?" she asked, remembering this morning's Communion hymn. Purposely she avoided Eileen's wide eyes and gazed into the garden, pausing for effect. Sarah Bernhardt, she knew, could not have timed it better. "Don't you think we should help the world to hammer its swords into plowshares?" She met Eileen's horrified stare with half-shut eyes. After a pregnant pause she shoved her bifocals up the bridge of her nose, turned, and left the room.

But not before she heard Eileen mutter, "Glory be to God, Mary Helen, what I think is, you must be getting right mad." Her brogue was as thick as Mary Helen had heard it for a long, long time.

Outside, Mary Helen took a deep breath and squared her shoulders. The wet fog felt cool against her flushed face. She had really worked herself up into quite a pitch. She looked around, feeling a little foolish. First chance she had, she must apologize to Eileen. The scene in the coffee room had been a wee bit overdone, but her point had been sincere. How could she expect the Prince of Peace to come until she'd done her level best to establish peace right here on her little patch of earth? And that was by helping Kate Murphy find Suzanne's murderer, of course.

Glancing at the lowering sky, the old nun dug her hands deep into the pockets of her Aran sweater. Thank God she had worn it to Mass this morning. She pulled the collar up around her ears. Hunched against the chill, she quickly skirted the college building and headed toward the convent.

She had become so emotional about Suzanne's death and spoken so confidently and so purposefully about helping

Kate Murphy uncover the murderer, she had forgotten all about determining just how.

Lest she be accused of being "heap big smoke, very little fire," Mary Helen decided the best thing to do was to go upstairs to her bedroom, sit quietly in her big leather chair, and figure out exactly what she would do. A little shiver ran through Mary Helen's mind when she thought of Kate Murphy. The last time she'd tried to help, the young woman had not been too receptive. Mentally she pictured Kate, blue eyes blazing. But that was in the beginning, Mary Helen reminded herself. Why, at the end everything had turned out beautifully! This time Kate would surely be delighted. On the phone last night when she called about Suzanne's emergency card, didn't she say, "We have a problem"? Who else could the we have referred to? Yes, Mary Helen assured herself, Kate would be delighted.

In the quiet of her small bedroom, settled in her comfortable chair, she would sort out her exact role. Mary Helen stopped mid-hill. Use your head instead of your feet, she admonished herself. Why walk up and down this hill twice? She turned. As long as she was this close to the college building, why not drop by Suzanne's office? Check the desk. Gather any clues she could for Kate. Poor girl would have her hands full searching Suzanne's apartment, questioning the other tenants, checking and double-checking for anything that might give her a lead. Why, she and Inspector Gallagher would probably not get to the college until Tuesday or Wednesday at the earliest.

Gingerly, Mary Helen let herself into the college building. Behind her the heavy door swished shut. A "school-y smell" surrounded her. A school-y smell would be hard to describe to a neophyte, she thought, but every seasoned schoolmarm, especially anyone who had taught as long as she had, recognizes it immediately. It is a curious mixture of disinfectant and chalk, perspiration and lunch pails; except in college, she reminded herself, they won't have lunch pails. She stood for a moment in the empty foyer. The long, narrow windows threw strips of dim light across the parquet floor and onto the white marble steps leading up to the second floor. Here and there, Carrara busts atop ornate pedestals stared at her with blank eyes.

As she crossed the entrance way, the parquet creaked. A shiver ran down her spine.

"Deck the halls with bows of holly," she began to hum. She didn't know where it came from, although these halls could surely use some decking.

"Fa-la-la-la-la-la-la-la-la" she sang aloud, making her way down the long deserted corridor.

The *la-las* echoed around her as she opened the door leading to the basement steps. Mary Helen didn't know why she was singing, but it made her feel better.

Eyes lowered, she quickly made her way down the concrete steps toward her basement office—hers and Suzanne's. Stopping every few steps, she listened. Nothing. Just stillness. The building was completely empty. Who in the world did she expect anyway? The ghost of Christmas past?

Her key made a great reverberating click as she unlocked the heavy oak door to the office. Automatically she reached in for the light switch. Fluorescent lighting illumined the two adjoining offices. Its familiar hum gave a friendly sound to the place.

Mary Helen looked around. Everything was exactly as she remembered it from Friday. The philodendron in its aqua pot was sitting on the file cabinet. A small wicker basket full of pencils and pens was on one corner of the desk, the beige metal "in" and "out" baskets, one on top of the other, on the other corner. The computer, disc drive, and printer were lined up along the wall, all neatly covered with see-through plastic covers. Yes, everything was just the same, except for one important factor. Suzanne would never be back to sit behind that desk. Never again would Mary Helen see her bent over the computer keyboard, her scrawny little neckbone showing where her straight black hair separated and fell over her shoulders. Plain, reliable, soft-spoken Suzanne was gone. Mary Helen could feel hot tears crowd her eyes. She forced them back. Now was not the time for sentiment. Now was the time for action!

Yet, for a few moments she stood reverently in the middle of Suzanne's small cubbyhole of an office, pondering the imponderable whys of life and death.

Then, adjusting her glasses on the bridge of her nose, she set to looking around Suzanne's office for a clue.

She had been correct about one thing. Obviously Inspectors Murphy and Gallagher had not yet arrived. Everything was in apple-pie order. Suzanne was—had been—so neat and tidy. That was one of the reasons Mary Helen suspected she might have been a nun; one you could put your finger on anyway. Thinking of her own desk, she amended her reasoning. The girl had been like a young nun fervent and fresh from her novitiate training.

She had mentioned her suspicions to Eileen.

"Take a look at our Anne," Eileen had reminded her. "She's a young nun, fresh from her novitiate, and there's not a thing neat and tidy about her office."

"She's creative," Mary Helen had countered.

"That may well be," Eileen conceded, "but the point I'm making is, it's best not to stereotype. *Neat* and *nun,* young nun, that is, are not necessarily synonymous."

Mary Helen had to agree. Yet, as she looked around Suzanne's office, she could not help thinking of it as "nunny-neat."

Carefully she opened the long wooden cupboards.

Nothing there. Not "nothing," really. Just supplies neatly stacked. In the metal file the alumnae folders were carefully labeled. Each folder followed the one in front of it with not a corner out of whack. The desk drawers were the epitome of order. Even the pencils in the wicker basket were freshly sharpened. Disgusting, Mary Helen thought, slamming the narrow top drawer shut. She was unable to find one personal or revealing thing.

Even the desk pad had the December calendar centered on the green blotter. Suzanne must have remembered to do that before she left on Friday. Now, that's efficient! Mary Helen shook her head. Why, there wasn't so much as a decent layer of dust on the desk. For no reason she could think of, or at least for no reason she would admit, Mary Helen pushed the pad askew. At least now the desk looked a little human. Feeling better, she smiled. Then she saw it; the corner of a snapshot shoved under the desk pad, as though someone had done it hurriedly. But why? She picked up the snapshot and studied it closely. A slight young man was standing behind Suzanne. The couple was posing in front of a rather scrawny tree. His arms were around her and his hands were resting on her—adjusting her bifocals, Mary Helen took another look—his wide square hands were actually cupping her breasts. What a pose, Mary Helen thought, scrutinizing Suzanne's face. The girl looked embarrassed, but not unhappy. No wonder the Polaroid wasn't framed and sitting on the desktop.

Squinting, Mary Helen tried to make out the young man's face. An overhanging tree branch lined it with shadows. She thought she detected a smirk, but that may have been her imagination. The fellow was thin, blondish, not much taller than Suzanne. What features she could make out were even. Something about him looked vaguely familiar. Had she seen him before? Mary Helen tried to concentrate. Was he a delivery boy, maybe? The bread man or the milkman? The fellow who filled the vending machines in the Student Union? Or was he just one of those people who have a familiar face?

She held the snapshot in a better light. The UPS man? Mary Helen tried to visualize the fellow's face in a brown suit with a clipboard in his hand. Nothing came clear.

She shook her head. One thing was certain, Suzanne had never brought him around the office.

A loud click from down the hall startled her. Catching her breath, she whirled toward her open office door. The hall outside was empty. Who could that be? she wondered, tightening her jaw. Who would be in an empty building at this time on a Sunday morning? Mary Helen listened, but all she could hear was her own heart beating. Cautiously she moved toward the doorway.

"Yoo-hoo," she called, her mouth dry. "Who's there?"

"Only me," Anne's low voice called back. "I'll be working in my office for a while. Did I scare you?"

Mary Helen ignored the question. *Scare* was too big a word. *Surprised* would have been more like it, she told herself.

"Look what I found." Relieved, she walked down the corridor toward the Campus Ministry Office with the snapshot.

Anne looked. "Should you be in there," she asked, "touching things?"

"After all, it *is* my office!" Mary Helen felt a bit huffy. It was amazing how cautious these young nuns were about some things! She caught herself. Was she beginning to sound like Therese?

Shocked at the sudden pique, Anne shrugged and looked again at the picture.

"Besides," Mary Helen added before Anne could say

anything else, "I was just about to call Kate Murphy. May I use your phone?"

"Sure." Anne cleared away a jumble of notes from around her Mickey Mouse phone.

"What do you think of the picture?" Mary Helen asked while she waited to be connected to the Homicide Detail. She felt a little silly holding the receiver from a grinning Mickey Mouse while she called the police.

"That's some pose." Anne handed the picture back.

"That's what I thought," Mary Helen said. Maybe there wasn't such a generation gap after all.

"Doesn't fit the Suzanne we knew, does it." Anne was making a comment more than asking the question. "What's that Eileen says about still water?"

"Still water runs deep." Impatiently, Mary Helen tapped the edge of the photo on the desk, wishing she could place that young man. Surely he'd be able to take some of the mystery out of Suzanne. What had Kate called her? A mystery woman?

She wondered for a moment if this fellow was what Suzanne had wanted to tell her about a month or so ago. Or why she had asked, just last week, if she was happy in the convent. Oh, how she wished she hadn't scared poor Suzanne off.

When she finally was connected, the inspector on duty told her that Kate Murphy was off today. "It's Sunday, lady," he said.

She called Kate at home. The line was busy. The second time she called she let the phone ring and ring, but no one answered.

Frustrated, she called Homicide again and left a message for Kate to call her back.

Kate woke early on Sunday morning. Before nine she was up, showered, and had breakfast under way.

"What's gotten into you this morning, Ms. Murphy-dash-Bassetti?" Jack asked when the aroma of lean bacon sizzling finally pulled him out of bed and led him downstairs into the kitchen.

Shivering against the morning chill, Jack pulled his old blue woolen robe tightly around him.

He could use a new robe for Christmas, Kate thought, watching him pad barefoot across the worn linoleum.

"Need any help?" He settled on a kitchen chair and yawned, then shivered again.

"You shouldn't come down here barefoot." Kate put a mug of coffee on the table in front of him. "You'll catch your death of cold."

"Okay, Ma," Jack said, playfully patting her slim hip.

My God, Kate thought, moving back to the frying pan, I am beginning to sound like my mother. What's worse, I'm beginning to sound like his mother.

"What are we doing today?" Jack ran his fingers through his tousled black hair. This was the first Sunday they had both had off in over a month and Kate was looking forward to it. She had made up her mind that nothing and nobody, not even murder and Sister Mary Helen, were going to interfere.

"First of all," she said, "let's eat and get out of this house so nobody can catch us on the phone."

"Agreed." Jack reached over and took the receiver off the kitchen extension. "That's in case they try." He winked. "I was afraid this Mount St. Francis homicide was going to wreck our Sunday." He took a sip of his hot coffee.

"For the moment, it's at a standstill." Kate placed a platter of bacon and eggs between them. "No one seems to know a thing about the gal. We've sent her prints to Sacramento. The coroner will need a couple of days with the body. No one saw or heard anything unusual. Damnedest thing!"

"The case of the mysterious woman . . . I can see the *Chronicle* now." Jack laughed.

Kate nodded. "Let's not think about it today, pal." She refilled both mugs with coffee.

"How about the ten o'clock Mass at St. Thomas's? Today's the first Sunday of Advent."

Jack nodded. Strangely, right after they were married they had begun to go back to church on Sunday. Neither had said anything about it. It was just one of those tacit agreements that happen. Kate had purposely avoided mentioning it to Mama Bassetti. She didn't want her mother-in-law to think that the marriage was becoming too traditional.

"Then let's go Christmas-tree hunting!" Kate's blue eyes sparkled with excitement. She loved Christmas, although somehow the preparation for it was almost more enjoyable than the actual event. Even as a child she had loved the anticipation: the Advent Wreath with its candles, the small sacrifices the nuns had taught her to make in preparation for the coming of Christ. For years she had practiced the ancient Kris Kringle custom of doing kind little things for someone anonymously. Kate had always chosen her father as her Kris Kringle and somehow he had never guessed that his "red-headed handful" was the one shining his shoes or pressing his tie. That made it even more exciting. She relished the long, purple vigil culminating in the splendid mystery that burst into light at Midnight Mass. Kate even loved shopping, wrapping, and hiding the gifts, and decorating. Although she wasn't quite sure how Jack's patience would fare while stringing popcorn for the tree, she thought she'd try it this year.

Standing at the stove, she felt his arms close around her. His chin rubbed her cheek.

"Why don't you go shower?" she said. "I'll clean up the dishes and we can get started."

Reluctantly, he let her go, but not before he nuzzled her neck, kissing it softly.

"Don't forget to shave," she called after him, her cheek and neck still tingling.

"Yes, Ma," she heard him call as he took the narrow stairs two at a time. I am going to have to stop that, Kate thought, biting her lower lip.

The day went beautifully. Even the weather cooperated. The fog remained wet and cold all day long. It kept a kind of sharpness that makes people walk quickly, then dash into stores to get away from the bite. All in all it was the kind of Sunday that made Kate tingle with Christmas.

The couple had quickly located a small Christmas-tree lot where a tubby little Italian man with a heavy black cigar stuck in the corner of his mouth took great pride in selling them a perfectly shaped tree. Jack had cursed a bit tying it to the top of their Toyota, but that was part of the fun.

They had talked and giggled and ducked into all the quaint little shops along Union Street so Kate could search for just the right ornament to mark this year.

By four o'clock, however, Jack declared he was starving. Maybe it was the early breakfast. Maybe he was running out of patience with the quaint little shops along Union Street. At any rate, he knew not only that he wanted to eat, but where.

"There's a new place the guys at the Detail were telling me about in Noe Valley," he said.

"Noe Valley?" Kate was surprised. There were a dozen restaurants on Union Street.

"Yeah. An old mortuary made into a bar and grill. Still has the stained-glass windows."

"Mortuary?" Kate shivered. For a moment she thought about Suzanne and wondered how Mary Helen was doing. The poor old nun! What a shock to have discovered Suzanne's brutalized body. And how peculiar that she had no emergency information on her secretary. That seemed out of character for Mary Helen. Kate winced when she thought of their phone call yesterday. She should never have said "we." She hoped Mary Helen didn't think she should get involved. Kate would be reluctant to stop her, since she had been so much help on the last case, yet murder was dangerous business. Much too dangerous for a nun, no matter how well-meaning.

"What are you stewing about?" Jack asked, interrupting her thoughts.

Kate dropped her hand. Unconsciously she had been twisting a thick strand of hair around her finger. "Nothing," she said. "Nothing that I'm not going to stop thinking about immediately." Today was her day with Jack and she had determined not to think about work.

Just as Jack had said, the Noe Bar and Grill was a renovated mortuary. The inside, except for the stained-glass windows, was a study in wood. The interior decorator had made every effort to make it look rustic and woodsy. As far as Kate was concerned, he had succeeded. She was grateful, however, she was not the one who had to water and feed all those hanging plants.

Seated at the corner table, they both had ordered the house specialty, eggplant parmigiana. Jack called for a bottle of expensive Italian wine while they waited.

"You enjoy today?" he asked, taking her hand across the table.

"Loved it."

"You really are crazy about Christmas, aren't you, hon?" Jack smiled that crooked smile.

"Love it," she admitted. "I'm just like a kid."

"Yeah, Christmas is really great for kids . . ."

Before he even finished his sentence, Kate could feel herself start to bristle. She hoped he was not going to bring up having kids again and spoil a perfectly beautiful Sunday together.

Jack must have noticed. He didn't say any more, just sat there silently holding her hand, smiling that long-suffering smile.

All at once she could feel the hot flush of anger rise in her face. Abruptly she pulled her hand away from his. Jack looked puzzled, but still said nothing. Kate wished he'd shout or rant or rage. But he simply picked up his tulip-shaped glass and took a sip of wine. How dare anyone have such an easygoing, pleasant disposition? It was infuriating. And furthermore, if they ever did have children, with her luck the poor little things would inherit her temper.

"What's the matter, hon?" Jack asked softly. "Did I say something wrong?"

"Not really." Kate felt a little ashamed. He'd hardly said anything at all. "It's just that 'kid' thing. I know you want a family and I'm just not ready, Jack. I can't give up my career just yet. Someday maybe, but not yet. And when you said 'Christmas is great for kids,' I guess it made me feel guilty. And you know how mad it makes me to feel guilty."

"Hey, hon." Jack reached across the table and took Kate's hand. She let him. "There's no reason to feel guilty," he said. "It's our decision. I agreed to wait till we're both ready."

With her free hand, Kate picked up her glass and took a big swallow of wine. Its warmth slid all the way down.

"That's it. You agreed to wait. Agreed. Didn't decide. And underneath, I know you want kids," she said.

"Yeah. But they will need a mother and I'd like it to be you!"

Kate ignored his attempt to lighten the mood.

"And Christmas is a family time," she went on.

"Agreed," he said, "but . . ."

"And we're not getting any younger."

"For God's sake, Kate, you're beginning to sound just like my mother." This time Jack let go of her hand.

"That's another problem, your mother." Kate pouted.

"What the hell has my mother got to do with this?" Exasperated, Jack ran his fingers through his curly hair.

"I know she's still upset about my insisting on being Murphy-Bassetti and using Murphy at work."

"Two Officers Bassetti at the Hall of Justice would have been a little much. I explained that to her and even she understood." Jack rolled his dark eyes toward her.

"And I know she must be upset that we've been married over a year and I'm not pregnant yet."

"Frankly, Scarlett . . ."

"Don't say you don't give a damn, Jack, because I know you do." Kate felt hot, angry tears sting her eyes. She turned her head away.

Jack fumbled for his handkerchief. "Of course I give a damn, but not about what my mother thinks about your being or not being pregnant. I give a whole lot of a damn about us. I love you, Kate."

Kate looked up.

"Blow," he said, handing her his handkerchief.

Kate blew. "Are you sorry you married me?" she asked, feeling a little foolish.

"Sorry? I practically had to force you, if you remember."

"Are you sorry you forced me, then?"

"Kate Murphy-dash-Bassetti." Jack reached over and his hands cupped her freckled face. "You are the most stubborn, strong-willed, hot-tempered damn Irishwoman I've ever met. . . ."

"I think that's what you said the night you proposed."

"And I think I also said I'm a damn lucky man to have gotten you."

"Do you still feel that way?"

Leaning across the wooden table, Jack kissed her full on the mouth. "Absolutely, hon. And furthermore . . ." He paused for effect, nodding his head. "When we do have kids, they'll be the luckiest damn kids in the whole world."

"How's that?"

"Because they'll have two crazy parents who love each other deeply, warmly, passionately." Jack kissed her again.

Kate couldn't help smiling. Sweet, patient Jack. Somehow he was always able to put oil on her churning water.

"I guess we do love each other," she admitted.

"Damn right. Deeply, warmly, passionately," he repeated. Kate noticed a special emphasis on passionately. She giggled.

"Want to go home and practice up for parenthood?" Jack asked, his hazel eyes dancing.

"I guess we owe it to the kids," she answered, feeling a familiar ripple of excitement.

Grabbing her hand, Jack pulled her from behind the wooden table. Their waitress did look a little surprised when they asked her to fix their eggplant parmigiana to go.

TUESDAY—FIRST WEEK OF ADVENT

Sister Mary Helen was relieved to hear herself paged from the college switchboard. Since Sunday she had been waiting, not too patiently, for Kate to return her call. She hoped this was it. She was eager to tell the young woman about the Polaroid shot she had found under Suzanne's blotter. Mary Helen was sure it would make good evidence. Although she did not recognize the young man, maybe Mimi or somebody else could. It would at least give a clue as to Suzanne's associates, take some mystery out of the mystery woman.

"Sister Mary Helen speaking," she said into the phone, hoping not to sound too expectant, afraid she might sound too disappointed if the caller wasn't Kate.

"Hi, Sister." Mary Helen recognized Kate's voice immediately. She felt a wash of relief, but before she could speak, Kate went right on.

"The autopsy report is back," she said. Kate certainly didn't waste any words getting to the heart of the matter. Mary Helen grimaced. The mental picture of Suzanne's supple young body being sliced and divided by the thin blade of the scalpel flashed through her mind. Opening her eyes wide, she breathed deeply. Someone had told her that if you kept your eyes open wide and took deep breaths, you could not gag. She prayed that was true.

"Yes?" she said, swallowing hard, hoping Kate would not notice the tightness in her voice.

"The cause of death was a single stab wound through the heart. The letter opener."

We certainly did not need a coroner to tell us that, Mary Helen thought, remembering the thin opener protruding like a silver sliver from Suzanne's breast.

"Does August eighth mean anything to you?" Kate asked, after a short silence. "August eighth, 1973."

August 8? Mary Helen searched her mind, first for historical events, then for birthdays of patriots, statesmen, and saints, finally for Hallmark's Dates to Remember. August 8? Feast of St. Dominic was all that surfaced. She wished she'd paid more attention to the trivia game the nuns had been playing in the Community Room.

"Well, August eighth is the Feast of St. Dominic," Mary Helen answered. "That's the only thing that comes to my mind, but 1973 was certainly not the year of his birth. Why do you ask?"

"That was the date engraved on the letter opener."

Mary Helen was taken aback, but Kate didn't seem to notice. "There were bruises around her face and neck, but it was the opener that killed her," she repeated. "Suzanne put up a good fight. The coroner found particles of human skin under her fingernails."

"Then you'll be able to find her killer," Mary Helen said, instantly wishing she hadn't. Certainly she had read enough mysteries to know that the police can't just go around scratching people for no good reason except to compare skin particles.

"It's not quite that simple," Kate said, dismissing her remark in what Mary Helen thought was a bit of a patronizing tone. "The coroner did tell us one more interesting thing about your secretary," she continued.

The way Kate said "interesting" made Mary Helen forget all about Kate's condescension and planted a feeling of dread firmly under her ribs.

"What's that?"

"Our Suzanne Barnes had had a baby."

Mary Helen stood silent for a moment, cradling the phone. She couldn't believe it! For years she had heard the expression "You could have knocked me over with a feather." At this moment, she understood the hyperbole perfectly.

Imagine Suzanne—a mother! Admittedly, the girl had been private, but to have worked with someone for over a year and never to have known she had a child! That had to be the ultimate in private. And if Suzanne was a mother, where was the child, not to mention the child's father? Suzanne had never even hinted at a baby! I told Eileen she was hiding something, Mary Helen thought smugly. But a baby?

And what about the fellow in the picture? Could that be the baby's father? She was so shocked by Kate's news that she almost forgot to mention the photo to her.

"I have a little bit of news for you too," Mary Helen said as soon as she could gather her wits and get her breath. Her news seemed pale by comparison, unless, of course, it could lead to more information about Suzanne.

"Oh?" Kate said. *Oh* sounded interested. Mary Helen went on.

"I was in Suzanne's office and I found a picture of her with a young man."

Kate didn't say anything, so Mary Helen continued. "I think it may be important. They seem rather . . . ah . . . ah . . . intimate!" she said for lack of a better word. "Maybe it would give you a clue into Suzanne's friends."

"Do you recognize the fellow?" Kate asked.

"No," Mary Helen answered, wishing she could place that face, "but someone might," she added quickly, relieved Kate hadn't asked her what she was doing in the office.

"Thanks." Kate was businesslike. "I'll pick the photo up this afternoon. And by the way," she added, "the body should be released by Thursday, in case you want to have the wake and Funeral Mass at the college."

Mary Helen hadn't even thought about that. Of course Suzanne should have a proper wake and a proper burial.

Replacing the receiver, Kate picked up her right earring from the desktop and cocked her head to replace it.

"Why the hell do you wear those things?" Gallagher growled at her from across the double desk. "Have to take the damn things off every time you use the phone. Seems to me they're more trouble than they're worth," he commented for the hundredth time.

"Glamour," Kate said with a quick smile. "A lady cop ain't nothing if she ain't got glamour, Denny."

Snorting, Gallagher took a deep pull on his stubby cigar. A wreath of smoke circled his bald head.

"What did the old nun say?" he asked.

"Nothing much," Kate answered. "She found a photograph in the victim's office. Wants us to see it."

"How come we didn't find it?" Gallagher asked.

"She must have beat us to it."

"Oh, oh." Gallagher shook his head glumly.

"What . . . oh, oh?" Kate asked.

"Sounds like she is getting involved again. That's all we need. We haven't got enough trouble!"

"Why do you think I didn't return her Sunday call or her Monday call?" Kate asked.

"That's Sunday and Monday calls, plural, no triple," O'Connor called from the next desk.

Kate ignored him. Slowly she twisted a thick strand of hair. What was she going to do? As unintentional as it was, she realized she had encouraged Sister by saying "we have a problem" when Mary Helen had returned her call on Saturday. Kate had picked that up immediately in the old nun's voice. She should have nipped it then. But she hadn't. And right now, she'd said "our Suzanne Barnes." She would have to stop that; tell Sister Mary Helen she couldn't get involved. But she was fond of the nun, and besides, the gal had an uncanny way of ferreting out the truth. Yet this was police business . . .

"This is police business," Gallagher said, repeating her thought. "She could get hurt. Besides, she's got no damn business nosing in it." Gallagher stood up and resolutely hitched his belt over his paunch.

"How are you going to tell her?" he asked.

"Gently, very gently," Kate said aloud. And very, very slowly, she thought.

By Tuesday noon, Mary Helen had checked with Sister Cecilia, the college president, and O'Mara's Funeral Parlor.

Sister Cecilia was in total agreement. Of course Suzanne should have a proper funeral and Mount St. Francis would be happy to provide it. O'Mara was gruff, but agreeable. "Our pleasure," he said after Mary Helen had explained the whole problem. She felt sorry for the undertaker. His mother-in-law was a longtime friend and benefactor of the Mount. His life wouldn't be worth living if he refused to bury Suzanne gratis. "I'll pick the deceased up Thursday," he said. "We'll have her ready Friday. Our pleasure," he repeated. Poor O'Mara.

Kate Murphy arrived right after lunch. Mary Helen handed her the photo of Suzanne and whoever. Kate just looked.

"I wonder who this guy is," she finally said aloud.

"I don't know, but I'm sure they were close," Mary Helen answered, belaboring the obvious.

"Where did you find it?"

"In Suzanne's office . . . under the blotter on her desk."

"Did you find anything else?"

Mary Helen was a bit annoyed by Kate's question, although she should have been gratified. She'd fully expected Kate to tell her to stay away from Suzanne's office. "If I had," she said with a bit of an edge on her voice, "I would have told you!"

"Just checking," Kate said, studying the old nun's face for a moment. "Oh, by the way, Sister . . ." She must be satisfied, Mary Helen thought, since she is going to change the subject.

". . . When we were going through Suzanne's car we found your prayer book."

Mary Helen could feel her face flush. Obviously Kate hadn't opened the book's cover! Someday soon she'd have to remind the young inspector that you cannot always tell a book by its cover, and that her plastic cover had served her well.

Today, however, was not the time.

"I thought you might need it," Kate said, "so I bent regulations just a little. I took it out of the car and gave it to Suzanne's next-door neighbor before anyone noticed."

"Mimi?"

"That's the name." Kate checked her notebook. " 'Mimi Heagerty, Apt. 206.' She was right there, so I slipped it to her for you to pick up later."

"Thanks," Mary Helen said. "I'd like to visit Mimi anyway. Poor dear was so upset."

WEDNESDAY—FIRST WEEK OF ADVENT

Wednesday morning, Mary Helen woke up early. She wasn't sure if it was the foghorns that woke her or the heavy lump of sadness she felt in her chest.

Dressing quickly, she stepped outside the convent. Thick fog encompassed the college like a wet cocoon. The weather was terrible, perfect for mourning. Six-fifteen, and it was still as dark as the proverbial pitch. This is when they could have used some of that daylight they were always saving, she thought. Or better yet, she could have stayed in bed. Isaiah had prophesied "Woe unto them that rise up early in the morning." At this hour she couldn't quite remember the rest of the prophecy, although she thought it was something about having too much to drink. Anyway, this morning the first part fit perfectly. It was a "woeful" morning.

The sharp wind pulled at her heavy Aran sweater and made her nose and eyes water. She could see her breath as she made her way across the deserted campus toward the chapel. She'd be early for morning office. Good. She needed a little time alone with God to think.

Mary Helen swung back the heavy brass door to the chapel. The lights in the sanctuary were already on, but the body of the chapel was empty. The steam heat made a friendly hiss. She walked up the middle aisle, genuflected, and settled into her high-backed pew. She could hear Always Prepared—Sister Therese's staccato footsteps hurrying about in the sacristy, setting out the purple satin vestments for the morning Mass. Everything seemed so peaceful, so ordinary.

It was hard to believe that at this moment conscientious, quiet Suzanne lay on a cold morgue slab, her thin body mutilated. And that buried within her was the secret of her killer.

And her baby. Mary Helen still could hardly believe that Suzanne had had a child—and where was the poor little thing now? Alive? Dead? Abandoned? It didn't seem right. Advent, when the world was waiting expectantly for the birth of a Child, while Suzanne had concealed hers. Why? Right after breakfast, Mary Helen determined, she would grab Eileen, visit Mimi, and find out a few whys. Besides, she had to retrieve her prayer book, didn't she?

California Street was festively decorated in greens, reds, and blues, but was nearly deserted when the two nuns pulled up to Suzanne's apartment building. It was so deserted, in fact, that Mary Helen could make a U-turn and park right in front.

When Mary Helen finally curbed the wheels and pulled the key from the ignition, Eileen let her breath out slowly.

"Glory be to God, Mary Helen," she said, "this detecting business must be going right straight to your head. You are beginning to drive like something right out of *The Streets of San Francisco.*"

"This is police business," Mary Helen said, hoping she didn't sound too officious, just officious enough.

"I hope you can explain that to the two officers coming down the street." Eileen pointed to a black-and-white patrol car moving slowly down California toward them.

This time Mary Helen was the one who let her breath out slowly when the black-and-white rolled right by.

"Look at the second floor." Mary Helen was still locking the car door. "Last bay window on the right."

Pulling her sweater collar around her ears, Eileen

looked up. "All I see are lace curtains, and it's Irish lace at that!"

"They moved," Mary Helen said. "As soon as I slammed the car door, I swear I saw them move."

Eileen's bushy eyebrows shot up. She shook her head in disbelief. "In all this wind and fog, you saw the curtains move, two stories up at that? You had better give me the name of your eye doctor, old dear. He must be a miracle worker!"

Ignoring her, Mary Helen adjusted her bifocals and marched to the doorway of the apartment building. She pushed the button beside Apartment 206.

After a moment, Mimi's sleepy voice came through the small speaker holes.

"Who is it?" she said.

"Sister Mary Helen. I'm sorry I woke you. I've come for my prayer book."

"Prayer book?" Even though she was half asleep, Mimi giggled. Or at least Mary Helen thought she heard a giggle.

Unlike Kate, Mimi had obviously opened the book.

"Come on up, Sister," she said, pushing the buzzer to release the front door.

"How, in the name of God, are you going to explain a prayer book cover on your murder mystery?" Eileen asked as soon as the two were in the stuffy vestibule.

"Some things are better left unexplained," Mary Helen answered. Someone important must have said something like that once, she thought. Or if they didn't, they should have.

Neither nun spoke until they reached the second floor. They needed every bit of breath they had to climb the steep, narrow apartment house stairs.

As soon as they opened the heavy door leading to the second floor, Mary Helen heard a latch click at the far end. She stopped and listened, giving her eyes time to adjust to the semidarkness of the hallway. Then she saw him, a tall hulk of a man outlined against the dull light of the hall window. Startled, she felt a little shiver of fear prickling down her spine. For a moment the man just stood staring.

Then, clutching a worn tweed cap in his hands, the burly frame lumbered toward them, looking for all the world, Mary Helen thought, like an unmade bed. As he drew closer she studied his face. Early seventies, she reckoned, with that ruddy Irish look. Examining the high color a bit closer, she noticed the thin network of surface veins that produced it. A less practiced eye might have attributed the healthy glow to fresh air and exercise. Mary Helen knew better. A small unlit cigar was lodged in one corner of his thin mouth. It looked like a permanent fixture.

"Morning, 'Sters," he said out of the unencumbered side of his mouth. "And a miserable morning it is too." He shook his balding head sadly.

"Now, don't get me wrong, 'Sters. I'm glad to be alive even on a miserable morning. Many's that wished they were." Dejectedly he twirled the old wool cap, melancholy oozing from every pore. He loved it. He shot a knowing glance toward the sealed door of Suzanne's apartment.

"Turrible business went on right here in our own apartment building. You must have read about it."

"Do you live in this building?" Mary Helen asked with a sweet smile, knowing full well he did. What else would he be doing in the building?

"Yes indeed. That last one is my apartment." He pointed to the last door on the far right. "I've a front window. Fine view of California Street."

And I bet you don't miss a single thing that goes on out there either, Mary Helen thought. She felt sure now that she had, most certainly, seen that curtain move.

"Turrible business," he repeated, shaking his head.

"Don't get me wrong, 'Ster, but The City just isn't what it used to be. Full of degenerates, perverts. Was a time I could leave my apartment door open. But no more."

I bet you don't miss much that goes on in the hallway either, Mary Helen thought.

"Have you lived here long, Mr. . . . ah . . . ?"

"Flaherty, Patrick Flaherty. Be honored if you'd call me Pat."

"How do, Pat." Eileen extended her chubby hand. Flaherty hesitated, staring uncertainly at Eileen's outstretched hand. Mary Helen wasn't sure for a moment whether he was going to shake it or kiss it. Probably trying to remember the protocol, she told herself. Most likely the last time he'd spoken to a nun she'd had both hands decorously tucked into her long black sleeves.

"Have you lived here long?" Mary Helen repeated her question, mercifully giving Flaherty a distraction. Eileen took the chance to move her offending hand up to scratch her head.

"Long? I've lived here since the folks passed away, God rest them." They all paused a moment out of reverence for the departed Flahertys.

"Right after the war. The big one. World War II. Both passed away. You know that Spam was awful hard stuff on the old people's stomachs. Sold the family home. Moved in here. Just stayed on after I retired from the Muni." Flaherty stopped to calculate. "Five years now.

"Don't get me wrong, 'Sters, but even the Muni isn't what is used to be. Was a time us motormen knew the passengers, waited for the regulars to cross the street. Now they'd just as soon shut the door in your face and run you over. Can't blame them, though, what with muggings, robberies, punks carving the seats. Turrible business." Flaherty paused again to reflect on the horrors of today's society.

Mary Helen shifted impatiently. "Then you must have known our Suzanne?" she asked, after what she considered a respectful silence.

"Girl in 204? Knew her by sight. Nodded when we passed. Nice polite girl. Lots quieter than the rest."

"Than the rest?" Eileen asked, with just enough interest in her voice to encourage Flaherty to go on. Although Mary Helen wasn't sure he needed much encouragement.

"My neighbors." Flaherty pointed to Apartment 203. "Skinny little thing lives here. Name of Iris Adams. Now, don't get me wrong, 'Sters, but I ask you, who would baptize an infant Iris? Why, that's a flower, not a saint."

Mary Helen was about to confide to Flaherty that one of her grandnieces had been christened Holly and the other Heather, but thought better of it.

"Iris is a haircutter. Calls herself a 'stylist.' Don't get me wrong, but in my books a haircutter is a haircutter.

"Next door to her, 201: Arnold Shultz. Wimpy-looking little guy, thick glasses, a librarian. Who ever heard of a man librarian? But don't let that fool you. Books aren't his only love. Girls, too. Every weekend, girls, and it's not always the same one. I even caught him pestering 204."

"Suzanne?"

"That's right, 204. But she passed him like a freight train passes a bum, if you get my meaning. Think it made him sore too. Not used to being turned down." Flaherty shifted the cigar in the corner of his mouth.

Watching him, an old couplet of Ogden Nash's popped into Mary Helen's mind:

"There are two kinds of people who blow
    through life like a breeze
And one kind is gossipers and the other kind
    is gossipees."

"Now, on the other side of the hall, 202." Flaherty

went on unabashed. "That's Ms. Farraday, a schoolteacher. First or second grade, I think. Gets mad as hops if you call her 'Miss' by mistake. Every Christmas, Ms. Farraday has a little open house for the floor. Nice party, good eats. A little cheer, if you get my meaning. Nice apartment, too, but like a jungle."

"Jungle?"

"Regular botanical gardens like in the park. Hanging plants all over, even in the toilet! Don't get me wrong, 'Sters, but what kind of woman hangs plants in a toilet?"

Mary Helen looked over at her friend. Eileen's gray eyebrows had shot up and her eyes were open wide. Mary Helen knew exactly what she was thinking! *How in the world does he know what Ms. Farraday has in her bathroom?*

"Then there's these two!" He pointed to Apartment 206. "In my day doctors was respectable, if you get my meaning. This one got a beard and a wild look in his eyes. Plus which, I don't mean to offend you, 'Sters, but he's living with a cute little lady that works in a café."

"You mean Mimi?"

"That's right. Mimi. Real name's Maureen Heagerty. With a good Irish name like that you'd think she'd be better brought up, wouldn't you, now?"

Without warning, Flaherty plopped his tweed cap on his head and tipped it toward the two nuns. "Don't get me wrong, 'Sters, but I've promised to meet with a few of the lads. Don't want to keep them waiting."

Mary Helen watched the heavy door close behind Flaherty's massive frame. "I'll bet the meeting's been called at the Would You Believe? on Geary," she whispered to Eileen. "What do you think?"

"I really don't know what I ought to think," Eileen whispered back, "but for one thing, I hope to heaven that we didn't get him wrong."

"Well, at least," Mary Helen said, "I hope we got his meaning."

Both nuns were giggling when a sleepy-eyed Mimi finally opened her apartment door. They didn't stay long. Mary Helen would have liked to, but Mimi, groggy-eyed and wearing only a long T-shirt, simply handed her the paperback.

"Didn't even suggest we come in and sit down," Mary Helen grumbled to Eileen as the two nuns started down the stairs.

"It's just as well." Eileen patted her friend's arm. "I really should get back to work. It is funny, isn't it, how life doesn't pause even for the cruelest of tragedies. And you'd better do a little something with yourself too," she added when they reached the lobby. "Leave this murder business to the police."

Mary Helen knew her friend was right. This was a job for Kate Murphy, but she couldn't stand going back to the alumnae office just yet. She couldn't go back to work as if nothing had happened, as if someone hadn't drained the life out of Suzanne. She clutched her paperback. How she wished she hadn't given up reading mysteries for Advent. Reading would at least be a distraction. Maybe she should relent a little. Read only on Sundays. After all, even the pre-Vatican Church had considered Sunday a day of relaxation from fast and abstinence. Heaven forbid she should be holier than the Church! Why, Christ Himself had condemned the Pharisees for keeping to the letter of the law and not to the spirit. God would surely want her to enjoy Sunday even during Advent, wouldn't He?

"Pardon me, Sister." A deep, almost hollow voice startled Mary Helen. Fortunately, it was a woman's voice. Sister Mary Helen was positive God was male, no matter what Sister Anne said.

She turned to face a short butterball of a woman with bright red chipmunk cheeks standing in the doorway of the manager's apartment. Her sharp blue eyes showed signs of recent tears. A crisp gingham apron enveloped her faded wash dress.

"I've something here," she said, waving a thin, inexpensively bound magazine. "Mailman just delivered it for Suzanne." She fumbled in her pocket for a tissue, found one, and dabbed at her eyes. "Poor girl. It's one of those religious magazines. But of course she's gone, so I thought one of you nuns might like to read it." She handed the publication to Mary Helen.

"Nothing like this ever happened before in my apartment building. And such a nice quiet girl too." She dabbed her eyes again and blew her short, stubby nose. "No sense standing here in the drafty lobby, blubbering. Can you Sisters come in for a cup of tea? I've just taken a loaf of bran bread out of the oven. I'm Mrs. McGrath, the landlady."

So Mrs. McGrath wasn't so interested in passing on religious literature as she was in having a bit of company. Mary Helen looked at her watch, then at Eileen. One look told her that the thought of fresh-baked bran bread had pushed the pursuit of duty right to the bottom of her friend's priority list.

Even on a dreary wet December day, Mrs. McGrath's apartment was warm and cozy. The aroma of fresh bread hung in the air. In no time at all the three women were seated around the kitchen table, chatting like old friends.

"We ran into Mr. Flaherty on the second floor," Mary Helen said as she watched Mrs. McGrath slice the round crisp loaf.

"That old busybody!" The woman slapped a generous cut of soft butter on the warm bread. "Bet you girls got an awful earful from him!" She handed the slice to Eileen, who wiggled with anticipation.

"I'd throw the old coot out, except he has no place to go, and besides, he's my husband Eddie's second cousin. God rest him!"

Mary Helen assumed she meant Mr. McGrath, not Pat Flaherty, who seemed to be in remarkably good health.

"Besides, as you know, blood's thicker than water."

Mouth full of bread, Eileen nodded. Mrs. McGrath continued. "Regardless, don't pay him no heed. A black Irishman, he is, sees the gloomy side of everything and everybody. Suzanne was a nice polite young girl."

"Did she have many visitors?" Mary Helen asked.

"Police asked me the same question." Mrs. McGrath drained her teacup. "Not too many that I know about. Palled with Mimi mostly. Had another fat, dark girl visit pretty regular. Don't know her name, but I'd know her by sight, I suppose."

"Ever see anyone suspicious-looking?" Mary Helen asked. Nothing ventured, nothing gained.

"Suspicious?" Mrs. McGrath's blue eyes twinkled. "If I'd listen to Pat, everybody looks suspicious."

"This fat, dark girl. You've no idea who she is?"

"None whatsoever."

Mary Helen was just about to ask if she'd noticed anything unusual on the night of Suzanne's murder when she felt Eileen kick her under the table.

"Why did you kick me?" Mary Helen asked indignantly when the two nuns were back on California Street.

"Glory be to God, you were beginning to grill that nice woman like a policeman. And besides, I thought you said you were not going to get involved in this murder business."

"If I remember correctly, you said I wasn't."

"Now don't be telling me . . ." Eileen stared at her friend incredulously.

Don't worry, I won't, Mary Helen thought. Politely but definitely, she changed the subject.

FRIDAY—FIRST WEEK

Just as Kate stepped out of the shower she heard the front door slam shut.

"I'm home, hon," Jack called up the front stairs.

She grabbed Jack's faded robe from the hook. Wrapping herself in it, she opened the bathroom door a crack. The sudden wedge of cold air jabbed the steam-filled bathroom and made her shiver.

"Up here," she shouted, quickly closing the door.

Kate slipped her feet into Jack's fur-lined slippers and pulled his robe tightly around her. She listened as her husband took the narrow steps two at a time, then opened the bathroom door just as he reached the top. No sense standing in the cold until you absolutely had to. A warm cloud of steam followed her into the hallway.

"I just finished," she said, pecking him on the cheek. "It's all yours, pal, but hurry."

"Hurry?" Jack looked puzzled. "Where the hell are we going?"

"Tonight's Suzanne's wake, Rosary at seven-thirty. Remember? One of us should be there. Check out who shows. I told Denny I'd go this time."

"Damn," Jack swore softly. Apparently he hadn't remembered.

"There are some celery sticks with peanut butter in the fridge," she said, "to tide you over. After, we can go out and—"

"You smell luscious," Jack interrupted. His mind was obviously not on celery sticks. "What is it?"

"Soap," Kate answered flatly. "Now, hurry," she added, "we don't have much time."

"Hurry and what?" Playfully, Jack enveloped her in a giant bear hug, pinning her arms tightly to her sides. His face nuzzled her hair, then he softly kissed her ear, her temple, her throat. The neckline of the old robe sagged.

"Pal, we've got to go," Kate protested weakly as his lips touched her breast.

"Why?" Jack asked, moving his mouth toward hers.

"Because I told Denny I would, and besides, I feel kind of guilty. I'm afraid we aren't going to be able to find the killer."

Jack's eyes shot open. He released his hold. "Run that by me again," he said.

"Suzanne's killer!" Kate walked into their bedroom, Jack close behind her, and sat on the edge of the bed.

Thoughtfully, she began to twist a strand of hair. "We've no real information on her, no one really knows who she is, where she came from. No one saw anyone or heard anything unusual on the night of her murder. So we have no real suspects. No place to go. And I feel bad about it. So the least I can do is to go to her Rosary and take you along, just in case you see something I don't. Does that make sense?"

Kate looked up. Jack stood above her, leaning against a poster of the old brass bed. His hazel eyes were patient, as always. I'm lucky to have him, Kate thought for the thousandth time. She reached for his hand.

"Does that make sense?" she repeated.

"Sort of." Jack took her hand and squeezed it. "But I'd hate to see you make it a practice to attend all the wakes of the unsolved murder cases in The City. Especially if you intend to drag me along."

"You know this is different." Kate rose from the bed. "This is my case—Denny's and mine. One of us has to go, and this girl was, after all, Sister Mary Helen's secretary."

"Almost like one of the family, huh?" Jack took off his jacket and began to loosen his tie.

"And that's another problem. I'm afraid Sister Mary Helen thinks she's going to help me solve the case. Denny was wild. Wants her to get the hell off of it. And he's right, you know."

"And he wants you to be the one to tell her she should get the hell off of it, right?" Jack smiled, visualizing Gallagher's dilemma.

Kate nodded.

"And tonight, I suspect?"

Kate nodded again. "Then there's the baby."

"Baby?" Jack asked, sitting on the edge of the bed and untying his shoes.

"Yes. The coroner's report showed that Suzanne had a baby. I thought I told you that."

"No," Jack said, removing his socks.

Kate sat down again and put her arm around Jack's hunched shoulders. "No one knows what happened to the baby. Seems sad, huh?"

"Which part?" Jack unbuttoned his shirt.

"All of it, but the baby especially. Giving birth is such a . . . a . . ." Kate fumbled for a word. "An awesome thing." As soon as the words left her lips, she wished she hadn't said them.

"Awesome, miraculous, joyful, wonder-filled, sacred. And all this can be yours, kid, for just the asking." Playfully, Jack pulled Kate over onto the wide bed, his body close beside hers.

She ran her index finger softly along his chin, then planted it on his lips.

"I thought you weren't going to bring up babies anymore," she said. "You know I'm not ready to settle into motherhood yet."

"Me!" Jack feigned shock. "If I remember correctly, you brought it up." He hesitated, then bent forward to kiss her. "But maybe I'm wrong. What with your warm body and that tantalizing aroma of soap, not to mention that glamorous robe, I could have lost my head." He kissed her again. "Can't blame a poor helpless cop, can you?"

Kate giggled. "We've got to go, pal," she said. "We'll be late."

"What's the rush?" Jack said, his voice low. "I have a feeling that your friend Suzanne isn't going anyplace."

Kate felt Jack move his hand slowly down her back. My God, she thought as he gently loosened the belt of her robe, this morning I forgot to take a pill.

The moment Sister Mary Helen opened the chapel door, she noticed Patrick Flaherty. Cap in hand, he stood against the back wall, right next to the holy-water font. That way he's sure not to miss a single mourner, Mary Helen thought, wondering for a minute why the old fellow was so interested.

Dipping into the marble font, she blessed herself, then nodded toward Pat, who had begun to fumble nervously with his cap.

"Evening, 'Ster." Pat shifted awkwardly. "Turrible tragedy," he muttered, apparently for lack of anything better to say.

"Yes, terrible," Mary Helen agreed.

"But she looks good, if you get my meaning. O'Mara's done a fine job."

In this case, saying something nice just didn't cut the

mustard. At a funeral, if you can't say something consoling, you shouldn't say anything at all. Mary Helen was just about to tell this to Pat Flaherty when Eileen pulled at her jacket.

"You had better hurry, Mary Helen," Eileen said, "if you intend to pay your last respects to Suzanne. Poor Cecilia is quite anxious about starting the Rosary on time."

"How do you know that?" Mary Helen asked her friend.

"Just look at her. She has a face on her like a frosty morning," Eileen whispered.

One look at Sister Cecilia assured Mary Helen that Eileen was one hundred percent correct. The college president stood in the front of the chapel, just in front of the sanctuary and to the right of the casket, stiffly greeting those who filed up to view the body. Her tense smile was firmly fixed in place. A frosty morning was putting it mildly.

Can't blame her, Mary Helen thought. Imagine a second murder case at Mount St. Francis. The horror of it will not set well with the board of directors, the trustees, the parents, the alums, let alone the students. Why, the poor girls were still uneasy about the murders on the hill last year. Not even the bravest wanted to roam around the campus alone. And you can't blame them, Mary Helen thought, shivering a little herself when she remembered her grisly discoveries.

A commotion in the vestibule announced the arrival of an on-the-spot television crew. Poor Cecilia! Her worst fears were about to be realized.

The two old nuns started up the middle aisle. The chapel was filling up quickly. People sat in clusters, visiting in hushed tones. Mary Helen recognized some students and faculty members. Some looked vaguely familiar, probably parents and boyfriends. Some were perfect strangers. For a moment she wondered angrily how many really cared and how many were merely curious. Several groups stopped mid-sentence when she passed. Probably wondering if I'm jinxed, she thought, trying to avoid their stares and the feeling that she might be.

She was glad to see Kate Murphy and her husband, Jack Bassetti, slip into the side pew. It was a welcome distraction. Kate looked a little flushed; probably rushing, since they were almost late. She waved.

Toward the front of the chapel, a small group huddled together. She recognized two of them immediately: Mrs. McGrath and Mimi. No Dr. Slater. He must be on call. She could guess who the others were from Flaherty's description.

The thin, stylishly dressed, almost masculine woman on the edge of the pew must be Iris, the haircutter. Everything about her was angular, everything, that is, that Mary Helen could see. Her honey-blond hair, cut like a Dutch boy's, her padded shoulders, even her short nose—all had a sharp, chiseled look.

Next to her sat a round, doughy-looking woman with curly henna-colored hair. Here and there strands of gray were beginning to push their wiry way into the red. Bright red lipstick gave her lips a rosebud look. Tiny jeweled Christmas trees dangled from her ears. Her loose-fitting all-weather coat was a mass of brightly colored sunflowers. In Mary Helen's opinion there were too many of them and they were too large and too bright for the roundness of the lady. That must be Ms. Farraday, she thought, lover of plants, although she didn't fit Mary Helen's idea of a Ms. at all.

The fifth member of the group was the slight young man who had held the door for her the morning she found Suzanne. She studied him closely. Thick, rimless glasses sat on the bridge of his prominent nose. Bearded, he looked like a young rabbi. Mary Helen took a second look. This must be

Arnold Schultz, the lady-wooing librarian. Well, there was no accounting for taste. Probably a good thing, too. . . .

Mimi recognized Mary Helen immediately and waved. The old nun waved back.

The front pew, the one usually reserved for family, was noticeably vacant. Its emptiness made Mary Helen's heart ache. No one, not one single relative or family friend, was there to mourn for Suzanne. It didn't seem right, especially at Christmastime, a time when the living yearn to surround themselves with family and old friends. Shouldn't the dead be given as much love?

Suzanne's body lay before the main altar. Six beeswax candles, like six sentinels, flanked the open casket. In their flickering light she looked so alive, so healthy, as though she had just fallen asleep on that soft white satin pillow. Mary Helen knelt on the prie-dieu beside the casket. She stared down at Suzanne, unable for a moment to comprehend the reality. She wanted to touch her face, hoping crazily that the girl would open her watery blue eyes and smile that bashful smile of hers. How Mary Helen would love to shout, "We made a mistake. Everybody go home now."

But as she gazed down at the frail young body that O'Mara had tastefully draped in soft azure, she knew it was true. Her mind shot back to the vivid scene. The bedroom a shambles, blood everywhere. Suzanne bruised and motionless.

Eileen tugged at her elbow and Mary Helen rose. Woodenly she slipped into a pew beside Cecilia. The college president knelt like a ramrod, looking for all the world like a TV commercial for tension headache. Poor Cecilia was trying to keep a stiff upper lip. Mary Helen suspected that before this was over not only her lip would be stiff, but her shoulder and her back and probably her bony knees too.

Father Adams entered the sanctuary, knelt on the bottom step. Behind her, Mary Helen heard the congregation rise, then kneel. The priest began the Rosary. Automatically she fumbled in her black leather case for her own worn set of beads. The steady rhythm and repetition of the ancient prayer slowly eased her tension and freed her mind.

"Holy Mary, Mother of God . . ." Who had done this terrible thing to dear Suzanne? Who could have done it?

"Truth will come to light; murder cannot be hid long." Hadn't Shakespeare said that? Mary Helen felt a bit better.

"Pray for us sinners . . . us sinners . . . us sinners." "Other sins only speak; murder shrieks out." Some seventeenth-century playwright or other had written that. From somewhere, it had popped into her mind. Suzanne's murder was shrieking at her. It must be explained.

After the Rosary, Sister Cecilia rose, walked rigidly to the pulpit, and announced a reception in the Student Union. The Mass of the Resurrection, she said, would be celebrated on Monday, since Holy Cross Cemetery did not bury people on Saturday. Meanwhile the body would be kept at O'Mara's mortuary.

By the time Mary Helen and Eileen arrived, the Student Union was crowded. Mary Helen shuddered. She didn't feel a bit like being sociable. The two headed for the punch bowl in the far corner.

"It's the one with the hooch in it," Eileen whispered on their way across the room.

"How do you know that?" Mary Helen whispered back.

"After years of college wakes, I can tell." Eileen winked. "It's always the one the faculty crowds around."

Mary Helen smiled in spite of herself. It was a mistake. A newspaper reporter, narrow pad in hand, sidled up to her. "Sister," he began, "is it true you found the body and the girl was your—"

Her well-practiced schoolmarm stare stopped him mid-question. Why not, she thought, watching the young man squirm. That same "school-face" had stopped generations of eighth-grade boys midprank.

The reporter was just beginning to summon up his courage for a second attack when Kate Murphy touched her arm.

"Excuse me, Sister," she said, "are you busy?"

"Kate." Mary Helen turned, leaving the reporter to find a new interviewee. "You don't know how glad I am to see you.

"And Jack too!" She gave the young couple an expansive hug and led them to the punch bowl. Out of the corner of her eye she could see the reporter heading straight for Sister Cecilia.

"How nice of you to come," she said as the three sipped spiked punch. "And how are we doing on finding poor Suzanne's murderer?" No sense wasting time on small talk. At these affairs, you never could tell how long it would be before someone interrupted your conversation.

Kate's face reddened. "We are trying," she said, "but it's very difficult with as little information as we have on the victim."

Mary Helen grimaced. She hated to hear Suzanne called "the victim." The victim is someone you don't know. "Then we'll just get some more," she said. It seemed simple to her.

Jack's hazel eyes twinkled. "I'll bet we will," he said, placing what Mary Helen considered undue emphasis on the *we*.

Kate was just about to say something when Mrs. McGrath joined the group. They made small talk for several moments before Kate and Jack Murphy-Bassetti excused themselves.

"I'm glad they finally left," Mrs. McGrath confided. "There's something I wanted to tell you privately."

Mary Helen led Mrs. McGrath to a far corner of the room, where, she hoped, they could talk without being disturbed.

"What is it?" Mary Helen was curious.

"You asked who came to see Suzanne?" Mary Helen nodded. "Well, I spotted her here." Mrs. McGrath cocked her gray head toward the center of the room. "Short, fat dark girl."

Mary Helen followed her gaze to, sure enough, a short, fat dark girl. "To Mimi's left?" she asked, just to make sure.

Mrs. McGrath nodded. "That's the one."

Mary Helen stared at Mrs. McGrath with new respect. The landlady had either been watching a lot of TV crime shows or was picking up the spirit of the chase. Whichever, it was fine with Mary Helen.

Quickly she elbowed her way across the Student Union until she stood right next to the girl. On closer look, she was really no girl. Her long, straight hair hanging loosely around her shoulders gave that impression. Close up, her face was weathered and hard. She was pudgy, no doubt about that. But the overweight was not the kind that comes from self-indulgence. It was the kind that you see among the poor or in boarding schools. The overweight that comes from too many starches and too many puddings—cheap filler-uppers.

Mary Helen would have been hard-pressed to tell anyone how she could tell the difference, but the fact of the matter was, she could.

"Hello," she said in a friendly conversational tone.

The young woman turned and greeted her with a sullen stare. No, maybe not sullen, more wary, Mary Helen thought, studying the woman's dark eyes.

"I'm Sister Mary Helen." The old nun introduced herself, then took a sip of her punch, waiting for the woman to give her name.

When she said nothing, Mary Helen made a second stab at conversation.

"Suzanne was my secretary," she said pleasantly. If at first you don't succeed . . .

Still the woman said nothing. She didn't even nod. Her eyes remained fixed on Mary Helen's face.

This was too big a fish to let off the hook without a fight. Mary Helen made a third attempt.

"I understand you were a friend of Suzanne's."

"Yeah," the girl answered. It isn't much, but it's a start, Mary Helen thought.

"And what's your name?" she asked, hoping the girl would go on.

"Reina. Reina Martinez."

Adjusting her bifocals, Mary Helen studied the young woman's face. Her straight bangs almost touched her brows. Her eyes were a liquid brown and cautious. They belonged to someone used to being used.

"Have you and Suzanne been friends long?" Mary Helen asked pleasantly.

"Long enough," the woman answered. Her chin protruded stubbornly, yet the nervous brushing back of her bangs gave her away.

"Were you school chums?" Mary Helen was trying to sound chatty.

The brown eyes scanned her from head to toe, then back up. "Sizing me up," one of Sister Mary Helen's private eyes would have said. Mary Helen wriggled uncomfortably.

"No," Reina answered. "I got to go now," she added. Mary Helen detected a little menace in her tone.

"Oh? Do you live in The City?" Mary Helen asked, undaunted.

"No, Calistoga."

"Calistoga! How interesting! Do you work there?" For a long moment Reina glared at the nun. Mary Helen was afraid she was going to say "What's it to you?"

"Yeah," she answered finally, turning away. "In the baths."

Frantically, Mary Helen searched the room for Eileen. Where is Eileen with all that chitchat when I need her? Mary Helen thought. By the time she spotted her friend, Reina Martinez had deftly slipped through the crowd and out of the Student Union.

"Glory be to God, what's up?" Eileen asked.

"Did you see the girl I was talking to?"

"I was too busy avoiding that reporter to be looking at who you were talking to," Eileen answered, obviously flustered.

"She's a friend of Suzanne's. Works in Calistoga. Maybe she's a lead."

"A lead to what?"

"To who knows what," Mary Helen said. "But it's one more lead than we had."

"We?" Eileen's gray eyes opened wide. "Did I hear you say 'we'? Shouldn't *we* let the police handle this investigation?"

Mary Helen chose to ignore the remark.

"When you had her cornered, why didn't you tell Sister Mary Helen to get off the case?" Jack asked Kate as the two drove home to 34th Avenue. "Politely, of course," he added.

"I was about to," Kate said, snuggling closer to him in the front seat of their car. "But I didn't have the heart."

"If you ask me," Jack said, putting his hand on her knee, "you didn't have the courage."

"Who asked you?" Kate said, and began to twist a lock of her red hair.

SUNDAY—SECOND WEEK OF ADVENT

The morning news woke Mary Helen early on Sunday. It came right through the wall from the Sister's bedroom next to hers. "Partly cloudy skies, with a chance of showers," the newscaster predicted just before he began a medley of Christmas carols.

Slowly, Mary Helen moved to the window of her bedroom and pulled back the curtain. It was just beginning to get light. The sky hanging over the college promised to be patchy blue with roaming clouds, heavy and black. A black-and-blue sky, just like Suzanne's bruised face, just like her own spirits.

She dressed warmly for the early Mass in her navy wool dress and heavy jacket. No matter which way the weather went, at eight o'clock on a Sunday morning the chapel would be cold.

Leaving the convent building, she walked slowly across the college campus toward the chapel. The campus was deserted and strangely silent. In the dull morning light, it appeared forlorn. The rose bushes bordering the formal gardens had lost their leaves and stood like barren clumps of black sticks. The azaleas, which could always be counted on for brilliant color, had not yet really begun to bloom, although if you looked closely, you could see clusters of buds and here and there one or two brave pink blossoms.

Even the statue of Saint Francis in the concrete bird bath looked abandoned. The saint was standing there all alone in the middle of the silent campus with his Franciscan robe trailing in the murky water. There was not so much as one single sea gull in sight.

Mary Helen was glad when she reached the chapel. The lights and heat were on and Sister Therese was busily arranging the altar for Mass. She was especially glad to see her friend Eileen already in the pew. Eileen always had a way of cheering her up. If not, misery loves company.

"Comfort, give comfort to my people . . ." The first reading at Mass for the Second Sunday of Advent prayed in the words of the ancient prophet Isaiah. Mary Helen wasn't sure exactly what his problem had been, but she knew she, too, could surely use a little comfort now. A little comfort and a lot of direction. Where should she start? Before they could begin to find Suzanne's killer, they must find out just who Suzanne really was.

After Mass and a quick breakfast, Mary Helen and Eileen decided on a walk.

"Clear our heads," Eileen had said. But Mary Helen knew better. Eileen was upset.

The two nuns started down Parker, cut over to Stanyan, and headed for Golden Gate Park. For several blocks they walked in comfortable silence.

The two stopped in front of the McLaren Lodge to study the hundred-foot Monterey cypress on the wide front lawn. They both knew they had really stopped to catch their breath, but neither one cared to admit it. Instead they kept up the mutual pretense of scrutinizing the huge tree. In a couple of weeks the San Francisco Fire Department and the Park and Rec tree toppers would string it with Christmas lights, just in time for McLaren's birthday and Christmas week.

"Feeling better?" Mary Helen asked, marveling once again that McLaren's mother had had the good grace to give birth to the great man just in time for Christmas.

"As well as can be expected under the circumstances," Eileen answered, "and how about you?"

"Same." Again they walked a ways in silence. The park was alive with joggers taking their run before the predicted showers began. Here and there glassy-eyed tourists stumbled along, cameras in hand, snapping pictures of the Dove of Peace in one of the rectangular flower beds outside the Conservatory, and the cactus-created Santa that had recently been planted in the other. Young couples walked along, holding hands or pushing strollers. Mary Helen enjoyed being surrounded with all this life, although she could never quite get used to seeing two clean-cut young men walking hand in hand.

"I just can't get Suzanne off my mind," Eileen said as they reached the Main Concourse. "Imagine you, of all people, Mary Helen, working with the girl for better than a year and not knowing anything about her!" She looked at Mary Helen as if she were seeing her in an entirely new light.

Mary Helen avoided her gaze. Instead she looked up at the two statues guarding the entrance.

Junipero Serra, robes flowing, held his cross high. Across from him, Unitarian clergyman Thomas Starr King kept his eye on the corner. No, she had not known Suzanne really. Who can really know someone else? Each individual is unique, so complex. Who can ever really figure out what makes someone tick. We are all so different.

Mary Helen studied the two statues more closely. These two men, for example. How different they were in their approaches to life, to death, even to God! She wondered, for a moment, why. Why did one man believe so wholeheartedly, so avidly, so sincerely, in Christ's divinity, while another man, just as wholeheartedly, just as avidly, just as sincerely, did not?

There were no real answers to that question, just as

there were no real answers to the whys of anyone's life and death. Why would one young woman be out looking for a killer, while another had become the killer's victim? And would that killer ever be found! In a brown study, Mary Helen turned around and headed for home. Eileen followed.

"Do you think Kate will ever be able to find out who killed Suzanne?" she asked, as if she had been reading her mind.

"I certainly hope so," Mary Helen said.

"But there are no witnesses, no suspects, no nothing."

Mary Helen told her about finding the snapshot under Suzanne's desk blotter.

"If we could only find out something," she added before Eileen could object. "Who her friends were, who the fellow in the picture is. If someone went home with her that night. Even what time she died. Anything would be helpful."

"I think I know what time she died," Eileen said.

Mary Helen stopped, astonished. "How in the name of all that's good and holy do you know that?"

"My Big Ben clock stopped," Eileen answered smugly.

"Your clock stopped? For the love of Pete, Eileen, what does that mean?"

"Well, old dear, there is an old Irish saying . . ."

Mary Helen groaned. Another old Irish saying. She wondered in amazement from where Eileen pulled all these sayings. Once again she half suspected her friend made them up.

"Yes, when a clock stops for no reason, the saying goes, someone has died," Eileen continued, unabashed, "and my clock stopped, for no reason, at three-seventeen A.M.! I'm sure that's when she died." She set her mouth. There was no use arguing logically with Eileen's set mouth. Besides, Mary Helen was speechless.

"But I wonder why someone would kill her so brutally." Eileen seemed unaware of Mary Helen's stare. "It must have been someone who was really demented, or who really hated her."

"Or really loved her."

"Loved her? How could you do something that horrid to someone you loved?"

"Wasn't it George Bernard Shaw, to quote another Irishman, who said, 'When we want to read of the deeds that are done for love, whither do we turn'?"

"To the murder column," Eileen finished the quote.

By the time the two arrived back at the college it had begun to drizzle. The soft gray rain covered the hill like a wet pall and blotted out The City. From here and there strings of colored Christmas lights gleamed through the mist. A flashing red star, hung on a far hill, reminded them that there was still life below.

The pall extended right through lunch. Everyone tried to be cheerful, but to Mary Helen the forced cheerfulness was much more wearing than downright honest gloom. Eileen must have felt the same. Right after lunch, she approached Mary Helen.

"I'm going to do something I haven't done for years," she said.

"What in the world can that be?" Adjusting her bifocals, Mary Helen studied her friend's face for signs of an erratic gleam in the eye.

"I'm going to take an afternoon nap!"

"That doesn't sound too bizarre to me."

"Frankly, Mary Helen, at our age it is probably not only not bizarre but a downright excellent idea. You should think about taking one too!" Eileen turned on her heel and left.

Just in time, too, Mary Helen thought, watching Eileen's round blue figure trot down the convent hall, then mount the narrow steps to the bedrooms. Imagine saying "at our age." Why, you are only as old as you feel! Everyone knows that!

Still annoyed, Mary Helen climbed the stairs toward her room on the second floor. Suddenly her legs felt wooden and heavy. She could have sworn someone had added a few steps. By the time she reached her room, she had to concede, but only to herself, of course, that maybe you are not so much as old as you feel, but as old as you are willing to admit.

Once in her room, Mary Helen was plagued with temptation. To read or not to read her murder mystery: that was the question. Life is too blasted short not to enjoy yourself, she thought, picking up the paperback and settling into her large leather chair.

Why, even if I did give these things up for Advent, God would want me to relax and enjoy myself on Sunday, she rationalized, running her hand over the plastic cover.

"You would, wouldn't You?" she asked, thankful once again that God did not answer aloud. She could imagine His horse laugh.

Feeling a little foolish, she shoved the murder mystery under her chair. Life is too short, too blasted short, especially at your age, she fussed, pushing herself up from the chair, to start fooling yourself.

Purposefully, she rummaged through her nightstand for something to read.

She was surprised to discover a copy of *St. Jude's Messenger* among her other books. For a moment she couldn't remember where she had picked up the magazine. Then it dawned on her. It was the one Mrs. McGrath had given her.

She turned it over. Sure enough, Suzanne's name and

address had been handwritten on the address label. But what had been crossed out? She scrutinized it closely. *Sister Mary Bonaventure,* the original said. *Aquinas Center, 95 East Lake Road, Erie, Pennsylvania.*

Who was Sister Mary Bonaventure? Mary Helen wondered, but not for long. Whoever this Bonaventure was, she would know something about Suzanne. She'd bet her eye teeth on that one. She could even be Suzanne. Or was that too much of a long shot? For a moment Mary Helen tried to visualize Suzanne in a white Dominican habit, being called "Bonaventure," but only for a moment. Then she went immediately to the phone.

Sunday the rates are low, she thought, dialing long-distance information in Erie. In her heart she knew the rates had very little to do with her making the phone call. She simply could not wait until Monday. She dialed the number the operator gave her.

The phone rang at least twenty times before someone picked it up. She had begun to lose patience after about ten rings and would have hung up except she suspected the place was full of nuns. If it was anything like Mount St. Francis, they all heard the phone and each one wondered, irritably, why some one else didn't answer it.

"Good afternoon, Aquinas Center," a soft, sweet voice answered.

"May I please speak to Sister Mary Bonaventure?" Mary Helen asked.

There was a long pause. "I'll connect you with Mother General," the voice responded.

Mother General! Mary Helen was surprised. She must have dialed the generalate of an order. With names like Bonaventure and Aquinas, it was no doubt Dominican.

She could lay odds that the place had once been called St. Thomas Aquinas Convent. Then things started going

"Center." The trend had so annoyed Therese that when their own order's motherhouse became a "Center," she had remarked, "This won't stop until they've changed O'Mara's mortuary to Dead Center!" Nobody thought that was as funny as O'Mara did!

After what seemed ages, a crisp, efficient voice answered, "Sister Thomasine's office."

"I'm sorry," Mary Helen said, "I wanted Sister Mary Bonaventure and the Sister who answered the phone told me she'd connect me to the Mother General."

"This is Mother General's office. May I help you?"

"I wanted Sister Bonaventure." Mary Helen was getting so frustrated, she dropped the *Mary*.

"To whom am I speaking?" The voice was annoyingly businesslike.

"My name is Sister Mary Helen. I'm with Mount St. Francis College in San Francisco and I want to speak to Sister Bonaventure."

"Sister, the Sister on the turret was absolutely correct. Mother General is the one to speak to about Sister Bonaventure. Mother General's name is Sister Thomasine."

"Then, may I speak to her?" Mary Helen asked, conjuring up in her mind what a "turret" looked like. "By the way," she added just for the ducks of it, "to whom am I speaking?"

"Sister Alberta. I'm Mother General's secretary. And I'm sorry, Sister Thomasine is at a meeting. We are not expecting Sister home until next Sunday. If you will give me your name and number, I'll have her return your call." Right after Sister Mary Helen did, without any further ado, Sister Alberta hung up.

For a moment Mary Helen stared at the receiver. Who was this Bonaventure? Why did she have to talk to the top banana about her? How were these women connected to

Suzanne? And the silver letter opener, the one that had killed Suzanne . . . Maybe August 8, Feast of St. Dominic, had not been such a farfetched guess.

Quickly she replaced the phone and hurried toward Eileen's bedroom. She could hardly wait to talk to her friend. On her way, Mary Helen tried to figure out how to tell Eileen she had probably been right about Suzanne and the nun's watch without coming right out and saying "I told you so!"

The Hall of Justice was almost deserted when Kate arrived on Sunday morning. Alone in the elevator, she cursed her luck. Right now she could be home in bed, warm and cozy, snuggling beside Jack. But this Advent murder business had caused a big stir in the media, and the chief wanted it solved yesterday. Can't blame him, Kate thought, imagining the calls he must be getting from the mayor's office, the supervisors' offices, probably even the fire chief and the superintendent of the Water Department, not to mention the general manager of Park and Rec. Everyone knew someone who was in some way connected with Mount St. Francis College for Women.

The light shining from Room 450 into the fourth-floor hallway told her that Gallagher had beat her there.

"Hi, Denny," she called, opening the half-glassed door of the Homicide Detail. Her voice echoed through the long, empty room. The faint aroma of tobacco smoke floated on the air. Denny had been here for a few minutes, Kate reckoned. Long enough to fumble with his matches and get his cigar lit.

"Hi, yourself, Katie-girl." Denny emerged from the coffee room, holding two steaming styrofoam cups.

"Lousy day, huh? Even downtown." He handed her a

cup. "Damn dreary." Blowing on his coffee, he gazed out the window at the James Lick Freeway already crowded with cars heading for the Bay Bridge and God knew what in the East Bay.

The fine drizzle mixed with the exhausts to give The City a worn, dirty look. The sky hung like a low gray canopy.

"I should have stood in bed," Gallagher said. He sat down hard on his swivel chair, facing Kate across the double desk.

She smiled, thought briefly of Jack, and tried to bring her mind back to the case. The sooner they solved it, one way or another, the better. Kate did not want this thing dragging on over the holidays.

"Where do we start?" she asked, spreading the paperwork out on her desk.

"With what we know for sure." Gallagher cleared his throat. "You're all business today, Katie-girl. What's up?"

"I'd like to get this damn thing solved," Kate answered. This is our first real Christmas together, Jack's and mine. Last year didn't really count. We'd only been married a month. And I'd like this Christmas to be special. I don't want a murder investigation interfering."

"There's a way to stop that." Leaning back in his chair, Gallagher hitched his thumbs in his belt.

"You mean quit the department?" Kate could feel her face flush.

"That's one way." Gallagher was annoyingly calm.

"I'm a detective and a damn good one." Kate slammed her fist down on the desktop. "I don't see why I can't be married and work at the same time. Lots of women do, you know. It's just that I don't want murder to interfere with Christmas."

"Murder is your work," Gallagher answered logically.

Kate stopped. She could feel her temper rising. She

knew she was beginning to sound irrational. Stop while you're ahead, she warned herself. This is your own fault. You brought it up.

"Sorry to be so vehement, Denny." Kate lit a cigarette, then sipped her coffee. "I guess it's something I'm working out myself. Didn't mean to take it out on you."

"What are partners for?" Denny smiled that old teddy bear grin.

Kate smiled back. Good old reliable Denny—sweet, fatherly, a real love. For a moment she wanted to get up and hug him. Kate resisted the urge. Why was she feeling so—so sentimental? It wasn't at all like her. You don't suppose I'm pregnant, she thought. A feeling of panic washed over her whole body. Could be. She'd know, for sure, in about two weeks. I can't worry about it now, she thought, struggling hard to force the possibility from her mind. Right now there is a murder to solve.

"As I was saying, let's start with what we know," Gallagher said, interrupting her thoughts. "What we know is, Suzanne is dead, stabbed to death with a silver letter opener. Before she was killed she was beaten . . ."

"And raped," Kate added. "From the looks of the apartment she must have put up a terrific fight."

Gallagher shook his head. "Hellava way to go," he said. "And by the way, I noticed you left that part out when you were talking to the Sister last Tuesday. How come?"

Kate shrugged. "I don't know, really. It's not what killed her, and rape seems so . . . so . . . debasing. I just didn't see any reason to tell her. Why do you ask?"

"Just wondering." Gallagher twisted his cigar around in his mouth. "So," he said, "we know her attacker was strong, violent, debasing . . ."

"And a man," Kate said.

"What we don't know for sure is anything about the

victim. Except where she lived, where she worked, where she was the night before, and that she bore a child." Denny ran his hand over his bald pate. "Sacramento has nothing on her prints so I sent them to D.C. If she has any on record anywhere, they should be back by the middle of next week."

"Let's list suspects just for the heck of it." Kate took out a pencil and turned over a report form for scratch paper.

"What suspects? If we had a suspect, we could run a skin test on him and . . ." Gallagher shook his head. "That is, unless he gets a good lawyer who advises him not to take it."

"Then let's list the men she knew," Kate said. "Good old what's-his-face should be the top of the list," she said, shoving the Polaroid snap toward Gallagher.

Gallagher studied the snapshot. "Shall we call him Lover Boy?" he asked.

Kate looked over at her partner. Disgust was written all over his face.

"Who else?" she asked.

"Pat Flaherty, Arnold Schultz, Lee Slater, from the apartment. Then, the owner of the Sea Wench, what's his name? Rosenberg?"

"And the place must have a bartender and waiters."

"Jeez, Kate, if you're going that route, what about all the professors, the gardeners, and the janitors at the college?"

Gallagher pushed back in his swivel chair. "Lover Boy would be my first guess," he said.

Kate stared out the window at the dull-looking city. Somewhere out there in the wet grayness a murderer was hiding. Was he frightened? Wary of every stranger he passed? Suspicious of every phone call? Panicky whenever his doorbell rang? Or was he cocky? Sure of himself? Certain no one had seen him and no one would suspect him? She wondered for a moment how it would feel to be the hunted rather than the hunter. The thought made her shudder.

"Do you think there's a chance we'll find the guy?" she asked finally.

"Sure, somebody's got to know who he is." Gallagher leaned over to study the list she was making. "But until we do, let's give Rosenberg a whirl. What's his first name? Punch? How about a trip to the Sea Wench? Ask him if he's remembered anything he forgot to tell us and how in the hell he got the nickname 'Punch.'"

Ghirardelli Square was freezing. A bitter wind whipped uphill from the Bay and cut through the brightly decorated courtyard like a whetted knife. Tourists ducked quickly into novelty shops or, better yet, into the long protected hallways of the old Chocolate Building. If the weather's good for nothing else, Kate thought, at least it's good for business.

As Gallagher and she crossed the courtyard, Kate shivered. She wished she'd worn her padded coat. It was at least a year out of style and made her look like a plum-colored polar bear, but the thing was warm. She was glad when they finally reached the door to the hall. Both sides of the passage were lined with the brightly colored display windows of the Kilkenny Shop, the Hammock Way, the Shoe Inn, Tutwiler's Brass. Each shop specialized in some one item; even the restaurants specialized.

Delicious aromas from Via Veneto, Gaylord's, and the Magic Pan filled the concrete hallway. Kate marveled that there were enough shops featuring just one thing to fill the entire building.

"Just like a medical complex," Gallagher answered when she mentioned it to him. Good old Denny! The life of the party, as usual!

Gallagher pushed the elevator button. While they waited for it to arrive, Kate stared into the window of the shop across from it. Baby Bunting Boutique. In the window, Santa Claus's sled was overflowing with satin layettes, frilly baby dresses, even designer diaper covers. Soon all these could be hers. Suddenly, she felt full of butterflies.

"Why so quiet?" Gallagher asked.

"Just looking. Isn't that adorable?" She pointed to a cuddly red and green Christmasy-looking quilt in the showcase.

"Thank God, Mrs. G's not with us." Impatiently, Gallagher pushed the elevator button again. "Since the grandkids started coming, I can't keep her out of these joints. It's costing us a king's ransom. Think I'll open one when I retire. Who but a grandmother would buy designer diapers for a kid to do his business in?"

Kate laughed. She could just imagine sedate, efficient Mrs. G going crazy Christmas shopping.

"Well, after raising five kids on a cop's salary, she's entitled," Kate said.

"That's what she thinks too," Gallagher said, "but I'm not too sure about what the daughter-in-law thinks."

For a moment Kate was taken aback. She couldn't imagine anyone objecting to a mother-in-law like Mrs. G.

"I get the feeling, she thinks the wife is butting in." Gallagher hitched up his trousers. "Never says anything, but I get the feeling. What the daughter-in-law doesn't get is that the wife's so used to giving, it'd kill her to stop." Gallagher glanced over at her. Kate could feel her face flush even though her partner had no idea how close to home he was hitting.

He pointed to the boutique window. "Hell, at those prices, I wish she'd slow down."

Kate was glad to see the elevator door open.

With one hand, Gallagher pulled open the heavy wooden door of the Sea Wench. With the other he covered his left eye. An old commando trick, he'd told Kate a hundred times. Helps you when you go from the light into a dark place. One eye adjusts.

It must be true, Kate thought, when Gallagher spotted Rosenberg. Her eyes were still trying to adapt to the bar's dim interior.

"At the end of the bar," Gallagher said. "Place is deserted. A bartender, couple of cocktail waitresses, one or two serious drinkers getting a head start on this afternoon's 49er game."

Rosenberg must have recognized the officers as soon as they opened the door. He left the barstool and came right over.

Grinning nervously, he extended a wide, hairy hand. "What can I do for you, Inspectors? How about a little libation?" Rosenberg sniffled. His wide nose was red around the nostrils. Above it his dark eyes studied them warily.

Both inspectors shook their heads. "Just a few routine questions, Mr. Rosenberg." Gallagher shook the extended hand. "Just routine," he repeated, trying to put the man at ease.

Rosenberg sniffled again and took a swipe at his nose with the back of his hand. "I told you guys everything I knew last time you were here."

"Maybe something you thought of since?" Gallagher and Kate followed Rosenberg to a small wooden table toward the back of the bar. The bartender came right over and put a tall glass of orange juice in front of Rosenberg. "Anything for you two?" he asked. Again both shook their heads.

"Got a hellava cold," Rosenberg explained, lifting the orange juice to his lips. "Full of vitamin C."

And vodka, too, Kate thought, watching Rosenberg fumble for his handkerchief.

"It's this business," the man continued miserably. "The place gets as hot as hell, then you go out in the middle of the night. Outside it's freezing. Even with the car heater on, I shiver all the way home. Lucky I don't get pneumonia. I can't wait to retire and get the hell out of here." He shook his head, dragged the back of his hand across his raw nose. "But you didn't come down here to listen to my troubles. What can I do for you?"

"As I said, sir, just a few routine questions." Gallagher took out his pad. "We have you down as 'Punch,'" Mr. Rosenberg. Could you tell us your real name?"

"Francis. Francis Xavier Rosenberg. My pop was Jewish, my ma Irish. I'm a regular 'Abie's Irish Rose.'" He smiled. Obviously, it was a much-used joke.

"Married?"

"Sure. Thirty years next June. Wonderful gal. Lets me be. You know what I mean?"

"Have you children?"

"Three boys, but they're not kids anymore. All graduated college." He fumbled in his back pocket, pulled out a wallet that looked like he'd been sitting on it for thirty years, and produced a color portrait of the family.

Kate studied the photograph. A younger Punch sat with his arm around a petite blond woman smiling sedately. The couple was flanked by three tall young men, all with their father's full head of curly hair. The trio could have passed for the offensive line of any high school football team.

She looked more closely at Mrs. Punch. The sweet smile did little to mitigate the look of absolute control in those large eyes or the determined set of the iron jaw. Kate had no doubt which Rosenberg ruled the roost.

"About the victim," Kate asked, handing back the picture. "How well did you know her?"

"Hardly at all, I told you guys that. It was that cute little Mimi talked me into giving her a chance. I'm always one to give a kid a chance. God knows where I'd be if no one gave me one." Rosenberg took a long swig of orange juice.

"The kid wasn't bad. Not much of a looker, but this place is dark. Anyway, she was built okay. Nice legs, cute little backside, not even bad in the boobs once they got the top of the costume tight enough."

"I thought this was a singing job." Kate could feel her temper rising.

Rosenberg stared at her openmouthed. "You got to be kidding, lady. Lots of people can sing. Here you got to be able to sing and wiggle. And nine out of ten times it's the wiggle that's hard to come by. Spend half my evening walking around patting backsides to remind them."

Kate wondered how he explained this part of his job to his steely-eyed missus.

"So you didn't really know Suzanne?" Kate asked again.

"Her name, address, phone, social security number. And that she was a friend of Mimi's. Now, there's a kid with a wiggle." Rosenberg sniffled.

"Nothing else about Suzanne?"

"Well, she only worked here one night. What more's to know?"

"Anything strange happen that night? Anything at all you remember?"

Rosenberg studied his orange juice, then shook his head sadly. "Really wish I could," he said, Kate thought, a little too earnestly. "Don't think I haven't been thinking about that poor kid. Only thing I can remember was a guy in the audience coming on to her, but that ain't unusual. Happens twenty times a night to twenty different gals."

"What happened?"

"Nothing happened. The kid, Suzanne, told me about it. She struck me as the timid type, you know. So I goes over to this guy. Told him not to fool with the merchandise. He was with a date anyway and she looked a little sore. Also, a little underage. So I told him to leave. Thought for a minute he was going to get feisty. Then I looks at the bouncer. The guy, he also looks. Next thing I know, he leaves. Nothing unusual."

"Do you remember what the guy looked like?"

"Like a hundred other guys that come in here. Medium height, sandy hair, nothing special about him. Actually, he smelled like my youngest kid, Todd."

"Smelled like your son? How?"

"The kid uses some goofy perfume. 'For men,' he says. I says, 'Real men smell like sweat.' Muriel, that's my wife, says, 'Real men can smell any way they want. Our Toddy is entitled to smell how he wants.' Damn stuff costs a fortune. Got a polo player on the front."

"Ralph Lauren," Kate explained to a baffled Gallagher.

"Today I couldn't smell a thing," Rosenberg said, then sniffled for emphasis.

Fortunately, Kate had stuck the photo in her purse.

"Could this be the guy?" she asked, handing him the snapshot.

Rosenberg stood up and took the snapshot to the bar to study it in the light.

Returning, he flipped the photo onto the small table. "Can't say for sure. Like I told you, this place is dark. Could be, but couldn't be too. The guy at the table had more hair. Much more hair. Besides, if they were this cozy, why would he have to come on to her? He already owned the merchandise!"

Kate put the photo back in her purse. "Do you remember anything else that may have happened that night?" she asked.

Rosenberg shook his head.

Kate noticed the color drain suddenly from his face and small beads of sweat break out on his upper lip. He looked like a man about to pass out. Quickly the bartender appeared with another tall orange juice. Rosenberg drank thirstily and some of his color returned.

"Anything else I can help you with?" he said after a moment. Smiling, he looked Kate up and down.

She wondered, hotly, if he was appraising her ability to wiggle.

"Just curious, but how come they call you 'Punch'?" Denny asked before she could say anything.

Rosenberg gaffawed. "Started out as a fighter," he said. "Middleweight. Only got in one or two good punches in my best bouts. Some smartass sportswriter started calling me 'One Punch Rosey.' The Punch part stuck."

Smiling, Gallagher shook his head. "This gal that got killed was a fighter too," he remarked casually, pushing back his chair. "Yeah, she put up a hellava fight, all right. Clawed the guy. We got skin particles if we ever nail the bastard." Rosenberg didn't respond, just smiled a tight smile. Kate noticed the color had left his face again.

"Why did you tell him that?" Kate whispered as Gallagher pushed open the heavy door.

"I think the guy knows more than he's telling," Gallagher replied. "I'm letting him know we also know more than we're telling. It'll scare the shit out of him. I hope," he added as an afterthought.

Outside, the weather hadn't improved. The day was still gray and overcast. A perfect afternoon to be at home with a roaring fire, settling in for the football game. That's exactly what Jack must be doing, Kate thought as she and Gallagher made their way across the courtyard.

"I'm starved," Gallagher said finally. He checked his watch. "Hell, it's way past our lunchtime. Want to eat here?"

"We may as well," Kate answered, mentally calculating how much money she had in her wallet.

The two officers followed their noses down the stairs into the Woolen Mill and into a small dark restaurant called Monk's Madness. Kate wasn't a bit surprised when the hostess greeted them dressed in a miniskirted Franciscan habit.

TUESDAY—SECOND WEEK OF ADVENT

When Sister Mary Helen awoke on Tuesday morning, she pulled the covers over her head and kept her eyes shut tight. No matter what the alarm clock said, she wasn't quite ready to face the day. She needed a few more minutes of darkness and quiet to sift through yesterday.

As she snuggled down in the warm covers, yesterday seemed like a bad dream. Mary Helen wished that was all it had been. Yesterday they had buried Suzanne.

During the Mass of the Resurrection a cold hard rain had poured sympathetically from the dark sky, pelting the narrow stained-glass windows of the college chapel.

Father Adams had intoned the ancient hymn for the dead: "May the angels lead thee into paradise. May the saints be there to welcome thee . . ." Mary Helen followed the casket down the middle aisle, then down the front steps where a slick black hearse waited. Below the college, The City was wrapped in a soggy mantle of wind and rain. She stared, oblivious of the large drops soaking her and blurring her glasses. "There's weeping in my heart, like the rain falling on the city." Some nineteenth-century French poet had written that. At no moment, Mary Helen thought, could it have been more true.

Eileen, Anne, and she had squeezed into the same limousine with Cecilia and Therese. The funeral cortege wound its way down to Fulton and along Fulton to the Great Highway. No one spoke. Sister Mary Helen had stared out the fogged windows, watching the blue-gray churning Pacific on her right. Huge breakers rose, then crashed down on the rain-soaked sand. A strong wind pummeled the limousine with angry rain, and wet sand blew across the black asphalt. The windshield wipers worked furiously to keep a fan-shaped clearing. Their steady rhythm began to resound in Mary Helen's brain: *Swish-swish, swish-swish, Suzanne's dead, killer's free. Suzanne's dead, killer's free. Who was she? Who is he?*

The procession had passed Fort Funston and the Olympic Golf Course and turned onto John Daly Boulevard, heading for the El Camino and its final destination, Holy Cross in Colma.

Colma is the city of cemeteries. Not only is the Catholic cemetery located there, but the Italian cemetery, the Jewish cemetery, the Chinese cemetery, the Greek cemetery, and a number of nonsectarian cemeteries. Mary Helen had wondered idly what Colma would look like on the Last Day, when the dead would rise to be reunited with their bodies.

"Even the weather seems to be in mourning," Eileen said, interrupting her thoughts.

"Is that a good omen or a bad one?" Anne asked, just to keep up the conversation, Mary Helen was sure.

"Good, I'd suspect. Aye, Mary Helen?" Eileen turned toward her.

Mary Helen had noticed that Eileen's brogue had thickened: she was upset too. She glanced around the limousine. They were all upset. Cecilia's face was strained and white, her thin lips pulled into a tight, firm smile. Therese nervously blinked back tears. Even Anne's usually ruddy complexion was drained. Of course they were all upset. Who wouldn't be? A young woman they had all known and loved had been brutally murdered. Rain beat down heavily on the roof of the limousine: *Swish-swish, swish-swish,* the windshield wipers taunted, *Suzanne's dead, killer's free. Who is she? Who is he?*

With one eye, Mary Helen squinted at her alarm clock. Like it or not, it was time to get up, to face Tuesday. Reluctantly, she left the warm bed.

Right after breakfast she made her way to her small basement office. On the way down the stairs, she passed a small tight cluster of students whispering. Although each one of the girls had tried to smile and nod as she edged by them, she noted the wariness, the tension, that hung over the group. She didn't have to guess what they had been whispering about. Suzanne's murder hung over the entire college like a giant purple mantle of sadness. Hesitantly, she put in her key and turned the lock. One hand was full of messages she'd picked up when she passed the switchboard. Although her office had been closed for over a week, the college was still in session. Somehow, as much as Mary Helen hated to admit it, life went on no matter what tragedies occurred.

She switched on the light. The small office was cold. It smelled damp. Suzanne's desk stood there, empty and bare. Looking at it, Mary Helen could feel her throat tighten. Involuntary tears stung her eyes. Blinking, she made her way into her own inner office, sat at the desk, and opened the first note.

Mary Agnes Van Der Zee wanted a list of alumnae for the class of 1940. They were planning a reunion. Mary Agnes was either very late for their twenty-fifth or mighty early for their fiftieth.

For a moment, she almost called Suzanne to ask her to take off the list on the computer. Suddenly she remembered, Suzanne wasn't here. Suzanne would never be here. Suzanne

would never run the computer again. A huge aching lump
lodged in her throat.

Reluctantly she went into the outer office. The computer had always been Suzanne's field of expertise. Mary
Helen had never even tried to run the thing. Suzanne had
done it so well and had been so proud of her accomplish-
ment. There was really no need for Mary Helen to learn.
Besides, if she was entirely truthful, she was scared to death
of the blasted thing!

For a few moments she studied the machine. Its blank
screen looked harmless enough. If timid Suzanne could mas-
ter it, why not she? It would take more than a machine with
a harmless name like Apple to intimidate her, she ruminated, refusing to give way to the gnawing thought that
something named Apple was said to have begun all man's
troubles. Resolutely, she sat in front of the computer. With
a minimum of hunting she found the "on" switch, then a
floppy program disc for making lists. So far, so good, she
thought, removing the disc and sticking the one labeled
"Class of 1940" into the disc drive.

A little square on the computer screen blinked by FILE
NAME. "Class of 1940" Mary Helen punched in. The disc
drive gave an odd whirr. Then flashed CAN'T FIND FILE onto
the screen.

Mary Helen punched in "Class of 40" and again the
disc drive whirred, then flashed CAN'T FIND FILE.

Mary Helen pointed to the disc drive. "I know it's in
there," she shouted at the computer, "I've seen Suzanne get
it out!"

Suddenly banging her fist on the computer keyboard,
she began to cry. A strange assortment of letters appeared on
the screen. INVALID SELECTION NUMBER. REENTER, the screen
remarked coldly. Mary Helen wasn't sure just why she was

crying: frustration, rage, grief. Whatever the reason, the release was welcome.

Slowly her tears dried. Her throat ached and her face felt hot and stiff. But not as stiff as her backbone. She straightened up, blew her nose, and wiped her bifocals. Takes more than this to get a good woman down, she thought, rising from the computer table. "When the going gets tough, the tough get going," she had read on a bumper sticker. And going she would get! Right out of here and straight to Reina Martinez to find out all she could about Suzanne. Determinedly, Mary Helen walked into her office and dialed Eileen on the intercom.

"Can you go with me to Calistoga?" she asked without any preliminary remarks.

"Go to Calistoga? You mean right now?" Eileen sounded incredulous.

"Right now." Mary Helen's tone was a bit bossier than she'd intended.

"I suppose I can." Eileen had apparently picked up the urgency in her tone. "Can you spare me a few minutes . . . say ten, to—to powder my nose?"

"Ten minutes would be fine. And ask Anne to drive us, will you?" she asked.

"Shouldn't we be notifying Cecilia if all three of us are going? Just in case someone might be looking for us?"

Mary Helen was piqued. It was sensible, of course, yes, even professional, to notify the college president when three of the staff were taking the day off. But she wasn't in the mood for any arguments.

Knocking on the president's door, she sincerely hoped Cecilia would not try to second-guess her. Sister Cecilia looked somewhat surprised to see Mary Helen, but quickly composed her face. It remained composed when Mary Helen announced her plans to go to Calistoga. So composed that she decided to mention her purpose: "To see what I can find out about Suzanne's murder," she said.

Cecilia's face did not flicker. She simply smiled and said, "Good luck!" Mary Helen was beginning to like Cecilia.

Miraculously, Eileen had been able to find Anne and persuade her to join them. Everything about Anne said she was reluctant to go but that she was more reluctant to let the older nuns go alone. Good, Mary Helen thought, we've got her where we want her, between the devil and the deep blue sea, to quote the well-worn phrase.

The midmorning traffic was light. Quickly the three nuns made their way across the Golden Gate Bridge, past Marin City, and crossed Richardson Bay. Strawberry Point stood out to their right. Mary Helen wondered, as she had a dozen times, why they called it Strawberry Point. Did strawberries grow there or did the land mass look to a fanciful cartographer like a gigantic unpicked berry? One of these days she'd have to find out. So many whys of things. But right now, the most important why was, Why was Suzanne killed?

The trio rode along in silence. A dull gray sky wrapped the whole Bay Area in gloom. Finally, passing the blue-roofed Marin Civic Center, Anne asked the question Mary Helen felt sure had been on her mind since they'd left the college.

"Why are we going to Calistoga?"

"Because there's a girl there who knew Suzanne."

"The dark, rather chunky one you were talking with at the wake?" Eileen asked. Mary Helen nodded.

"I saw her too," Anne said. "Ladies, she was no girl.

She's definitely a woman." Once again, Mary Helen had forgotten that age is all relative.

"Yes, of course," she said. "Anyway, this woman's name is Reina Martinez. Seems she visited Suzanne at her apartment. So, their friendship was more than a casual, live-in-the-same-apartment-building type of thing. Maybe she can tell us more about Suzanne. Lead us to who might have wanted to kill her."

"Did you mention her name to the police?" Anne asked.

"Well, of course I fully intended to." Mary Helen didn't dare look at Eileen. "But," she continued with as much conviction as she could muster, "there is absolutely no sense alerting them unless this Reina knows something."

"Glory be to God!" Eileen stared at her friend. "Does it never occur to you that she might know too much? Like not only why someone killed Suzanne, but who?"

Frankly, it hadn't, but Mary Helen certainly was not going to admit that. Not at the moment anyway. "Look," she said, pointing out the car window at an old cemetery right next to a shopping mall. "Doesn't that say something about the proximity of life and death?"

"No more than traveling with you does, old dear," Eileen muttered.

Anne headed east on Highway 37. At Sears Point she turned north and somehow found a two-lane highway that would lead them to Napa, then through St. Helena and into Calistoga. Mary Helen was glad the young nun was at the wheel. It gave her the leisure to enjoy the drive. The countryside rolled with small gentle hills. Miniature cows grazed in fields turned lime-green by yesterday's storm. Gnarled grapevines, stripped of fruit and leaves, ran in squat rows down to the road. Here and there a farmer had plunked down a small square pile of white wooden beehives. It seemed impossible that this rustic countryside lay less than an hour's distance from The City.

On the last stretch they drove past the wineries: Beaulieu, Franciscan, Charles Krug. The sprawling stone buildings were set back behind wide fields of now-bare vines. Beyond them, a stubborn fog hung on forest-green hills.

"What's our plan?" Anne asked when they spotted the sign announcing WELCOME TO CALISTOGA.

"Find Reina Martinez and talk to her," Mary Helen answered. It seemed simple enough to her.

"And just where do you suppose we are about to find her?" Eileen asked.

What a time for her to turn practical, Mary Helen thought. She studied the narrow main street carefully as Anne drove slowly through the town.

"We know she works in one of these places," she said, pointing to the signs advertising mud baths, mineral springs, and massage that dotted both sides of the street.

"And just what do we do if the woman is working and doesn't feel she can take the time to chat?" Eileen asked, her brogue beginning to thicken.

For a moment Mary Helen was silent. She studied the expectant faces of her two friends, searching for just the right words to use in divulging her plan.

"Oh, no," Anne groaned before Mary Helen could begin.

Eileen's bushy eyebrows shot up; her gray eyes widened.

Mary Helen did not need to go on. From the looks on their faces, she knew they had both guessed.

On the third try they located the spa where Reina worked.

The three nuns sat on hard cots in three adjoining alcoves in Doctor Long's Mud and Mineral Spa. Each was wrapped, mummy-like, in a white flannel sheet. Steam heat gave the whole place a warm, sticky feeling.

"You never mentioned this when you asked me to drive," Anne whispered from the middle alcove.

"Frankly, dear, I had no idea," Eileen whispered back in self-defense.

"Lucky the place wasn't crowded," Mary Helen whispered. "We were able to get right in."

Neither nun answered.

Silently attendants led the three from the alcoves toward the baths. Mary Helen managed to juggle around so that Reina was her attendant.

"Nice to see you again," she commented, following the silent woman down the narrow stone hallway.

Reina said nothing. When they reached the entrance to the baths, the woman turned and faced Mary Helen. Her eyes were hard. But there was something else, a look beyond hardness. A look Mary Helen had not seen often. With a sudden jolt, she realized what it was—pure unadulterated hatred. Momentarily shaken, she steadied herself against the rough wall.

"Go in," the woman commanded, pulling back the white linen curtain covering the entrance to the baths. Reluctantly, Mary Helen obliged.

After a hot shower in mineral water, the three were eased into large rectangular tubs of oozing brown mud. For a moment Mary Helen's body floated on the thickness. Then the slimy mud began to slip and flow, wet and sticky, between her toes, under her arms, around her trunk. Slowly it was pulling her down. Mary Helen felt helpless. She couldn't sink and she couldn't float. Mud oozed into every crevice of her body. She tried to pull one arm out of the mud. She couldn't. She felt for all the world like an elderly tar baby.

Above her, unsmiling, Reina grabbed up soft, sticky clods and roughly dropped them onto her body. Obviously the young woman did not have a vocation to mud-bath giving. She did, however, seem to be enjoying pelting Mary Helen with the clods. Soon only the old nun's head was above the deep brown mud. Reina turned on a tap, filling the tub with steamy-hot mineral water. Mary Helen's bifocals fogged. The pungent odor of sulfur rose from the tub. She wrinkled her nose. Slowly, two strong hands cupped her shoulders and pushed her still deeper into the tub. She squirmed, pressing her foot against the bottom, but it slipped. Hot mud covered her chin. She felt a sudden sickening lurch of fear.

"Will you please wipe my glasses?" she asked, tasting mud on her lower lip. Deliberately she kept her voice steady. Strong, thick fingers snatched them from her nose. The hairs on her neck prickled as the edge of the hand rubbed across her neck and stayed there just a moment too long. The prickle ran down her backbone as she sat there in the tub, the world around her a blur. After a few long moments, her glasses were returned, smeared but at least clear. Mary Helen pulled in a deep breath and let it out slowly, forcing herself to relax.

She turned her head sideways. How glad she was to see the heads of Eileen and Anne in the two adjacent tubs.

"How are you doing?" she asked cheerfully.

"If you are wise, you won't ask," Eileen grunted.

"This is wonderful!" she heard Anne exclaim. "It's like getting in touch with . . . with Mother Earth. Oh, Mary Helen, I'm so thrilled you asked me. I feel one with all of nature."

Ah, youth, Mary Helen thought, trying unsuccessfully to wiggle her toes. Too bad it's wasted on kids.

Above her, Reina stood, sullen and brooding. With strong hands she lifted Mary Helen from the tub and began to scrape off the caked mud.

"Well. It's nice to see you again." Mary Helen tried, again, casually to start up a conversation while Reina was putting her through the after-mud mineral bath.

"What do you want?" Reina almost growled. Roughly she rubbed the last of the clinging earth from Mary Helen's back.

"Just wondering how you knew Suzanne. I was hoping you could help me find out who would have wanted to kill her," Mary Helen said calmly but bluntly. Reina did not seem the type who would appreciate a subtle approach.

"Listen, nun. Suzanne is dead. Let her rest. Don't you know whoever killed her is loco?" She pointed to her head. "He could come after you. After me. What can we do for Suzanne? Huh? I ask you. Best to let it go. Go to your church. Pray to your God. That's enough. And me? I know nothing. Do you understand? Nothing!" Reina wadded up the washcloth, threw it into the water, and left the room.

Mary Helen's fingers were beginning to look like prunes when another attendant returned, wrapped her in a hot flannel sheet, and turned her over to the massage department.

Well, that was a road to nowhere, Mary Helen thought, settling herself on the massage table. Or maybe somewhere. Obviously Reina knew something she was afraid to tell and hated Mary Helen for trying to make her tell it.

"Relax and enjoy," the short, chatty masseuse advised her. When the woman attacked the knots in her neck and shoulders, Mary Helen had no choice but to comply. Or at least try to.

About two o'clock the phone on Kate's desk rang. Gallagher didn't seem a bit surprised when she handed it to him.

"Rosenberg for you," she mouthed.

Expectantly she watched him. Concentrating hard, Gallagher ran his hand over his bald pate and nodded his head as though Rosenberg could see him.

"He wants to meet us at the Old Mission, the little graveyard on the side," Gallagher said, slamming down the receiver.

"Just like playing cops and robbers," Kate muttered, following him out of the detail.

Punch Rosenberg looked old and tired slouched on the corner of the large flat marble tombstone toward the rear of Mission Dolores Cemetery. A winter sun had broken through in the Mission District and flooded the small cloister with brightness and the smell of damp loam.

Dew still clung like tiny crystal tears on the edge of half-bloomed roses. Headstones cast plump shadows on the damp grass. A well-fed Angora cat licked her paw and kept a suspicious eye on the whole scene.

Kate could hear the gravel crunch under their feet as Gallagher and she crossed the silent garden. They sat beside Punch Rosenberg.

And "punch" looked exactly like what someone had done to the man. His puffy face was pale. When he looked up, dark circles under his eyes met just above his raw, red nose. His thick head of curly gray hair looked as if it hadn't been combed in days. Slowly, almost painfully, he straightened his shoulders.

"I got something terrible to tell you guys," he said, fiddling nervously with the diamond ring on his little finger.

"About Suzanne Barnes?" Gallagher asked. Punch nodded his head and looked as if he were about to speak.

"Hold it a minute, fella. I better read you your rights." Gallagher fumbled through his pocket for the card and his reading glasses.

"I know my rights," Punch exploded. "I know I got to get this off my chest. It's killing me. Can't sleep. Can't eat. Look at me!" He stuck out a shaking hand. "I'm a goddamn nervous wreck!"

"You're going to have to be a nervous wreck for two more minutes," Gallagher said, then began to read the familiar formula.

"I didn't kill her," Punch burst in the moment he had finished.

"You dragged us clear down here to tell us that?" Gallagher patted his pockets, searching for his cigar. He looked around guiltily. Then he struck his match on a rough corner of the stone and puffed quickly. Kate was sure the two Ruffinos, resting under the large square of marble since 1872, wouldn't mind.

"I thought you said you had something terrible to tell us," she said, watching the smoke curl around the graying headstones.

"I do." Punch choked on the words, then swallowed hard. Kate stared in amazement. The cocky, tough-talking, bottom-watching Mr. Rosenberg looked as if he was about to cry. Fighting for control, he began.

"I took the kid home," he said miserably. "She was scared and I took her home."

"Go on," Gallagher urged, brushing ashes from his sleeve.

"Well, we gets to the apartment, see, and I'm feeling

lousy. This damn cold." Rosenberg took a swipe at his red nose. "I'd been drinking orange juice all night laced with a little vodka and the damn stuff sneaks up. Lousy Communists!" Rosenberg looked accusingly at Kate, as if she were part of a worldwide conspiracy.

"Anyway, the kid, Suzanne, opens the door, wiggles her fanny a little, and goes in. I don't know what comes over me, but it turns me on. I'm old enough to be the kid's father and she turns me on." Rosenberg shook his head in disgust, then felt in his back pocket for a crumpled handkerchief.

The trio sat for several moments in silence. A round black bee hovered over an open rose. Rosenberg blew his nose loudly and wiped his eyes.

"Then what happened?" Gallagher hitched up his pant legs and shifted uncomfortably on the hard marble.

"Then . . ." Rosenberg hesitated, replaced his handkerchief, and began to fiddle with his ring, like someone stalling while he worked up enough courage to go on.

"Then something inside me goes 'bang'! Don't ask me what happened. I don't remember everything. But I know I come on to her. She wouldn't go for it. I went crazy. Smashed stuff. Knocked her around. But I know I didn't kill her. You got to believe that." His eyes blinking, nervously, searched Gallagher's face for reassurance.

Gallagher's look was cold and hard. "How do you know? You said you don't remember anything. How can you be sure?"

"I said I don't remember everything. Some things I remember. And I'm sure I didn't kill her. I wouldn't kill anybody. Besides, I remember the sobbing. The poor kid was sobbing when I left. That's what brought me to my senses, Officer. The sobbing. I can't stand to hear a kid cry."

"Why didn't you tell us all this when we saw you on Sunday?"

The color drained from the man's face. "Muriel," he said.

"Muriel?" Gallagher asked.

"Muriel. My wife. She'll kill me when she finds out. I thought I could pull it off, but I can't. Muriel knows something is wrong. Keeps asking me what. But I didn't kill her."

Gallagher stood. "I hope you've told us everything, Mr. Rosenberg," he said. "We will need to contact you, so don't leave town."

"Leave town! I won't hardly be able to leave the house when Muriel gets finished with me," Rosenberg said.

"If you're not guilty, you won't object to taking the skin test, then?" Kate asked. Although she couldn't see any scratch marks on Rosenberg's face, perhaps there were some under his shirt sleeves or on his chest.

"Sure. Anything, miss. Officer, miss." He corrected himself quickly. "I'll do anything to clear this thing up."

"By the way," Gallagher asked, "I'm just curious. Is there any reason you wanted to meet us at Mission Dolores?"

Rosenberg smiled a wry smile. "Yeah, Officer. I got a reason. Went to church here when I was a kid. Thought I'd tell you guys, then I'd go to confession, and then I'd go home and come clean with Muriel."

"I will never be able to understand how a man can fear his wife more than he fears either the police or God," Kate said as Gallagher and she made their way across Dolores Street to their parked car.

"Yes, you will, Katie-girl," he replied. "You just haven't been married long enough yet."

"I'm starved," Anne announced as soon as the trio began the ride home from Calistoga. They stopped at an out-of-the-way restaurant north of Oakville that looked for all the world, Mary Helen thought, like a wayside chapel.

The place was made of brick, and the booths, she would swear, were old church pews. Stained-glass windows flanked either side of an ornate bar. A large carved statue of Saint George, sword raised, slaying a ferocious dragon, stood atop the roaring fireplace.

Everyone studied the menu silently. Eileen hadn't spoken one word since they'd left Calistoga. Nearly twenty miles of silence was a lot for Eileen. Mary Helen was frankly worried. She felt certain that a mere mud bath wouldn't break up a fifty-year friendship, but she had great respect for that one straw that broke the proverbial camel's back. She must remember to order a carafe of wine with the meal. That would relax the atmosphere.

After they ordered, Mary Helen gazed around the room at the large nudes on the walls. Each figure was painted with a different background, Roman, Egyptian, Oriental. Each face and bare body, however, was exactly alike.

"Some model surely must have had a lot of work," Mary Helen said for lack of anything better to say.

"How could you?" Eileen asked, eyes narrowed. She was seething.

"You didn't enjoy it?" Mary Helen feigned surprise.

"Enjoy it? Enjoy it? I detested every bloody minute of it. Furthermore, unless I live another twenty years, which seems unlikely, running around with you, I will never be able to get my toenails clean."

Anne stared, openmouthed. "I just loved it," she said. "It was a marvelous experience, so real, so earthy, so . . . so holistic. I felt in touch with my entire being. I wish everyone could share the experience."

"They can most certainly have my share," Eileen said with uncharacteristic sarcasm.

Halfway through the meal Eileen had regained some of her usual good humor. "Did you get what you were after?" she asked, taking a sip of white wine.

"Not a thing," Mary Helen said, congratulating herself on ordering the carafe. "But that girl obviously knows more than she's willing to tell."

"It could be she has something to hide."

"It could be. But how am I going to find out what?"

"That is exactly why we pay the police. So that they can find out the whys." Eileen took another sip of wine. "Can't I convince you, old dear, to let them do it?"

"I guess I'm going to have to," Mary Helen conceded, "since I couldn't get a thing out of her myself."

"You know," Anne said, "I've been thinking. I've just assumed that a man killed Suzanne because the killer seemed to be so strong and violent."

Mary Helen and Eileen nodded. "But you know," Anne continued, "when I watched Reina, so quiet and so— so surly, shoving all that heavy mud around, pulling a dead-weight body from the tub, it occurred to me that maybe, just maybe . . ."

She didn't need to finish her sentence.

"I'll mention her to Kate Murphy first chance I get," Mary Helen said, mentally calculating how long it would take to get home.

By the time they got there, a dull haze was covering the Golden Gate Bridge. The round winter sun had begun to set behind the fogbound Pacific. Commuter traffic to Marin was heavy. Mary Helen was happy they were going the other way. She was eager to put her call in to Kate Murphy and tell her about Reina Martinez.

She crossed her fingers, hoping Kate would still be at the Hall of Justice. Ugh! she thought, Eileen and her blasted superstitions are contagious.

The phone rang just as Kate was about to leave the Homicide Detail.

"For you, Murphy," O'Connor called across the room, "Sister Mary Helen."

Impatiently, Kate checked her watch. Five o'clock. If she didn't leave immediately, she'd never get to Mama Bassetti's by five-thirty. Since her husband's death, the dinner hour was nearly a religious experience to Jack's mother, and being late for it was akin to sacrilege. Maybe if she took surface streets, she'd be able to get out to the Sunset district on time.

"Yes, Sister?" Kate picked up the receiver and made her voice all business. Fortunately, all the old nun wanted was to tell her about a Reina Martinez in Calistoga. A friend of Suzanne's. Mary Helen felt the young woman might be of some help. Kate wrote down the woman's name and a description. She'd run it down first thing in the morning. Could be this gal would lead them to Lover Boy. Even though Gallagher didn't think so, he seemed like the best bet to her. Especially if Rosenberg was telling the truth. When she had more time, she'd tell Mary Helen about Punch.

As soon as Kate turned off Judah, she spotted Jack's car in front of his mother's house. Good, he was there, calming Mama's nerves, fixing the ritual predinner old-fashioneds, and assuring her that Kate would arrive any moment and not spoil the roast.

Kate took the narrow brick steps two at a time. Jack's mother must have had an eye out the window, because she opened the front door before Kate reached it.

"Well, hello, stranger," Mrs. Bassetti said as Kate pecked her soft flushed cheek. "Come in."

Kate bristled. Stranger! Why, they had been here for dinner two weeks ago. "Ignore her" was Jack's advice about his mother. For his sake, Kate would try.

"Sorry I'm late," she said, taking off her coat and hanging it on the coat tree in the entrance hall.

"I'm glad to see you anytime you come," Mrs. Bassetti answered. Kate caught the little dig. "Jackie's here in the kitchen, making us a drink. Sit down, Kate. Put your feet up." She pushed over a hassock. "You work all day. You must be tired when you come home. Both you and Jackie working all day long . . ." She shook her head sadly. "Both tired. Who makes you a good meal? Huh? You both look to me like skin and bones.

"Jackie, Kate's here," she called unnecessarily toward the kitchen. In the compact six-room house, even a stone-deaf person could not have missed her arrival. "And bring in the antipasto," she added. "I'll try to fatten you two up." She patted Kate on the top of her head, then pushed back a damp piece of gray hair from her own forehead.

Kate sipped her old-fashioned and wondered, as she did every time they came, what she was doing here. Why did she torture herself? She breathed deeply. No sense being negative. The woman was Jack's mother, her mother-in-law, and she had taken her, along with Jack, it seemed, till death did them part. So the only practical, sensible thing to do was to learn to love and appreciate her.

"So, what have you been up to?" Mrs. Bassetti smiled and looked brightly from Jack to Kate. Quickly Kate shoved a thin slice of Italian salami into her mouth. Let Jack answer. She was his mother.

"Nothing too spectacular." Jack sipped his drink. "Pretty busy at work. What's new here?" He threw the conversational ball back to his mother's court, where both he and Kate knew it would stay.

"You remember your cousin Enid's boy? The youngest son, Joey?" Jack's mother began, her hands moving as rapidly as her mouth.

The poor woman is just lonely and, like Mrs. G, used to giving, Kate thought, reaching for a few olives. And, she reminded herself, taking another sip of the old-fashioned, there's no doubt she loves her son and whoever his wife would have been. Kate glanced toward the dining room. Mrs. Bassetti had set out her best china and crystal. In the center she had placed a lovely red Christmas candle surrounded with holly picked from her own backyard.

"Jackie, *mangia.* Have a bread stick. They're the kind you like," his mother insisted. Kate smiled. I guess you never get too old to mother your child, she thought. Surreptitiously she touched her own stomach, wondering if she was beginning to nurture life.

A rush of excitement flooded her body. She could feel her face flush. Whether she wanted a baby now or not, she must admit that the thought of carrying life delighted her. Maybe it was time. Even if this proved to be a false alarm, maybe they should start a family. The photograph of Mrs. Rosenberg with her proud husband and surrounded by three handsome sons popped into Kate's mind. Now, there was a woman who looked fulfilled.

"Jackie, make us another drink while I check on the meat." Her mother-in-law's voice interrupted her daydream.

Obediently, Jack left the room, his mother close on his heels, still talking.

Or would she turn out like Mama Bassetti? Well-intentioned, but overbearing and possessive. She wondered for a moment what kind of mother she would make. . . . And Jack. What were his ideas of fathering? Maybe they should discuss that. Kate began to twist a piece of her red hair around her index finger, then press it into a curl. And her career. What about a pregnant detective? Did she really want to give up Homicide when she'd worked so hard to get there? Someday, of course, but now? She wasn't sure. A child must be wanted. She thought for a moment about Suzanne's baby. Where was the poor little thing? No, it was only fair that a child be wanted. Jack wanted one, she knew. But did she?

"Hey, pal, what are you thinking so hard about?" Jack asked, handing her the icy glass.

"Nothing much," she answered, taking it in both hands.

"She's tired, that's what!" Mrs. Bassetti interrupted. "Poor girl! She shouldn't be doing this hard police work. What kind of a job is that for a married woman? What's wrong with you, Jackie? What kind of a husband are you? Is that how I brought you up? Your wife working her feet off?" She pointed dramatically to Kate's raised feet. "She should be home, making the house nice." Kate could feel her backbone stiffen, but the older woman wasn't finished yet. "Keeping her husband happy, having a family, not out chasing down—"

"Whoa, Mama," Jack cut into the tirade, "go easy! Kate can stay home whenever she wants. We'll start a family when we decide the time is right. Did you finish the story about Enid's Joey?"

"When the time is right? Look at your age." His mother ignored the change of subject. "The sooner the better is the right time, if you ask me."

"Mama," Jack said kindly but firmly, "we didn't ask you."

"Right! What do I know?" Tears filled Mrs. Bassetti's eyes. "What do I know?" she repeated. "I'm only your mother."

"You know how to put on a heck of a good dinner." He kissed her gently. "And I'm starved."

Dabbing her eyes, Mrs. Bassetti hurried to the kitchen.

"Sorry." Jack sat down next to Kate and put his arm around her. Gently he kissed her forehead. "It's just Mama's dying to be a grandmother. She can hardly wait to talk about Jackie's oldest . . . whoever."

"I know," Kate said, plucking an imaginary speck of thread from Jack's pant leg, "and I know that you want a family too. But I don't know if I'm ready yet. Be patient with me, will you?"

"Love is patient. I read it on a poster." Jack hugged her. Kate relaxed against his body.

"I love you," she said, "no matter what kind of a husband your mother thinks you are."

"And I love you, too, my poor overworked wife. But to be honest, Kate, I agree with Mama on one thing she said."

"What's that?"

"You should be making your husband happy!"

Kate giggled.

"*Mangia!*" Mama called from the kitchen. "And hurry so nothing gets cold. Nothing worse than cold food. Kate, sit, Jackie, pour the wine."

The two rose from the sofa. On the way to the table Kate decided not to tell Jack there was a chance she might be expecting. She loved him so, no sense getting his hopes up, then having to disappoint him.

THURSDAY—SECOND WEEK OF ADVENT

Right after breakfast on Thursday morning Sister Mary Helen decided to go to her office. No more putting it off, she told herself firmly. She would have to get back to work. Suzanne was dead and nothing she could do would bring the young woman back. That efficient little Kate Murphy and her partner, old reliable Gallagher, were on the case. She smiled, imagining the two of them. Probably right this minute they were finding out all they could about Reina Martinez with her hard hate-filled eyes, and following the lead. Her lead, she thought with a surge of satisfaction.

The best thing you can do, she reminded herself, leaving the Sisters' dining room, is to get to work. "Doing the duty of the present moment," the old spiritual writers had called it. For a moment she wondered flippantly if any one of them had ever found his scribe murdered.

The hallway outside the dining room was strangely quiet. Yesterday the college had broken for Christmas vacation, and none too soon! With this murder business everyone had needed a vacation. Bits of curling ribbon torn from early Christmas gifts lay in the empty hall waiting for the janitor to sweep. The passageway had that eerie, deserted stillness of an empty school.

Imagine, Mary Helen fussed, her footsteps echoing on the parquet, breaking for vacation on a Wednesday. Whoever heard of such a thing? Cecilia had said something about class hours and scheduling. As she took the narrow staircase down to the basement, Mary Helen could already smell the dampness of the concrete floor. Why couldn't they arrange things to finish on a Friday and begin on a Monday the way they had when she taught school, she wondered, fumbling for her keys. So much more sensible.

She smiled, remembering how she had once looked forward to vacation time. Now she could be on vacation all the time and she wanted to work! She shook her head. If you ask me, people ought to retire at forty when they feel overused and go back to work at sixty-five when they feel useless, she thought, sticking the key into her office door. But so far no one had asked her.

Silently the door swung open, letting out a blast of cold air. The skin along her shoulder blades tightened as she stepped into the office, patting the wall for the light switch.

The long fluorescent-light tubes blinked on, flooding the small room. Their steady hum added a bit of warmth and a bit of familiar coziness.

Purposefully, Mary Helen walked to Suzanne's computer, switched it on, and inserted the disc for 1940. She'd conquer the blasted thing yet! Besides, what she didn't need was another phone call from Mary Agnes Van Der Zee.

"Ignore her," Eileen had advised. "When she went to school here she was Aggie Kelly from 14th Avenue. Just remember that!"

Nobody's what they seem, Mary Helen ruminated, staring at the menu on the computer screen. Not Mary Agnes Van Der Zee, not Suzanne Barnes. She punched in "Class of 40" with an apostrophe before the 40. CAN'T FIND THE FILE, the computer stated.

Mary Helen could feel her blood pressure rising. The file was in there. She knew it. What she couldn't figure out was how to get the confounded thing out. It was all a matter of hitting just the right combination of keys. After she'd found them, the solution would seem simple.

Just like Suzanne's murder, she thought, staring blankly at the screen. If she could just hit on the right combination of person and motive and opportunity, the solution would seem simple. Cradling her chin in the palm of one hand, she adjusted her bifocals and glared at the screen as if her schoolmarm glare would make it come clean.

The information was in the computer. She knew it. How had it been entered? She'd figure it out.

Suddenly an idea, which had been stuck down in her mind as tight as cotton in the top of an aspirin bottle, came loose. How had the murderer gotten into Suzanne's apartment building? How had he made it past the front-door buzzer? No one had mentioned breaking and entering.

Someone must have buzzed him in. Therefore someone must have known him.

Mary Helen could feel her spirits begin to perk up. Maybe she was on to something. Maybe Mrs. McGrath or someone on Suzanne's floor had heard the buzz. No harm in asking. She'd get Eileen and the two of them could go right over.

Turning off the computer, she crossed the office toward the light switch. "What about the duty of the present moment?" Mary Helen's conscience asked. "What about minding your own business?" she could hear Eileen ask. Eileen was always more direct.

Mary Helen was struggling with what to do, when her phone rang. "Hello," she said, picking it up on the second ring.

No one responded.

"Hello," she repeated. Ever since the phone company split up, the service had been terrible. Here was more evidence of it. Maddening!

Still no one.

"Hello," she tried a third time. She was about to hang

up when she heard it: slow, heavy, ragged breathing, as though a warm wet mouth were pressed close to the receiver.

"Sister," the low voice rasped, "how would you like to . . ." The skin across Mary Helen's shoulders and up her neck tingled. She slammed down the phone. Her whole body shook. An obscene phone call, she thought, feeling the goose bumps racing up her arms.

How would anyone know she was in her office? She stood stock-still and listened. Was there someone else on the basement floor? She strained for a sound. Everything was quiet, deadly quiet, so quiet that the hum of the lights and the electric clock seemed thunderous. Could someone outside have spotted the light from her narrow office windows?

She switched off the overhead light, cautiously edged toward the door, and listened. Nothing, except the sound of her own heart beating in her ears.

Shoulders hunched, eyes down, Mary Helen raced along the corridor toward the staircase. If someone was going to leap out of a doorway and attack her, she didn't want to see him coming. She'd die of fright before he ever grabbed her.

The thud of her feet hitting the stone floor reverberated and filled the hallway. Quickly she climbed the stairs, almost tripping herself in her haste. A scream was rising in her throat. She closed her mouth, tight, to keep it from escaping.

Mary Helen bolted across the deserted vestibule. The blank eyes of the Carrara marble busts stared ahead coldly as she pushed open the front door.

Leaning against a stone lion guarding the entrance, Mary Helen tried to catch her breath. This is ridiculous, she told herself. Whoever called is miles away in some grubby phone booth. Before her, the empty campus glistened in the crisp winter sun. Just recently she had read that San Francisco had an average of 16.7 sunny days in December. Thank God this was one of them. Nothing seems as frightening in the bright sunshine. In the distance she heard a car motor turn over, then start. At least another human being was near in case she had to shout for help.

She stood a moment with her eyes closed, waiting for her heartbeat to calm down. She could feel the sun warm and soothe her whole body. Consciously, she slowed her breathing.

"What in heaven's name . . . is wrong?" Eileen's voice startled her. Mary Helen's eyes shot open. Eileen was coming up the front stairs toward her. "You look white as a ghost," she said. "Are you all right?"

A few minutes later, sitting in the warm, cozy coffee room off the kitchen, Mary Helen told Eileen about the phone call.

"Who could have known I was there?" she asked her friend.

"It was probably just a coincidence," Eileen assured her. "Some lunatic going through the phone book. You know the college is listed, and your office number is under it."

"Why would he say 'Sister'?"

"It was probably just a lucky guess." Eileen refilled their coffee mugs from the large stainless steel urn.

"But I have never had one in my office before." Mary Helen was not convinced. She took another swallow of coffee. "An obscene call, I mean."

"How in heaven's name would you know whether you did or not? Suzanne always answered your phone," Eileen answered brightly. "Now, calm down, old dear." Smiling, she patted Mary Helen's hand.

Suzanne! Mary Helen remembered what she had been thinking about just before the phone rang.

"That reminds me." She was beginning to feel a little more like herself. "Before that—that—lunatic rang, I was on my way to get you."

"What on earth for?" Eileen's gray eyes studied her friend suspiciously. Once burned is twice shy!

"I had a thought about Suzanne." Eileen opened her mouth, but Mary Helen rushed on before she had a chance to say anything.

"Let me ask you, how did the murderer get in?" She pointed a finger at Eileen. "Can you tell me that? No one mentioned the front door having been forced, did they?"

Blinking, Eileen shook her head.

"So someone must have buzzed him in, right?"

Eileen nodded.

"So someone must have heard the buzzer, right?"

"I suppose you are right." Eileen stared at her friend, dumbfounded.

"Now, it would do no harm and I suspect a lot of good, if we could discover someone in the building who heard that buzzer. Right?"

Eileen's eyes widened. "But how on earth would we . . ." she left the question unfinished. "Who would have?"

"Mrs. McGrath, of course. She's the most likely. Right there by the front door. We could just drop over for a cup of tea, then introduce the subject casually."

"Just drop over, unannounced, and invite ourselves for a cup of tea?" Eileen's brogue was beginning to thicken. "Then, you say, introduce the subject casually?"

Mary Helen nodded.

"No harm, you say, and a lot of good?"

Adjusting her bifocals, Mary Helen nodded again. She could tell by the expression on Eileen's face that her friend was struggling with the suggestion. Tea would probably mean some fresh-baked bread, a temptation Eileen could hardly resist.

"And I suspect the next thing you'll say is, 'Far be it from us not to do a lot of good.' " Eileen raised her bushy eyebrows.

"It would be downright foolish." Mary Helen slammed her fist down on the tabletop for conviction.

"Well, there're no fools like old fools." Eileen smiled and patted her closed first.

Mrs. McGrath greeted the two nuns warmly and ushered them straight into her sunny kitchen. Mixing bowls, spoons, and a fine dust of flour covered the sideboard. Several round loaves of Irish bread sat cooling on the windowsill, plump dark raisins protruding from the thick golden crust. The aroma of fresh-baked bread filled the small room.

"Brightest room in the house," Mrs. McGrath said, motioning for the nuns to sit down. Smiling, she wiped her hands on the corner of her apron, then reached in the cupboard for teacups without even asking if they wanted any.

"Eddie, my husband, God rest him, loved this kitchen." She set three delicate white Belleek cups on the plastic tablecloth. "Said he'd rather have his tea in here than in any other place in the house."

Gingerly she moved a loaf of bread from the sill onto the table. "Said it cheered him up." With the skill of a highly trained surgeon, she cut into the bread, extracted two thick wedges, and deftly set one down before each of the nuns. With another flick of the blade she topped each slice with a dollop of rich, creamy butter.

Mary Helen's mouth began to water.

"If you ask me, what really cheered him up"—Mrs.

McGrath settled in for a cozy chat—"was being this close to the stove and the icebox."

The three women sat for a few moments in comfortable silence. Motes of dust spun down the golden beam of sun that settled on the tabletop.

"And what brings you good Sisters here so early on a Thursday morning?" Mrs. McGrath asked finally.

So much for dropping by and acting casual! Mary Helen wondered for a moment why she'd ever thought she could fool Mrs. McGrath. She sipped the hot tea. "Well," she began slowly. "It's this business of Suzanne's murder. I've been thinking about it—"

"I've been thinking of nothing else since it happened," Mrs. McGrath interrupted. "A terrible pity." She shook her head sadly. "A sweet young thing like that just snipped off before her life could ever come to full bloom."

The landlady shivered in spite of the warmth of the kitchen. "Imagine," she said, "someone coming right into this building, bold as brass, and murdering her. Why, it's enough to scare a body to death."

"Precisely my point," Mary Helen said. "No one mentioned anything about breaking and entering. So how did the murderer get in?"

Mrs. McGrath banged down the teapot and put her hands on her broad hips. "Police asked me the same thing, and damned if I know!" Suddenly realizing what she said, she blushed. "Excuse me, Sisters, but this whole bloody thing gets a body very upset."

Eileen patted her hand and smiled sweetly. "No need to be embarrassed, we understand exactly how you feel."

This was murder they were talking about. Mary Helen didn't have time to even acknowledge profanity. She pressed the point. "Did you hear a buzzer any time that night?"

"The blasted thing goes all day and half the night, if

the truth were known. They say the murder took place between two and four in the morning." Mrs. McGrath hesitated for a moment. "I was asleep, of course, but . . ."

Mary Helen nodded encouragingly.

"I'm a light sleeper," Mrs. McGrath continued. "I'm sure I'd have heard a buzzer at that ungodly hour."

"And did you?"

Mrs. McGrath shook her head. "Last one I heard was about eleven-thirty. I told the police that, too. Johnny Carson had just begun and I was dozing. Woke me up with a start." Mrs. McGrath cut two more slices of Irish bread and placed them on the nuns' plates.

"Delicious," Mary Helen said, nibbling at the bread and trying to hide her disappointment.

"It's a muddle, isn't it?" Mrs. McGrath brushed a few stray hairs from her flushed face. "Suzanne was murdered. The murderer got in. We know that. All I can figure is that either he came home with her or, God preserve us"—she blessed herself—"he lives right here under our very roof."

Leaving the apartment building, the two nuns ran into Patrick Flaherty in the entryway. He was fumbling with his front-door key.

"How do, 'Sters." Red-faced, he raised his cap, tipping it slightly. Mary Helen caught the faint odor of alcohol heavily camouflaged with minty breath-freshener. Most likely for Mrs. McGrath's benefit, she thought.

"Good morning, Mr. Flaherty," Eileen answered cheerfully. "And isn't it a beautiful morning for December? I see by your rosy face that you've been out for a walk already."

Flaherty flushed even deeper. Frowning, Mary Helen looked at Eileen with disbelief. Walk, my eye, she wanted to say. He's been out for his prelunch nip! But the twinkle in Eileen's eye told her the comment was unnecessary.

"We've just been visiting Mrs. McGrath," Eileen continued. "Lovely woman."

Flaherty shook his shaggy head in agreement. "My cousin's wife," he said. "Good woman, Delia. Don't find good women like you used to."

"We've been asking her about the night of Suzanne's murder," Mary Helen blurted out impatiently. She couldn't wait any longer for Eileen's chitchat to get to the point.

Blinking, Flaherty focused his myopic eyes and stared at her silently.

Mary Helen held her breath, regretting her impatience. Perhaps the shift in conversation was too abrupt. She didn't want to scare him into not talking.

"Turrible business," Flaherty muttered after a moment or two. "Beautiful girl. Hell of a shame, if you get my meaning."

Mary Helen let out her breath. Thank goodness, nothing seemed to stop Flaherty from talking.

"What we were wondering," she said, "is if you heard or noticed anything unusual on your floor that night?"

"Everything on my floor is unusual, 'Sters. Everything! Now, don't get me wrong, but just take Shultz, the librarian. Looks like the old ninety-eight-pound weakling. Remember those ads? The ones with the tough guy kicking sand in the little guy's face?"

Eileen nodded.

"Only this guy's got a beard, right?" Removing his cap, Flaherty scratched his head. "Month or so ago a turrible sound started coming out of his room. Drove me nuts. Would remind you of someone pounding sand into a rat hole. Steady, heavy banging." Flaherty thumped his clenched fist against the doorjamb to illustrate. "You get my meaning?"

Mary Helen nodded. Although she could never remember hearing anyone pound sand into a rat hole, she did get his meaning.

"Know what it was?" Flaherty paused just long enough to whet their curiosity, yet not lose their interest. A born storyteller, Mary Helen thought.

"I'll tell you what. Come to find out the guy was lifting weights. Don't get me wrong, but I ask you, 'Sters, why would a librarian need to lift weights? Not a book in the whole damn library that heavy, if you get my meaning." Flaherty laughed at his own joke. "Yet every night bang, bang, bang." He thumped the doorjamb three more times.

Mary Helen was just about to ask him if he had heard anyone buzzed into the apartment building on the Friday Suzanne was murdered when Mrs. McGrath's door swung open and she stepped into the hallway.

"Who the hell's banging the—I might have known it was you," she shouted as soon as she spotted Flaherty. "Not twelve noon yet and already you're hitting the walls! Have you no shame! Get in here before the neighbors see you. I'll feed you."

"Easy, Delia." Flaherty took off his cap and twirled it nervously in his hands. "I'm just here talking to the nuns."

The long, awkward silence confirmed Mary Helen's suspicions that Delia McGrath had not seen them standing in the darkened hallway.

"Nice visiting with you, Mr. Flaherty." Eileen smiled as though she hadn't heard a thing. "And you, too, Mrs. McGrath. And thanks again for the delicious tea."

Sheepishly, Flaherty closed the door behind them.

"Poor devil's going to catch it," Eileen said as the two nuns moved up California Street toward their parked car. The large red plastic wreaths hanging on the telephone poles rustled in the breeze coming in off the bay. Two sea gulls scavenging for food glided on black-tipped wings over the garbage cans.

"Well, we learned something, I guess," Mary Helen said when they finally reached the car. "Although I never did get around to finding out if Pat Flaherty heard someone come in."

"Oh, we did learn something." Eileen beamed. "Some of it, however, we could have guessed. Like Patty's tippling and Delia's fuse running a bit to the short side."

Straightening her skirt, she settled into the passenger's seat. "We learned that the last visitor was admitted at eleven-thirty."

"Hours before the murder," Mary Helen said.

The two nuns rode down California Street toward the college. A long gray bank of fog walled The City, just waiting to roll in; yet the sun was still bright.

"Another thing we must remember." Eileen turned toward her friend. "The librarian lifting weights."

"What about that?" Mary Helen asked, although she knew the answer.

"He'd be another person who is strong enough to have brutally murdered Suzanne."

The call came just before quitting time. Kate hung up the phone and stared at Gallagher. "You're not going to believe this," she said, feeling along the desktop for her right earring.

"Try me." Gallagher, who was pushed back in his swivel chair, loosened his loose tie still more.

"That was Bob Fitzpatrick from Sacramento about the Martinez woman, the one Sister Mary Helen called about."

"Yeah?" Gallagher sat up. "Go on," he said, an edge of impatience in his voice. The pair had spent most of the day on paperwork.

"Nothing much on her. A few juveniles. A bad check or two since. Nothing serious. But, this is the good part . . ."

"For crissake, Kate, get to the good part so we can get the hell out of here."

Kate blinked innocently at Gallagher, slowly replacing her earring. "The woman is a regular 'con doll,' " she said, shocked at her own callousness. She remembered well the outrage she had felt the first time she'd heard these women referred to in that way.

"Everyone calls them that, even the cons," a fellow officer had explained, baffled at her indignation. "And you'll notice these guys usually choose fat, dumpy, plain-looking gals. No competition from outside," he said. Kate was appalled.

"Why would a woman put herself in that position?" she had asked Gallagher later.

"Mother instinct? Masochistic? Savior complex? Born losers?" Gallagher had shrugged. "Who knows, Katie-girl. Furthermore, what poor dumb slob can ever explain what makes a woman tick?"

"Well, I'll be damned." Gallagher's low curse brought her back to reality.

"Yeah," she said, "her boyfriend is at Vacaville doing fifteen for second-degree murder. She visits faithfully. Makes sure the old man has cigarette money, et cetera."

Gallagher shook his head. For a moment he stared out the fourth-floor window. "Sounds like my kind of gal," he said. "I wonder if I could get Mrs. G to hustle in Calistoga getting my cigar money." He laughed. "Speaking of whom, I better beat it, Kate. I told you, tonight's one of the grand-kids' birthdays. Close to Christmas and all. The missus makes a big fuss so the kid won't feel left out. Can you imagine one of her grandchildren feeling left out?" Gallagher checked his watch. "I'll catch hell if I don't get out of here on time.

"How do you think she got friendly with Suzanne?" he asked, turning over his ashtray into the battered wastepaper basket beside the desk. To Kate's knowledge, it was the only attempt her partner ever made to clear the top of his desk. She watched the gray ash rise, then gently settle along the edge of the desk. Gallagher looked around for something to wipe off the dust. For a moment Kate was afraid he was about to use his tie. Instead he settled for the edge of his hand, which he then wiped on his pant leg.

Mrs. G would kill him, she thought.

"Huh?" Gallagher looked at her quizzically.

Kate pulled her mind back to real murder. "I don't know," she said, remembering his question.

"How about first thing tomorrow we take a ride up the country and talk to the gal? If she's a friend of Suzanne's, she may be able to give us a lead on Lover Boy. From the looks of things, he and Suzanne were plenty friendly. Maybe friend introduced friend." Gallagher gathered his jacket from over the back of the chair. "Although I'm still putting my money on old Punch," he added.

"Fitzpatrick said he thinks there's a child involved," she added.

"So, she's married to the guy in Vacaville?"

"No." She was betting that would stop him.

"No?" Gallagher halted midway across the empty detail, and turned. "A baby and not married?"

Kate smiled. "Honest to God, Denny, sometimes you sound like something right out of the ark. You know, don't you, that a woman doesn't necessarily have to be married to have a baby?" Kate rummaged through her purse for her package of cigarettes and took one out.

"After five kids, now you're going to start telling me the facts of life?" he snapped, his eyebrows raised. Apparently doing paperwork all day had shortened his temper.

Kate could feel her own temper begin to short. "No," she said, "just the facts of life now. Lots of women are deciding to have children and remain single."

"Jeez, Kate! If your father, God rest him, heard you talk like that, he'd roll right over in his grave. God knows, I thought when we got you married . . ." He shook his head.

Kate couldn't tell if it was from exasperation or disbelief. Whichever, she couldn't resist saying, "It's too late for me to make that decision, but it is conceivable in today's world that one of your own daughters might . . ." That was as far as she got.

Gallagher's face reddened.

"You watch your mouth, young lady." Shaking his finger toward her, he cut her off midsentence, much as her own father might have done. She closed her eyes, her whole body tense. How dare he speak to her like that! Gallagher was not her father, he was her partner. She opened her eyes ready to fight, but it was too late.

The detail door slammed behind Gallagher. The rattle of the pebble-glass half reverberated through the empty room. She could hear his heavy footsteps echo down the corridor. Kate stood there holding her unlit cigarette, feeling humiliated. No, maybe that wasn't the right word. Maybe *foolish* was more accurate. Gallagher had spoken to her as he would to a twelve-year-old, rather than to his partner, his equal. She could feel her face flush. As much as she hated to admit it, she had baited him, the way a twelve-year-old might.

She sat behind her desk, lit a cigarette, and stared out at the traffic crawling along the James Lick Freeway toward the Peninsula. Dusk was settling over the downtown high-rises.

What had gotten into her? She and Gallagher had not had a flare-up in months. Actually, it was almost a year. She smiled, thinking of all the arguments they used to have about her living with Jack. Denny had heartily disapproved of their "arrangement" and considered it his bounden duty to tell her so.

They had so many heated battles that their fellow officers had started calling them "dennybrooks" instead of donnybrooks. But that had all stopped when Jack and she were married.

What caused today's flare-up? she wondered, lighting another cigarette, her last. She crumpled the empty package and tossed it into the battered wastepaper basket. Its force made a little cloud of Denny's ashes rise.

One thing she knew for sure; she had provoked it. But somehow she couldn't resist. What was wrong with her nerves? Was it this latest murder, or having Mary Helen involved again, or the fact that the victim's baby was nowhere to be found?

Slowly she inhaled, then blew out a steady stream of smoke, watching it rise, spread out, then float in heavy clouds on the room's stale air.

If she were honest with herself, she'd have to admit it was not her job that was making her so testy, although the pressure did not help. It was her uncertainty, her mixed emotions about starting a family. If she were perfectly honest, she'd have to admit that she wanted both her job and a child. But right now, as unnatural as it sounded, she wasn't sure which she wanted most. And there had been the slipup with the pills. What if she were pregnant, right now? Guiltily she stubbed out the cigarette. She should stop smoking regardless. Maybe that's why she was feeling so jittery. Her whole system might be adjusting to support new life. Or maybe . . . Kate pulled out her purse calendar and tried to calculate. She cursed aloud, wishing she weren't so careless about marking the days.

The phone rang. "Hi, hon." It was Jack. "Will you be home soon, or do I have time for a quick affair with Bridie the cleaning lady?" he asked.

"I'll be right home, you jerk," she said. "Don't you dare start a quick affair with Bridie or anybody else when you can have one with me, or Gallagher will be investigating your murder."

"Ah, you're so romantic, my love. Hurry home, my sweet." Jack made kissing noises into the phone. "I can hardly wait till you get here. And, by the way, would you pick up a quart of milk on your way? I need it for the mashed potatoes."

As soon as Kate opened the front door, she could hear Jack on the phone.

"Okay, Ma. I really don't know, Ma. We'll see. . . . Okay, Ma. Cripes, Ma. Okay, Ma." The last *okay* sounded resigned. "I'll ask her."

What in the world does his mother want now? Kate wondered, realizing that the slow, traffic-filled ride home had done nothing to improve her disposition.

"What's up?" she asked the moment her husband put down the receiver.

Turning, Jack ran his fingers through his hair. "Same old crap," he said.

"Which old crap?" Kate took the quart of milk from the paper sack and placed it on the kitchen table.

"Thanks, hon," Jack said. His lips brushed her cheek as he grabbed for the carton.

The halfhearted kiss put the phone call in second place. "Aren't you the same guy who not a half an hour ago was blowing passionate kisses over the phone?" Kate asked.

Jack grinned, set the carton back on the kitchen table, and put his arms around her. This time he kissed her in earnest.

"What did your mother want?" Kate asked again when they finally settled down in the living room after dinner. The lights on the small Christmas tree in the corner filled the darkened room with red and blue and muted gold. Their glow gave a blush to the white wine in the half-filled glasses on the coffee table. Kate felt soft and cozy. She had resisted asking the question through the whole meal.

"My mother?" Jack tried to sound as if the call had slipped his mind. Kate wasn't fooled. Whatever it was, it was bothering him. It had bothered him all during dinner. So much so that he'd asked about Suzanne's murder. Kate was surprised, since early in their relationship they had decided to try not to bring their work home. Murder and rape added nothing to a relaxing evening. But tonight Kate was glad for the distraction. At the moment, murder had seemed more relaxing than dealing with Jack's mother.

Unfortunately, the conversation had only added to her frustration. All she had were questions. Who was Suzanne? And the blond guy in the snapshot? Whoever he was, he was an essential link. Did he have a motive for killing her? Or was Rosenberg the killer? How did Reina Martinez fit into the picture? And the most poignant question of all, where was Suzanne's child? Tomorrow, maybe she and Gallagher would find some answers.

Gallagher! Kate winced at the thought of him. First thing tomorrow morning she'd apologize.

"Yes, your mother," Kate said, taking the bull by the horns. Today had been a bad day. No sense counting on a cozy evening. Might as well ruin the whole day, she thought, start fresh tomorrow. "You know, pal, just before dinner. What did she want?"

"I thought you'd forget." Jack put his strong arms around her and pulled her close to him on the couch.

Kate snuggled in. She loved his faint spicy smell when she rested her head against his shoulder. She could feel his lips and his warm breath in her thick hair.

"A good detective never forgets," Kate answered dreamily.

"Why did I pick a smart redhead when I could have easily had a dumb blonde?"

"Who?" Kate sat up suddenly. "You never mentioned a blonde before," she said.

"Only kidding." Jack pulled her back toward him, but the mood was broken.

"Your mother?" she asked. Kate could feel the heel of Jack's hand moving slowly up her backbone. Poor fellow was trying to calm her. For whatever reason, it was working.

"All she wanted was to settle Christmas."

"Settle Christmas? What's to settle? When is it anyway?" Kate asked, suddenly aware of how much of her time and attention this case had absorbed.

"It's usually December twenty-fifth." Jack's fingers massaged her neck and shoulders.

This man is in the wrong profession, Kate thought, the tension across her back relaxing. "You know what I mean," she said, feeling like purring.

"Let's see, today's Thursday. Christmas is a Tuesday." Jack figured for a moment. Kate yawned.

"A week from Tuesday," he said.

"A week from Tuesday?" she repeated, jerking awake. "I don't have any cards written. And presents . . . I need to wrap the presents. This Christmas should be special . . ."

"Down, hon. Calm down." Jack refilled their wine glasses. "The weekend's coming. We can split it up. I'll address, you wrap."

Kate sipped her wine. Lying on her side, she pulled her bare feet up onto the couch. Sleepily she rested her head on Jack's knee. He kneaded her back gently all along her angel wings.

"I love you," she said.

"I'm never sure if it's me or my massage." Jack bent over and kissed her cheek, his hand resting on her hip.

"What did your mother want to settle?"

"Jeez, Kate." Jack sounded frustrated. She was sorry. She knew her timing was all off. She'd make it up to him.

Jack drained his glass. "If we'll come for Christmas dinner," he said.

"Why not?"

Jack looked surprised. "Well, I know how special Christmas is to you. I almost lost these talented fingers stringing that lousy popcorn." He pointed toward the tree. "And I know my mother is bugging us. Only because she loves us, that's how she shows it. But I don't want her to spoil it for you. I thought we might want to start some of our own traditions. If we ever have a family—"

"Do you think I'd make a good mother?" Kate rolled over on her back.

Jack stared down at her in amazement. "Aren't you the same gal who didn't want to discuss—"

"Do you?" Kate cut in again.

"Of course I do," he answered. His hazel eyes studied

her. She could tell he was puzzled. Kate was puzzled too. She didn't know what had gotten into her tonight. Maybe the wine, maybe the Christmas lights, maybe the stirrings of motherhood.

"Would you make a good father?"

"Best ever."

"What do we know about raising children?"

"Same as every other couple who has a first child."

Kate reached up and touched a lock of Jack's hair. She curled it between her fingers. "I'm serious," she said. "What do we know about discipline, for example? Who was the disciplinarian in your house?"

"Ma, who else?" Jack smiled. "Fastest wooden spoon in the West," he said. "And speaking of whom, do you want to have our own Christmas Eve here? Just you and me and whoever will come along . . . Then hit the Bassetti clan for Christmas dinner?"

"Sounds good," Kate said absently. She had begun to twist a thick strand of her own hair around her index finger. "Listen, pal. What do we know about developing a good self-concept, for instance, or about love . . . The right kind of love for kids, that's important."

Bending forward, Jack kissed her urgently on the lips. His hands caressed her body.

"Not that kind." She ran a single finger down the back of his neck.

Playfully Jack scooped her up in his arms and struggled up from the couch.

"I know the best thing a father can do for his children." Holding her tightly, he nuzzled her hair.

"I suppose you read it on a poster."

"Where else?" Jack said.

Slowly he started up the narrow staircase.

"What is it?" Kate asked.

"The best thing a father can do for his children is love their mother."

Kate giggled. "At least that's something we can practice ahead of time," she said.

"Damn right," Jack answered, turning the corner into their bedroom.

FRIDAY—SECOND WEEK OF ADVENT

"You think it'll be sunny downtown?" Kate hollered down from the upstairs bedroom.

Jack didn't answer. Kate heard the steady clank of dishes being emptied from the dishwasher. This was Jack's week. He probably can't hear me, she thought, swilling an extra jet of hair spray over the front of her heavy hair. Kate had trouble keeping that wedged front piece in place, especially on a long day, and today promised to be a long day.

"A woman may work from sun to sun, but a houseman's work is never done," she heard him shout as he trudged slowly up the narrow staircase.

"You think it'll be sunny downtown?" Kate repeated.

Jack looked out the front bedroom window. Heavy damp banks of early-morning fog rolling in from the beach wet the pavement. All the cars heading toward downtown had their headlights on and the windshield wipers going. Across Geary the windows of the houses shone like so many squares of light suspended in gray space.

"Doesn't look like this will burn off too soon," he said, although both of them knew you could leave the Avenues banked in fog and emerge downtown twenty minutes later to a sunny day. This phenomenon always amazed newcomers, but the natives took it for granted.

"Besides, aren't you going to Calistoga? This time of year it's always cold up there."

"You're right, pal." Kate hesitated, then grabbed her

beige London Fog from the closet. She hated to wear it. The trench coat looked too much like she was trying to play cop.

"See you at the Hall?" she asked Jack.

"You'll probably be gone by the time I get there. What did you decide about tonight?"

"I think I will ask Sister Mary Helen and Sister Eileen to dinner, if I can get them. Maybe have a little Christmas party. A few crackers and cheese, nice dinner. You are right. We need to start celebrating or Christmas will pass us right smack by."

"Whose Friday is it to cook?" Jack asked, strapping on his shoulder holster.

"Guess." Kate winked, kissed him on the cheek, and started down the stairs.

"Where do you think I put that blonde's number?" she heard Jack call as she slammed the front door shut.

Mary Helen was surprised and a little apprehensive when Kate Murphy called. She half expected to be upbraided for "returning to the scene of the crime," as Eileen so dramatically put their latest visit to Mrs. McGrath. So the dinner invitation was an unexpected pleasure.

Leaving the small phone booth, she hurried down the convent hall past Anne's bedroom. The great fragrance of white jasmine filled the narrow corridor. Mary Helen stopped to sniff. Sister Anne was no doubt pretzeled on her green yoga pillow in a reflective stance. The first time she'd heard Anne say that, it took Mary Helen a full minute to figure out she meant she was thinking. Or perhaps the young nun was burning incense and centering herself, whatever that meant.

Whatever it meant, Mary Helen had to admit that it seemed to work for Anne. And with Suzanne's brutal murder laying such a pall over the college community's Christmas preparations, Mary Helen was not ready to knock anything that worked.

"Any port in a storm," she had told Therese last week when she heard her complaining about the offensive odor of the incense.

But the platitude had fallen on deaf ears, although Mary Helen was never sure just how deaf. Therese had a way of hearing whatever you didn't want her to hear.

"Odious odor," Therese had snapped, hurrying by Anne's room.

"Has a nice ring to it," Mary Helen said, just for ducks. "Eau de Odious Odor!"

"Pure corny, old dear!" Eileen had commented later, pulling her soft, round face into a distasteful pucker.

A full chorus of men's deep voices burst from behind Anne's closed door.

"The people who walk in darkness . . ." they sang, "will see . . . will see a great light."

Anne must be listening to an Advent tape. Weston Priory or St. Louis Jesuits probably, Mary Helen wasn't sure which.

"Will see, will see a great light," the phrase resounded in her mind's ear. Blast it! Mary Helen thought, descending the stairs as quickly as her bifocals would permit. Now that confounded tune will be stuck in my head all day long. She stopped for a moment by the community room door to see if Eileen was in there. At the far end of the large room, two of the younger nuns were busy twisting paper and stacking kindling in the large stone fireplace. Soon the room would be warm and cozy with a big roaring fire. For a moment, she was tempted just to settle in one of the stuffed easy chairs and wait for Eileen to appear, forget everything for a while; but she knew she couldn't.

Mary Helen paused by the coat closet next to the front door long enough to pull out her heavy camel's hair coat. When she opened the convent door, she was glad she had.

Great waves of thick wet fog billowed across the campus. The hill was gray and silent; not even one light shone from the college building. She hurried up the driveway, turning on the road leading to the dining room. She hoped Eileen was still there. Moisture formed on her bifocals, the cold made her nose run, and she could see her own breath.

Downright eerie, she thought, digging into her pocket for a Kleenex. In the distance she heard the hum of a car engine. She stopped, listened. The sound seemed to be coming closer. She peered uncertainly into the grayness of the foggy road. No headlights. Just the steady hum becoming louder and louder.

Was a car coming up the hill? A delivery truck perhaps? Would it break through the fog momentarily? Cautiously she moved to the side of the road and waited. Suddenly, the engine sound died. She waited to hear a car door slam. Nothing.

"Yoo-hoo," she shouted into the fog. Her words tumbled down the silent hill. A prickly chill ran up her neck. "Wrapped in a cloak of gray mystery," some turn-of-the-century poet had described fog. At the moment, Mary Helen couldn't agree with him more.

Wiping her glasses, she turned back toward the convent. The large stone building had disappeared in the deep wetness. One or two small hazy bedroom lights were the only proof that the building still existed.

In the distance she heard the slow, heavy crunch, crunch, crunch of footsteps on the macadamized road.

"Yoo-hoo," she called again. "Who's there?"

She listened. Silence. The footsteps had stopped. Was she just imagining them?

All at once they started again. But this time the rhythm was different. The crunch was quick and steady and somewhat familiar. She squinted into the fog, but she could still see no one.

It's got to be one of the nuns, she thought, deliberately trying to steady her wobbly knees.

She strained to hear. The footsteps were drawing nearer. Then she heard it—a light, high-pitched tinkle. A tinkle? It took her a moment to place it. Of course, Christmas bells! Relieved, she wanted to laugh aloud. Certainly no one wishing to do you bodily harm would come stalking with a Christmas bell.

"Yoo-hoo," she called again.

"Yoo-hoo to you too," Eileen called back, emerging from the fog. Sure enough, on her lapel was a large holly corsage complete with three red Christmas bells.

"You scared me," Mary Helen said. "All I could hear were footsteps and those silly bells."

"You think I gave you a fright?" Eileen's eyebrows shot up. "How, in the name of all that's good and holy, do you think I felt when I heard the footsteps stop?"

"You heard footsteps stop?"

"Of course I did. You stopped, didn't you?" Eileen studied Mary Helen's face. "I really did give you a fright, didn't I?"

For a moment she wanted to tell Eileen about the second set of slow, heavy footsteps she thought she had heard and the car engine stopping, but maybe she was just fantasizing. Her nerves, no doubt. Probably just a delivery boy lost on the hill.

Mary Helen smiled. "If I had a heart, I'd be dead," she said instead.

Both nuns laughed. As the sound rippled into the fog,

Mary Helen could not help wondering if there was a third person groping unseen somewhere out there.

Over coffee in the small alcove off the kitchen, Mary Helen relayed Kate Murphy's dinner invitation.

"We're both invited," she said. "Kate made that quite clear. Are you busy?"

"I won't go so far as to say I was busy." Eileen hesitated. "But . . ."

Mary Helen was surprised at the hesitancy. Eileen loved to go out to dinner. "But what?" she asked.

"Do you think our going out to dinner seems . . . seems . . . I don't know what word to use exactly."

Mary Helen bit her tongue. Imagine, Eileen lost for words!

"Seems . . . right, I guess," Eileen said finally.

"Right?"

"Yes, what with Suzanne buried only a week and the murder still unsolved, should we be more . . . more respectful?"

"Of Suzanne or the murderer?" Mary Helen was clearly annoyed.

"You know very well what I mean." Eileen narrowed her gray eyes into slits.

For a moment the two friends glared at one another. But only for a moment. "Getting a bit testy, are we, old dear?" Eileen asked.

Mary Helen had to admit it. Eileen was right. She did feel impatient and edgy. She was provoked! "Shall see . . . shall see a great light . . ." the chorus from Anne's tape played over again in her mind's memory. She took a sip of her coffee before answering. No sense in backing down too quickly.

"I guess so," she admitted finally. "But who isn't these days? This tragedy is so . . . so tragic." Silly as it sounded, Mary Helen couldn't think of a better word to describe the situation.

Eileen patted her friend's hand. "Maybe *respectful* was the wrong word to use about going out to dinner," she said. "Maybe I should have said we need more time to mourn. There's an old saying at home, you know . . . 'Who lacks time to mourn, lacks time to heal.'" Mary Helen might have known!

"The murder itself is horrible enough," Mary Helen continued, as if she had not heard Eileen, "but now we find out we never knew who Suzanne really was in the first place. So we have scant idea of who could possibly have a motive.

"And that blasted computer. Do you know what I thought of yesterday when I tried to pull out the alumnae list for Mary Agnes Van Der Zee?" She looked at her friend accusingly.

Eileen's eyebrows shot up. "I haven't the foggiest notion," she said.

"That if we hit upon the right combination of person, motive, and opportunity, we could find Suzanne's murderer."

"Did that computer of yours mention anything about leaving it to the police?" Eileen asked, her brogue beginning to thicken. Apparently she had had second thoughts about playing detective.

Oh, oh! Mary Helen swallowed hard. She couldn't lose Eileen. She needed her for backup. Why, every Holmes has a Watson, every Nick a Nora! She'd have to lay it on thick.

She hurried on. "Do you know, this morning, when I walked by Anne's room, she was playing an Advent tape and it's been running through my mind all morning? Do you know what the words were?"

Eileen shook her head.

" 'The people who walk in darkness,' " Mary Helen sang. Her voice quivered a bit. She figured the quiver must add a touch of drama to her presentation, since Eileen listened wide-eyed. " 'Shall see a great light'!

"Don't you think that's an omen?" she asked. Get Eileen where she's vulnerable.

Her friend simply frowned.

Mary Helen refused to be discouraged. "Now, at this moment, who is more in the darkness than we are? The light will come. We will find the murderer who's running loose somewhere out there"—she waved her hand vaguely toward Marin County—"and we will apprehend him so we can once and for all put Suzanne to her proper rest."

"Maybe we should just mourn," Eileen suggested sheepishly.

"Do you know what Shakespeare says about that?"

"About Suzanne, the murderer, or mourning?"

Mary Helen knew Eileen couldn't resist making fun of a misplaced antecedent. "About mourning," she said, remembering once again with greater clarity why she was so fond of Eileen, why they had been friends for over fifty years. They were a perfect match for one another!

"Moderate lamentation is the right of the dead; excessive grief the enemy of the living." Mary Helen paused with satisfaction.

"Will you translate that or shall I guess?" Eileen asked flatly.

"You know what I mean. The police are doing a fine job, of course. The best way they know how. Kate and Inspector Gallagher will be going to Calistoga, if they haven't gone already."

Eileen made a face, which Sister Mary Helen chose to ignore.

"That we owe Suzanne something more than mourning. We owe her vindication." Mary Helen paused dramatically. Eileen rolled her gray eyes.

"That a deadly unincarnational pall"—Mary Helen knew Anne would approve of the term *unincarnational*, although she wasn't sure there was such a word—"has fallen over the nuns and the college's Christmas spirit."

"And what are we supposed to do about that?" Eileen asked, blinking her big gray eyes.

Eileen was softening. Mary Helen could tell by the blinking eyes. Now was the moment to play her trump card.

"We must become involved! It is only the decent thing to do," she said. "We owe it to all of them: Suzanne, the police, the nuns, the Church."

"You mean the Holy Roman Catholic Church?" Eileen asked in disbelief.

"Of course I do! Shouldn't we observe the liturgical year and shouldn't Advent be a time of joyful waiting, not a time of sadness and fear?" Mary Helen didn't wait for Eileen's answer. "We owe it to all of them," she said, slamming her fist on the table. The coffee cups rattled.

"To all of them," she repeated, for emphasis, "to help apprehend the murderer!"

"And you have a plan of how we are to do just that, I suppose." Eileen pursed her lips.

"Darn right I do," Mary Helen said, relieved she'd won yet another hand.

"What am I doing here?" Anne muttered to no one in particular as she drove the convent car slowly down the college hill. To her right, Mary Helen peered out the window. The dense fog had begun to lift.

"You can go straight up to California, then turn left.

You know, dear, by Children's Hospital?" Eileen hung over the back of the seat. The trio drove down Parker, across Geary, to California in silence.

Even this early in the afternoon, the streets were a tangle of traffic, all thinking they had the right of way without even looking. Shoppers toting heavy plastic shopping bags hurried across the intersections. Vacationing kids on Mongoose dirt bikes jumped curbs and chased each other in and around parked cars.

A veritable army of little old ladies with tightly permanented gray hair, sitting low in their heavy 1960s model cars like so many Sherman tanks, made left turns at whim.

"They're natives," Eileen had explained. "Why, most of these ladies have lived on the Avenues since they were nothing but sand dunes. By now they figure that they own the whole neighborhood. And who in their right mind is going to argue with them?"

"What are we doing here?" Anne asked when they finally parked the car. "Do you have a plan?" She turned to face Mary Helen, her hazel eyes blinking nervously behind the purple-rimmed glasses.

"Of course we have a plan," Mary Helen said with more confidence than she felt. No sense shaking Anne's faith any more than it was shook. To be perfectly honest, Mary Helen had to admit *plan* was a rather overblown word for what she had in mind. *Shot in the dark* might have described it more accurately.

"As we explained, when we asked you to come . . ." she began.

"Is that the imperial 'we' you are using, Mary Helen, or are you including me in concocting this caper?" Eileen asked from the backseat.

Mary Helen shot her friend what she considered to be an icy stare, and continued.

"As I was saying, since Kate Murphy and Inspector Gallagher are no doubt in Calistoga interrogating the Martinez woman . . ." She paused, pleased that she had remembered to use the word *interrogating*. It sounded so much more official than *talking to*. "And as they can't be everyplace at once, the only decent thing to do seems to be to help them out."

"Help them out?"

"Of course. By donating a few hours of time talking to the people on Suzanne's floor. Finding out what they know."

"It seems to me the police must have questioned them already." Anne nervously twisted the wide-band turquoise ring on her finger.

"That's where you come in." Mary Helen patted her on the knee. "People who would be reluctant to talk to the police may open up to you. You're young, attractive, and you look . . . look so . . ." Mary Helen struggled for the word.

"Unconventual!" Eileen prompted, a twinkle in her eye.

Mary Helen nodded in agreement. What a perfect way to describe Anne in her faded blue jeans, Mount St. Francis sweatshirt, argyle wool socks, and Birkenstocks.

She had traded in her Paiute moccasins for Birkenstocks right after the Holy Hill murders. Mary Helen was not aware if the shoes had worn out or had been retired. Anne never said.

"So, my plan is for you to ring Mimi and her doctor friend's bell. Chitchat, see what you can see. Then maybe talk with the hairdresser, if she's home. Eileen and I will"—she paused for breath—"cover the rest of Suzanne's neighbors."

"Glory be to God!" Eileen whispered as the trio darted across California Street. "For a moment I had the dreadful feeling you were going to say 'case the joint.' "

Anne's buzz admitted the three of them to the apartment building. The two older nuns stood on the stairwell until Mimi opened the door, and the silence in the hallway suggested a successful entry.

"See how easy it was to get in?" Mary Helen said.

"Just as the murderer must have done." Beside her, Eileen shivered.

Mary Helen nodded in agreement.

"Now that we're in, old dear, what in heaven's name do we do?" Eileen hissed.

From the stairway door Mary Helen surveyed the second floor. The coroner's seal was still affixed to Suzanne's door, not that Mary Helen ever wanted to go back into that apartment again. The violence and horror of the scene welled up in her memory. Suzanne's sprawled, stiffening body, battered and flung across the crumpled bed. There had been no dignity in the young woman's death, no repose. Well, Mary Helen would see to it that at least she would be avenged.

Taking a deep breath, she squared her shoulders and marched to the first door on her right and pressed the bell of Apartment 201.

She was taken aback when Arnold Shultz threw open the door. Somehow she had not expected him to be home. Or if he was at home, to answer his doorbell more slowly so she'd have time to rehearse her introduction.

Arnold Shultz must have been surprised too. He just stood there in his trunks, mouth gaping, large eyes blinking behind his thick steel-rimmed glasses, hand gripping the doorknob.

Mary Helen remembered seeing the young man at Suzanne's funeral, but at a distance. This close he reminded her of a younger Barbra Streisand with a short, well-trimmed beard. Totally dressed, Mary Helen realized, he would have somewhat of a gentle rabbinical look.

"Hi," he said, regaining his composure. She was startled by the deepness of his voice.

"Can I help you?" His free hand ran across his bare chest and twirled the few straggly hairs he found there.

"I hope we didn't disturb you." Mary Helen looked down at the trunks.

"No, I was just working out," he said, following her gaze. "What can I do for you?"

Fortunately, Eileen launched into an explanation of their friendship with Suzanne and their interest in the case. Before they knew it, Shultz had seated them on two chairs and had gone to a back room for a T-shirt.

Mary Helen studied the living room. A gleaming steel set of weights, barbells, and gym apparatus for developing who-knows-what dominated one side of the high-ceilinged room. As if an imaginary line had been drawn down the middle, three comfortable chairs flanked the brick fireplace. Built-in bookcases on either side of the mantel bulged with a haphazard combination of hardbacks, paperbacks, and magazines. Mounted on the wall over the mantelpiece was an old rifle that could have belonged to Daniel Boone, a wickedly curved samurai sword, and a rusty used-looking bayonet.

Obviously he is a collector, Mary Helen was about to remark to Eileen. But Eileen, in true librarian form, had busied herself studying the bookshelves.

"Lucky you found me home," Shultz commented as he entered the room, wearing a worn Bay to Breakers T-shirt. "I was just getting ready to run." He stood in front of the fireplace, put the palms of his hands against the mantel, and slowly shuffled backward. Mary Helen could see the muscles on the back of his legs strain.

"We were very fortunate," Mary Helen agreed, wondering why in the world he was home at all.

She didn't have to wonder long; Shultz volunteered the information. "My month to work Saturdays," he said. "So I get Fridays off." It seemed reasonable enough.

"How well did you know Suzanne?" Mary Helen began. When a runner is into warming up, she knew enough not to beat around the bush.

"Not very," he said, putting his hands on his hips and leaning first left, then right. "She had a good body, though. Nice tight stomach and buttocks, well-developed thighs, strong calves. Could have used a little work on the pectorals. Told her so too."

He put his toes on the hearth, then leaned forward. Sister Mary Helen wasn't sure what he was limbering, but she thought it might have something to do with his hamstrings.

"She got all bent out of shape, if you'll excuse the pun." Shultz blinked through his thick glasses at the two nuns to see if they got it. Both laughed appreciatively.

"Would have been good for her too," he added in a low-pitched tone that sounded almost somber. "The woman was depressed. Running counters depression, lessens anxiety, heightens mental acuity. Downright mystic experience." Shultz was pulling in deep breaths and letting them out in short deliberate puffs.

"Have you any idea why she might have been depressed?"

Shultz stopped suddenly and stared at her, as if he could not believe that anyone could be so ignorant. In the silence Mary Helen's heart began to race. Maybe they had finally hit on something. Some secret cause of depression that Shultz had discovered, which would give them an insight into Suzanne and why she was troubled.

"Like I said, not enough exercise, not enough stimuli in her life." Mary Helen felt a sag of disappointment as Arnold Shultz warmed to his subject. "Body must be full of toxin. The woman left home and came back home as regular as clockwork. Never any deviation. Not much action at all across the hall. Stagnates the mind, you know? Who wouldn't be depressed? I tried to tell her."

If the man didn't know Suzanne's innermost secrets, he certainly knew enough about her outward activity.

"Not many visitors, hum?" Mary Helen asked hopefully.

"One, two maybe." Shultz had begun to run in place. Mary Helen knew her questions were numbered.

"Could you recognize them?" He nodded. She must remember to get that photo of Suzanne and the blond young man back from Kate.

"Did you hear or see anything unusual the night she was murdered?"

He shook his head. "By that time of night, I was sound asleep. . . . Sleep like a baby. Body's like a fine-tuned instrument, you know." Arnold was beginning to huff a bit. "Keep it up and it works perfectly."

"Did you by any chance have a visitor around eleven-thirty that night?" Mary Helen asked, still wondering about the buzz Mrs. McGrath had heard.

"You've got to be kidding." Arnold looked almost offended. "I don't like anyone enough to let them interfere with my rest."

He jogged toward the door. The two nuns took the hint.

"Thank you for your time," Mary Helen said. "I know you're eager to go."

Picking up the pace, Arnold Shultz opened the front door to let the pair out. Following them, he slammed the door shut and without breaking stride headed across the hall-way and down the steps.

Mary Helen listened to his wake rising from the stair-well.

"Cheerful little fellow," Eileen said.

"A regular running antidote for what ails you," Mary Helen replied.

"He doesn't seem like the murdering type."

"Maybe, but we can't let that influence us. Did you notice that he was very knowledgeable about Suzanne's activities? Didn't seem to miss a trick. And did you notice all those weapons above the mantel?"

"God helps us, Mary Helen, you can't accuse a man of murder just because he's a busybody or because he's a collector, for that matter." Eileen puckered her face.

"And let's not forget that Friday, the day she was murdered, was his day off."

"For the love of all that is good and holy, he would have been off any day of the week at that time of night."

"Besides," Mary Helen added, not to be thwarted, "Shultz reminds me of a description I just read: 'He was a spare little man, full of dash and supremely confident in his own ability.'" She paused triumphantly.

"Now, where did you read that?" Eileen asked.

"In the mystery I was reading just before Advent, just before Suzanne was murdered."

"Was that the description of the murderer?"

Mary Helen could feel her face redden. "No," she admitted, as much as she hated to, "it was the description of the police inspector."

The two nuns crossed the hallway. Before Eileen could protest, Sister Mary Helen had rung the bell to Apartment 202.

"This one is right next to Suzanne. If any of the neighbors heard anything, surely this one did," she whispered out of the corner of her mouth.

Short, round Sarah Farraday swung open her front door and greeted the nuns with a broad smile.

"How nice," she said, as though she were expecting them. "Please, come in."

Eileen opened her mouth to begin an explanation, but it was unnecessary. Ms. Farraday ushered them right into her living room. Healthy philodendron and graceful spider plants hung in baskets from the ceiling and met rubber plants and ferns growing up from the floor. The flowered chintz-covered furniture added to the "jungle" look Patrick Flaherty had mentioned.

"Is it too early for a touch of eggnog?" Ms. Farraday asked pleasantly, tilting her head so her dangling Christmas-tree earrings swung back and forth.

"Never too early for a little Christmas cheer." Shaking her index finger at the pair, she answered her own question.

With a swish of her long Christmas-print mumu, Ms. Farraday disappeared behind a wooden swinging door that undoubtedly led to her kitchen. The two nuns were left alone.

Mary Helen looked around. In her opinion, *jungle* was a bit overdrawn as a description of the room. She could understand, however, why Flaherty had chosen that term to describe Ms. Farraday's apartment. Right now, if anything, it looked like Christmas in the jungle. In one corner a living Christmas tree was colorfully decorated with children's handmade ornaments. A bank of poinsettias filled the fireplace hearth. Candles and ribbons ran along the mantel.

The apartment, at least as much of it as Sister Mary Helen could see, was decorated to the nines. She would bet good money that Ms. Farraday was one of those primary teachers who walked wonderingly through life and whose creative classroom displays delighted the principal and frustrated the dickens out of the local fire chief. Her apartment was an extension of her classroom; her exuberance, an extension of her attitude of awe and amazement.

"I bet she's getting ready for her annual Christmas party," Eileen whispered, following Mary Helen's gaze around the room.

"If you ask me, the woman acts like a continual party getting ready to happen," Mary Helen whispered back.

"Isn't that saying, 'accident getting ready to happen'?"

Mary Helen shrugged. "Can't fault a person for trying to spruce up an old cliché."

The wooden door burst open and Ms. Farraday hurried in with a tray. "From one of my children," she explained, placing the beautifully wrapped plate of cookies on the coffee table.

Their hostess pursed her rosebud lips for a moment, but only for a moment. "I'm so glad you came," she began. "I'm sure it has to do with Suzanne, poor little Suzanne." Sarah Farraday rushed on, talking in great detail about Suzanne and her comings and goings, and her feelings about the sudden tragedy. Nothing in the monologue seemed to Mary Helen to be of any significance.

Eileen kept nodding politely. Mary Helen suppressed a smile. At last Eileen had met her match. Sarah Farraday was what might be dubbed the Muhammad Ali of talkers. She stopped only briefly to sip eggnog. Mary Helen studied Eileen, who opened her mouth several times synchronously with the sipping, but never could manage to get a foothold in the conversation.

Small dimples of annoyance were beginning to form on either side of Eileen's mouth. What was the old proverb? "Two great talkers will not travel far together." Mary Helen speculated that this would certainly be the case with Eileen and Ms. Farraday, whom they had just been invited to call Sarah.

"Suzanne was a teacher, too, you know," Sarah commented, nibbling on a sugar cookie decorated with pink frosting and small silver sprinkles.

"Pardon me?" The sudden bit of information burst in on Mary Helen's mulling. Her "pardon me" was so loud, it startled even her. Sarah stopped short, earrings dangling.

Scowling at Mary Helen as if she were an unruly first-grader, Sarah repeated, "Suzanne was a teacher. Or at least studying to be one."

"How do you know?" Mary Helen asked.

"She told me so." Sarah pouted slightly. "I asked her in one Friday night and we had a little wine. We talked about it."

"Did she say where she was studying?"

"No. Actually, Suzanne said very little about herself. She was a very private, quiet girl."

At the rate Sarah chattered, Mary Helen wondered for a moment how she could tell the quiet girls from the talkative ones.

"But a nice person." Sarah was off and running. "I knew that the moment she moved in. That was about a year ago. Moved in all by herself, you know. No one helped her.

"I tried to befriend her. At first it was hard. She reminded me of a sweet little puppy who has been hurt or abused. Frightened.

"Mimi tried too. Do you know Mimi?

"Lovely little thing, a regular little pixie. You can't help loving Mimi, although if I were her mother, I'd turn her right over my knee for letting that doctor move in with her."

"Mimi and you tried?" Mary Helen asked, wanting desperately to keep Sarah on the track.

"Mimi and I were succeeding, I think, Sister—I mean in drawing Suzanne out of herself. Then things changed."

"Changed how?" Mary Helen intruded once again into the monologue, hoping to steer the flow of conversation.

Sarah blinked and sipped her eggnog. "Changed. I don't know how to explain it really. Things were going fine. Then, all of a sudden, about a month ago, I could tell she was upset about something. Don't ask me what. As I said, Suzanne was a very private person."

"Well, did you notice anything unusual? Any new visitors?" Mary Helen prodded.

Sarah thought for a moment. "No," she said, "about the only visitor Suzanne ever had, that I saw, was that dark girl. And she's been coming since the beginning."

"Reina Martinez?"

"I think that was her name."

"You don't have any idea what happened?" Mary Helen asked, trying to jog Sarah's memory.

"Not really," Sarah answered, pulling at her round little mouth. "But, if I had to make a guess . . ."

"Yes," Mary Helen encouraged. A guess, even a wild one, was better than nothing.

"I'd say it was he . . ." Sarah motioned with her thumb toward Apartment 201.

"Arnold Shultz?" Eileen broke in.

"Yes. He's such a bold young stump." Sarah tugged at her mumu. Arnold must have had a field day reviewing Ms. Farraday's stomach and thighs, not to mention her pectorals, Mary Helen thought.

"I heard him say something to Suzanne one day, too, as

if anyone else's muscles were his affair. Suzanne was offended, as she had every right to be. And shortly after that I noticed she was uneasy."

"About how long ago was that?" Mary Helen asked.

"Let's see." Sarah Farraday pulled at her bottom lip. "I had just taken down my turkey color charts and put up those darling little snowmen with the colored top hats. The second to last week in November."

Mary Helen was so distracted by the image of multicolored turkeys that she almost missed Sarah's answer.

"Hum," she said wisely, determined to file that bit of information away with the rest of the little-known facts about Suzanne.

The three stopped to sip eggnog. The room was perfectly quiet, yet Mary Helen was surprised at how clearly she could hear Anne's and Mimi's voices float in from the hallway.

"Anne must be about ready," Eileen said, putting her empty glass back on the tray.

"She sounds like she's right outside the door," Mary Helen commented.

"No, not really," Sarah offered. "You can often hear voices from the neighbors, if you are inclined to listen."

"Could you hear from Suzanne's?"

"Not what was said, of course, only voices. But with Suzanne that really was no problem. She was alone most of the time."

"Did you hear anything the night she was killed?" Mary Helen asked, grasping for any straw that might lead them to Suzanne's killer.

"It's funny you should ask." Sarah emptied her glass. "I did wake up a couple of times that night. First I heard a buzz around eleven-thirty. Probably one of Arnold's girl friends." She pursed her lips in disapproval. "Later, banging

or pounding of something woke me. I was sure it was something out on the street. Suzanne was always so quiet. I was
groggy, so I really can't be sure, but the more I think about
it, the more I remember hearing a voice. But I could have
been half dreaming."

"Can you remember anything at all about the voice?"
Mary Helen could feel her pulse start to race as she waited
for Sarah's answer.

"No, not really. You know how it is when you wake up
out of a deep sleep." Sarah paused for a moment so they
could all remember how it was when you woke up out of a
deep sleep. "One thing I vaguely remember thinking,
though . . ."

"What was that?" Mary Helen prompted.

"That the voice was very, very deep."

"What did you find out from Mimi?" Mary Helen
asked as soon as the three nuns were settled back in the car.

"I'm not sure." Anne's eyes were wide behind her large
purple-rimmed glasses. Her knuckles were white as she
gripped the steering wheel.

"Then tell us what she said and we'll figure it out."
Mary Helen tried to keep the impatience out of her voice.

"What did you say first?" Eileen prompted, scooting up
and hanging over the front seat so she wouldn't miss a word.

"Well, she opened the door and I said, 'Hello,' " Anne
began slowly. Much too slowly for Mary Helen.

"Skip that part." She resisted the urge to shake the
young nun. "If you don't, we'll be home before you get to
the couch," she muttered, wondering once again why Anne
couldn't talk faster and drive slower.

"Go on, dear." Eileen patted Anne's shoulder and narrowed her eyes toward Mary Helen.

Much to Mary Helen's chagrin, Anne related all the initial pleasantries. Mimi, it seemed, knew immediately why the young nun was there. She herself had been ruminating over Suzanne's murder. So far, Mimi had come up with very little.

"Did she know anything about Suzanne's life before she moved into the apartment?" Mary Helen cut straight to the point.

"That came up," Anne said. "Suzanne never offered much information. Mimi didn't press. Everyone is entitled to their own space."

"Her own space," Eileen corrected automatically. Anne just blinked.

"But Mimi did read pain in Suzanne's aura, pain and separation and sadness."

"In her what?"

"Aura. Mimi can read auras. She sees colors radiating around people and these colors tell things about the people," Anne explained, as if she were now the one talking to two first-graders. "Lots of folks can read auras," Anne concluded.

"Can you?" Mary Helen wriggled a little self-consciously in case the answer was yes. Her aura would undoubtedly be purple with impatience. One look at Eileen told her that her friend would radiate the luminous white of shock.

"No," Anne answered, much to Sister Mary Helen's relief.

"Maybe this reading auras has something to do with her eyes," Eileen ventured. "You know—one being blue, the other brown."

Mary Helen stared at Eileen in disbelief. Eileen squirmed. "There's an old superstition," she said, hastening to change the subject, "that 'the corpse will bleed in the presence of the murderer.'"

"What has that to do with anything?" Mary Helen asked.

"Well, maybe a person who reads auras can read murder," Eileen answered brightly.

Mary Helen was willing to grasp at straws, but that was too much. "In that case, you don't need a police force, all you need is a few aura readers," she commented sharply.

"Which makes every bit as much sense as what we're doing." Eileen paused, having made her point, which Mary Helen of course chose to ignore.

"Does Mimi have any idea who might have murdered Suzanne?" Mary Helen asked. Enough beating around the proverbial bush.

"None." Anne did not elaborate.

"Did she know Suzanne had had a baby?"

"Yes."

"How?" Mary Helen asked, hoping the conversation would not revert back to auras. "Don't tell me Suzanne volunteered that!"

"Lee told her."

"How do you suppose he knew?" Eileen asked, speaking more to herself than to Anne.

"Mimi didn't say, and I didn't want to pry. Everyone needs their own space," Anne repeated.

"Her own space," Eileen corrected once again.

"For the love of all that's good and holy, Anne, we sent you up there expressly to, to . . ." Mary Helen couldn't bring herself to say "pry." "To make inquiry." She tried not to look exasperated. After all, it was her own fault for sending a boy on a man's job, to use a sexist phrase that she knew Anne would deplore.

Sister Anne parked the car behind the college building. The afternoon fog was surging in from the Golden Gate in great wet rolls. Below them the cupola of City Hall loomed like a giant green copper bubble over a thick sea of white.

Threading her long jean-clad legs, Anne turned in the driver's seat to face her companions.

"There are several things I did find out." She folded her thin arms and thrust out her lower lip. It was the closest thing to a pout that Mary Helen had ever seen on Anne.

"Without prying or violating anyone's space," she continued, hazel eyes flashing. "And if you give me a chance, I'll tell you."

Neither older Sister spoke.

"Mimi was close to Suzanne, as close as anyone in the building. She had the feeling that part of Suzanne's past was secret because Suzanne had been in an institution of some sort."

"Institution?" Mary Helen blurted out. Thinking again of the nun's watch, she couldn't help herself. Ignoring her, Anne continued. "Perhaps a mental hospital, a sanitarium, maybe a prison. Something she tried to hide. Mimi wasn't sure, but she had a strong intuitive feeling."

"A feeling?" Mary Helen attempted to hide her disappointment. What she needed to make any progress was not intuition but a few strong, unshakable facts.

"You're the last one in the world who should be turning up her nose at intuition, my friend," Eileen reminded Mary Helen, who reluctantly agreed.

Adjusting her bifocals, she tried yet another tack.

"Did she mention any other friends?"

"Just the teacher, Sarah Farraday, who lives across the hall. And Reina Martinez."

"No men?" Mary Helen asked, suddenly remembering the snapshot. She must get a copy of it back from Kate.

"No," Anne said, "but she did say something interesting about Reina."

"What?" said Mary Helen, who was beginning to liken this conversation to pulling teeth.

"Reina had the same kind of an aura as Suzanne, gave the same kind of intuitive feeling of a secret hidden life."

Drat it, Mary Helen thought, auras once more. Intuition was hard enough to explain to Kate Murphy, but auras were something else again.

"You know what has really been needling me?" Eileen jumped into the conversation and onto another subject. "Why did Suzanne take that job at the Sea Wench? It was so—so—out of character."

"Mimi shared that with me." Anne turned toward Eileen. "Apparently, she and the teacher—"

"Sarah Farraday." Mary Helen couldn't wait for Anne to remember the name.

Anne continued unabashed. "They were trying to bring Suzanne out of herself. Mimi actually talked her into the job, persuaded the boss, Mr. Rosenberg, to hire her. Now she feels guilty."

"Guilty about what?" Eileen asked.

"Maybe if Suzanne had stayed at home and not gone to the bar—"

"That's ridiculous," Mary Helen interrupted. "You can't blame her death on one night's work at the Sea Wench."

"Mimi has a feeling that something—"

"What could possibly have happened in eight little hours?"

Eileen frowned. "For the love of all that's good and holy, Mary Helen, will you let her finish at least one sentence?"

Mary Helen clamped her mouth shut and shoved her glasses up the bridge of her nose. Of course Eileen was right. It was not that she meant to be rude, it was just that she was so anxious to have Suzanne's murder solved and things put right before Christmas. Somehow it didn't seem fitting that the Prince of Peace should come into such unrest.

"Sorry," she said. "Mimi had a feeling about what?"

Poor Anne looked close to tears. "Just a feeling, she said, that Suzanne's murder may be somehow connected to that night at the Sea Wench."

"Could the owner, the one who was patting the girls, be involved?" Mary Helen asked with distaste.

"Mimi didn't say."

For the love of heaven, why didn't you ask her? Mary Helen was about to say, but bit her tongue instead.

"What did she say, dear?" Eileen prodded encouragingly.

"Only that she had a feeling."

Mary Helen was about to ask Anne if she'd mentioned the eleven-thirty buzz to Mimi when she remembered she hadn't mentioned it to Anne.

"Did she hear anything unusual from Suzanne's apartment the night of the murder?" she asked instead. Mary Helen had had about all of the feelings she could handle. What she needed for Kate tonight was facts.

"Mimi's a light sleeper, so she puts in earplugs to keep out the street noises. She said she was so tired that night, she took a glass of milk. Slept like she was drugged. She didn't even hear Lee come in. Lee claims he didn't hear a thing either."

So much for the buzzer. "Isn't that unusual?" Mary Helen wondered aloud. "The apartments are so close and Suzanne's was so ransacked, you'd think—"

It was Anne who interrupted this time. "I wondered about that too. But Mimi said Lee's so exhausted when he finally gets off duty that he sleeps like a dead man. Says he probably wouldn't even hear Gabriel's horn."

The unfortunate thing, Mary Helen thought, is that he didn't hear who it was that caused Gabriel to blow his horn for poor Suzanne.

Mary Helen and Eileen were quiet as they drove along Geary, across Park Presidio, past St. Monica's Church toward 34th and the Avenues and dinner. The traffic was heavy and the ride full of starts and stops. Mary Helen felt her mind starting and stopping just like the jerking vehicle. Anne had suggested a strong woman, and it could have been. Yet somehow Mary Helen felt sure it was a man. Sarah Farraday had heard a deep voice. A woman could have a deep voice, too, and Kate had not mentioned anything about rape. She'd ask her for sure tonight. She had read somewhere that most people are murdered by someone they know. So Suzanne's killer probably lived in the building or was someone she knew, since no one had forced entry. On the other hand, there are a lot of ways to enter. Ring another bell, slip in. She had seen it done dozens of times on TV. If she could pick up the technique, why couldn't a potential killer? As a matter of fact, Eileen and she had slipped into that very apartment building this morning behind Anne. But why pick Suzanne? The killer must be someone who had a reason and an opportunity. Flaherty. He had plenty of opportunity. It didn't seem likely, though. Still, everyone has heard stories of a dirty old man. And there was the famous biblical story of another Susanna and the elders. Flaherty—frustrated and a little drunk? Hardly likely, but maybe.

What about Rosenberg? He could have slipped out of the club. Followed her home, come in for a nightcap. Possible, but somehow Mary Helen felt he wasn't the type. Mimi and the other waitresses at the Sea Wench, she had noticed, were tolerant of the fellow and not a bit frightened. It was as if they sensed that the man would never intentionally hurt them. But what about unintentionally?

Lee. He certainly had the opportunity, right next door and Mimi sleeping so soundly. Being a doctor, he would, of course, have been able to run the letter opener through Suzanne's thin breast with the precision of a surgeon. And there was something unsettling about the coldness of his steely blue eyes. As if he was trying to hide something, or cover up something. They were so objective, so seemingly without compassion. But were they the eyes of a murderer? Mary Helen could not quite decide. And then, too, how did he know about the baby? She wished Anne had asked.

But the motive. What possible motive? Lee seemed perfectly content with Mimi. Cold, but content. That was the one thing missing with all her suspects, if you could call them that. Motive. And the fellow in the photo. How did he fit in? Tonight she must remember to ask Kate for a copy of the snapshot.

"Did you notice Arnold Shultz's bookcases?" Eileen asked out of nowhere.

Mary Helen had to admit she hadn't. She had been too fascinated with the weaponry over the fireplace to notice what was on either side. "What about them?" she asked.

"It is a very strange collection of books for a health fiend, if you ask me." Eileen's gray eyes were wide. "There are books on fitness, of course, nutrition, a couple of best sellers, a whole half shelf of mysteries."

"Nothing strange about that," Mary Helen answered, hoping she didn't sound too defensive.

"This is the strange part." Eileen shook a pudgy forefinger for emphasis. "Several how-to books and magazines—"

"How-to?" Mary Helen interrupted. "What's so strange about that? Maybe the man was just handy," she said, although she had to admit his apartment didn't show it.

"Will you please let me finish?" Eileen sounded exasperated. "The how-to books and magazines were a far cry from home improvement, old dear."

Mary Helen was puzzled. "How-to's on what, then?"

"On sex!" Eileen blurted out, then reddened.

For several blocks the pair rode in silence. Mary Helen mulled over Eileen's discovery. Arnold with sex manuals! Arnold who claims he goes to bed early and who Sarah Farraday claims has late-night women visitors. Surely there is more to poor Arnold than meets the proverbial eye!

"Let's make a list before we get to Kate's," she said.

"A list of what?" Eileen shifted to look at her.

"Possible murderers."

"Glory be to God, you are serious!"

"I think it would be helpful." Mary Helen tried to sound like Inspector Mallett of Scotland Yard. It must have worked, because Eileen foraged through her purse for a notepad and pencil.

"List Patrick Flaherty," Mary Helen dictated. "Then, Mr. Rosenberg, Lee Slater, and, of course, Arnold Shultz."

"What about Reina Martinez?"

"If you ask me, this is not a woman's crime. But put her over to the side. We'll find out about her when we talk to Kate."

Mary Helen made a U-turn at 35th and Geary and began the search along the boulevard for a parking place.

"And let's not forget the one suspect we must always put on the list. The one who is the most dangerous of all."

"Who do you mean?" Eileen tapped the end of her pencil against her front teeth.

"X," Mary Helen answered, "the unknown quantity. It is fatal to forget him. Whenever you make a list of possible criminals, you are apt to put yourself in blinders and forget that anyone else exists outside your list. Always put in X and keep a sharp lookout for him."

"Where did you hear that?" Eileen's eyebrows shot up. "It sounds like a quotation if I ever heard one."

"It is. Right out of the same whodunit I was reading just before Advent. The book I left in Suzanne's car. The reason, if you remember, why I stumbled on the body in the first place. . . . The inspector said it."

"Did he find the murderer, the X?" Eileen asked while Mary Helen attempted to parallel park.

"I don't know," Mary Helen grunted, pulling the front wheels tight into the curb, "that's as far as I ever got in the story."

The clock on the mantel struck ten. Kate Murphy yawned, then snuggled closer to her husband. "We'd better clean up," she said without moving.

Jack grunted. "I think the mess looks festive," he answered, rubbing his stocking feet together.

Slowly he adjusted his position on the couch.

"You okay?" Kate asked.

"Arm's asleep."

Kate moved her head from his shoulder to his lap and stared absently at the dying fire. A small bright burst of flame from a smoldering ember lit the darkened room. Right after the nuns left, Kate and Jack had decided to sit down and relax for a minute. They had been there ever since.

Kate looked up at her husband. The colored lights from the Christmas tree added a rosy glow to his face. In the background KABL softly played "The First Noel." Kate felt warm and cozy. The evening had gone so smoothly after such a hectic day.

"Feeling good, hon?" Jack asked, running his fingers through her thick hair.

Kate nodded, almost afraid to speak for fear any noise might break the spell.

"Hope this case winds down for you," he said, "so we can really enjoy Christmas."

She did too.

Gallagher, she was sure, was putting his money on Rosenberg. And she was hoping he was right. The whole thing seemed so logical, and so much more possible than locating the guy in the snapshot. Rosenberg: drunk, ex-fighter, frustrated. They had both been a little disappointed when they returned from Calistoga to find that Rosenberg had come in to give skin samples.

"What in the hell did he do that for?" Gallagher growled.

"Maybe he's stupid or his lawyer is," Kate answered hopefully.

"Stupid or innocent." Gallagher chewed the end of his cigar. "And goddammit, Kate, I'm not so sure which."

Although today's visit to Calistoga had not solved the case, it was a step in the right direction. As if under a giant moving lens, the people were beginning to come into focus and the whole picture become clearer and clearer. Poor Reina Martinez. They had had no trouble locating her. Kate had felt sorry for the woman the moment she saw her in the spa. Strands of black hair, limp with moisture, clung to her face and neck. Dark mud caked her arms, and long brown smears stained her loose white uniform.

Reina was barely thirty, yet she looked at least fifty. The fat, dumpy body and the slovenly clothes didn't help. But it was really her face. It was fixed like a rigid, hostile mask. Kate had seen that face many times before on prostitutes, battered women, women who had been used. Hatred had become their bulwark against hurt.

"I was just thinking about that poor girl we questioned today," Kate said.

"What about her?"

"How hard and belligerent she looked when Denny and I identified ourselves."

"Just hates cops? Or do you think there's something there?"

"It's hard to tell really. She admitted knowing Suzanne. She claims, however, she met her when Suzanne first came to The City and they both rented rooms in the Mission. Denny is going to verify that tomorrow. Although I really don't know what good the information will do us." Kate sighed. "Then Reina got a job in Calistoga, moved there. Suzanne went to work for the college and moved out to the apartment on California.

"She denied any knowledge of a baby, although everything about her said otherwise. Admitted she has a child of her own."

"Think it could be Suzanne's?"

"Again, that's hard to tell. But I don't think so," Kate said slowly, staring into the dying fire. "Yet I have the feeling the baby is significant. Maybe some link into their pasts—I don't know. Anyway, there is something Reina didn't want to talk about."

"Hum," was Jack's only comment.

"I think, however, we struck pay dirt when we showed her that photo."

"What did she say?"

"It's not so much what she said, Jack, but how she looked. Something like fear or at least wariness flashed in her eyes. If anything, her face became even paler than when we first arrived, and more unyielding."

"You think she recognized the guy?"

"Only a mind reader would know for sure, pal, but if I had to make a guess, I'd say definitely."

"What does Gallagher think?"

Kate giggled. "He thinks the same as he always thinks. That I put too much emphasis on gut feelings, read into things. Says 'We need hard facts, Katie-girl. Proof. Stuff like that can be written.' Besides, he's hoping Rosenberg did it."

Jack smiled. "You sound just like him. What did you think of Sister Mary Helen's list?" he asked.

"I hate to admit it," Kate said, moving her head back to Jack's shoulder, "but she's probably right. And X may just be this unknown fellow in the snapshot."

"By the way." Jack frowned. "I was surprised when you said you'd give her a copy of the picture. I thought you were working up to telling her to butt out."

"This was hardly the time or place," Kate said, knowing the excuse was shabby. "Besides, she may show it to just the right person."

"Isn't that an awful long shot? Who the hell is going to identify the guy?"

Kate began to twist a strand of her hair around her index finger.

Jack recognized the sign immediately. "Sorry I brought it up," he said. "No brooding tonight, save it for the office. Let's get back to now. How'd you like our party?"

Kate let go of her hair. Jack was right. No point spoiling a lovely evening speculating about murder. And it had been a lovely evening in spite of the fact that Suzanne's murder had definitely been a part of it.

Kate smiled thinking about Sister Mary Helen. She was quite a gal. She hadn't even flinched when Kate told her about the rape. If anything, she had straightened her shoulders and looked more determined.

Both older nuns were in rare form relating their afternoon's adventures. Once again, they had rushed in where angels fear to tread, yet they were a far cry from fools.

In fact, Kate sincerely valued the nuns' insights into the case, particularly Mary Helen's, although she hesitated to act very appreciative. If Sister Mary Helen had become this involved without any encouragement, God knows what a little gratitude might cause. And how would she ever explain it to Denny?

She would, however, look into the eleven-thirty visitor. Wondering for a moment why Mrs. McGrath hadn't mentioned it to her, Kate snuggled closer to her husband. Enough of this murder business. Tonight she felt euphoric, like those contented cows Gallagher and she had seen grazing on the Napa Valley hillsides.

"Dinner was good," she muttered.

"Thanks," Jack answered. Kate waited for him to elaborate on spending hours over a hot stove. Surprisingly, he said nothing more.

"How did you manage it?" she asked, suddenly suspicious.

Jack simply grunted.

"Sutro Super?" she asked, remembering the store did offer cooked turkeys as a special customer service. It must have cost him a fortune.

"Your turn to clean up." Teasing, Jack changed the subject.

Must be the price, Kate thought.

"I'll do it in the morning," she said. "I'm taking tomorrow off." She stretched, yawned, and for a moment relished the thought of a free Saturday to putter around in the kitchen. "Think I'll play domestic all day tomorrow." She grinned at her husband. "I'm really looking forward to it. Maybe I'll even wax the kitchen floor."

Jack hugged her tightly. "You could play domestic all the time if you want," he said. "You just say when."

Kate grimaced, hoping they weren't going to start fighting again about starting a family. It was her own fault, however. Why had she mentioned being domestic?

Slowly she ran her index finger up the back of Jack's neck. "Let's not spoil a perfect evening," she said, gently kissing the bridge of his nice straight nose.

"Darn right," he answered. His strong arms drew her closer. Gently his lips caressed her breast, her neck. Eagerly his mouth sought hers, and was pressing hard when the phone rang.

"Goddammit," Jack swore softly. He drew away and ran his fingers through his dark hair. Reluctantly he moved toward the hall phone.

Kate checked the clock: almost eleven. Who could be calling at this hour? she wondered.

"Yeah, Ma. No, Ma. That's okay. We were up." She could hear Jack answering his mother, a note of impatience in his voice.

"It was great, Ma. Thanks. No—not too dry. Delicious . . . Yeah . . . Everyone enjoyed it. Thanks, Ma."

The dinner! Of course that was what Jack had done. It wasn't from the Sutro Super at all. It was from his mother's. She should have guessed.

Kate rose quickly from the couch. Exasperated, she pulled out the Christmas-tree lights and flipped off the stereo. The mood was broken. Damn her, she thought, picking up her shoes. Bending forward, she angrily stirred the dying embers with the poker, watched as a shower of sparks fell on the hearth. Maybe I should stay home, she thought. That way I could make the dinner. Best of all, that way we could make love without any interference from Mama!

Sister Mary Helen wasn't home from Jack and Kate's more than five minutes when Sister Therese knocked on her bedroom door.

"Telephone," she announced, loudly enough to be heard up and down the convent corridor. "It sounds like a nun."

Irked, Mary Helen opened the door. Therese, still muttering to herself, was already three doors down. The slap of her mules echoed down the long narrow hallway.

What does a nun sound like? Mary Helen knew anyone but a nun would ask. And it would be very hard to explain. Yet somehow one nun could always tell another. Was it the tone of voice, the manner? Mary Helen was still mulling this over when she picked up the receiver.

Indeed, Sister Therese was right. The caller was a Sister Mary Thomasine.

"Yes?" Mary Helen answered, trying desperately to place a Sister Thomasine.

"My secretary said you called Erie. About Sister Mary Bonaventure."

That Sister Thomasine, the Mother General. Mary Helen never expected she would call so soon.

"Yes, Sister," she said, "I was just wondering—"

"I'm in San Rafael for a meeting," Sister Thomasine interrupted. Mary Helen was a little annoyed but let it go. Mother Generals were used to being in control.

"I'll be free on Sunday. I could meet with you then if you wish," Sister Thomasine said.

Mary Helen was overwhelmed.

"I think it would be wiser if we discussed Sister Mary Bonaventure face-to-face rather than over the phone," Sister

Thomasine continued. "Would three o'clock Sunday afternoon be convenient for you? There at St. Francis College?"

"Yes, Sister, that's fine."

"I'll see you then."

"I'm looking forward to it," Mary Helen said, but too late. Sister Thomasine had hung up.

Sister Mary Helen stared at the dead receiver. A whole conversation and she'd said less than ten words. She couldn't believe it. No one else would either. She could hardly wait to meet this woman.

Mary Helen had been asleep for about an hour when a soft knock came on her bedroom door.

"Are you awake?" Anne whispered.

"Yes," Mary Helen answered, reaching for her glasses on the bedstand. She checked the alarm clock! Twelve-ten. What on earth?

"Phone call for you," Anne whispered, then padded silently down the hall. The older generation could learn plenty from the younger, Mary Helen thought, rummaging through her closet for her worn chenille robe.

Pulling it tightly around her, she stepped into the deserted corridor. Who could this be? she wondered, fighting down the dread late-night phone calls always caused. It is probably just Sister Mary Thomasine calling back for directions, she thought, knowing full well that even a Mother General would wait until morning.

Small night-lights cast fan-shaped shadows along the long dark passageway. All the nuns' bedroom doors were shut. Not one light shone from under a narrow crack. Even Anne was back in bed. Mary Helen stood for a moment listening to all the night sounds, the ones missing during the day when the building was full of life. The hum of the new furnace, the buzz of the electric clock at the end of the hallway, the wind scraping a branch against a window. In the silence, the bleating of the foghorns on the bay sounded closer and clearer and much more ominous.

Mary Helen shivered. Turning on the light in the tiny phone room, she picked up the receiver.

"Sister Mary Helen," she answered as cheerfully as could be expected at midnight. For a moment, nothing. Then came the sound of slow, heavy breathing into the receiver. A long cold finger of fear ran up her spine. Could this be another obscene—

"Sister Mary Helen?" a deep, guttural voice interrupted her thought.

"Yes?" she said. Again the heavy breath pulsed into the receiver.

"Why don't you leave me alone?" a low, sad voice asked.

"Leave you alone?" Mary Helen's heart seemed to turn over, then beat so loudly she was afraid the caller might hear it. "What do you mean leave you alone?"

"Just, leave me alone." The voice broke, sobbing. "I loved her. I didn't want to hurt her. Just love her. Now you're torturing me."

"Young man," Mary Helen began in her most reasonable schoolmarm voice. The caller sounded like a young man. "I know how you must be hurting. Why don't you let me help you? Find someone you can talk to. Someone who can help you heal your pain."

The palm of her hand, moist and clammy, held the receiver tight as she strained hoping to hear his answer. All she heard was a soft pathetic whimpering like a sick child's, and the steady click, click, click of the telephone wires.

"Young man? Are you there?" she asked as gently as she could. "Can I help you?"

"Leave me alone!" The voice grew louder, more agitated, shrieked a string of obscenity, and then slammed the phone in Mary Helen's ear.

A feeling of nausea rose inside her. Involuntary tears stung her eyes as she stood there still clutching the receiver. With her free hand she pulled her robe tight around her throat.

Who was he? she wondered sadly. She strained to place the low, deep voice, but she couldn't. Whom had she upset with her probing? Most assuredly someone with a very sick mind. But who? And, more importantly, what should she do about it? Certainly not tell Kate Murphy. Kate would surely insist she give up her questioning.

Still clutching her chenille robe tightly to ward off the chill, Mary Helen made her way back down the dimly lit corridor to her bedroom. Pulling back the corner of her drape, she peered out at the deserted campus. All was darkness, except for the floodlights illuminating the main building and changing its tower to a ghastly green.

She searched the blackness for something unusual; strained her ears for a strange sound. Nothing. She was about to give up when over to her right on the access road, a pair of headlights snapped on. Silently, the car coasted down the hill. A feeling of panic welled up inside her. Deliberately she forced herself to take a slow deep breath. Probably just a couple of kids making love, she thought. The light from my window must have scared them off. She let the drape fall back into place.

Crossing the room, she locked her bedroom door. In the distance, an eerie foghorn bleated a warning. Its groan filled the silence. Mary Helen shivered and crawled into bed.

Outside, heavy, hanging fog must already be shrouding the bay. Somewhere in all that fog and darkness Suzanne's murderer lurked. Mary Helen felt utterly certain that tonight she had spoken to him.

SUNDAY—THIRD WEEK OF ADVENT

The theme from the morning's liturgy had echoed in Sister Mary Helen's head and heart all day and had managed to raise her spirits considerably. Even the weather cooperated, promising another crisp, sunny December day full of blue sky and billowy clouds.

"He has sent me to bring glad tidings to the lowly . . . to heal the brokenhearted," this morning's reading had declared. Certainly it was an omen. Surely, Sister Mary Thomasine's visit must be bringing some glad tidings. And who would feel lower than she had when she had awakened this morning?

Much as she hated to admit it, Friday's phone call had really upset and frightened her, so much so that she had told no one about it, not even Eileen.

The caller had known her name. Somehow, being called by her name had made her feel responsible and vulnerable.

She shook the dread from her mind, yet it clung to her like static electricity.

Besides, with Christmas just nine days away, it was about time for a breakthrough in this case, about time that Suzanne's murderer should be apprehended, those brokenhearted who had known her healed, and some peace and joy restored to the season.

At quarter of three, Mary Helen was already in the convent front parlor, looking for the hundredth time at her wristwatch and hoping the holiday traffic would not make Sister Thomasine late.

From their one phone conversation Mary Helen knew that on her own, Sister Mary Thomasine would never be late. If anything, Mother General Thomasine would be early.

At five to three, Mary Helen peeked through the parlor curtains and was not surprised to see a dark blue Citation pull into the visitors' parking space. She opened the heavy front door before the bell rang.

Sister Thomasine didn't blink. Obviously the woman was used to having doors opened for her. Instead, she simply stuck out her large right hand to be shaken.

Mary Helen grabbed it. She half expected her visitor to say "Dr. Livingstone, I presume." Fortunately she didn't. Mary Helen was afraid she'd never be able to suppress a laugh, and this was no laughing matter.

"I'm Sister Mary Thomasine of the Dominican Sisters of Erie," the visitor said instead. "You are undoubtedly Sister Mary Helen."

Mary Helen smiled as pleasantly as she could and watched without surprise Sister Thomasine's blue eyes slowly appraising her. She, meanwhile, was doing a little appraising of her own.

Sister Mary Thomasine, Mother General of the Erie Dominicans, looked every bit the part. She was a tall, wiry woman with broad bony shoulders, large hands, and long narrow feet. She had the look of a tennis player. Mary Helen tugged at her own jacket and vowed once again to get more exercise.

The white scapular of Sister Thomasine's Dominican habit hung straight but did little to hide a firm waistline held in by a black belt.

Sister Thomasine's short black veil covered all but the

very front of a thick head of graying hair. The woman's tanned face had an ageless look, but from years of experience Mary Helen judged her to be mid-sixtyish. The most dominant feature on her rather long plain face were her eyes. They were a bright, almost jay blue, and penetrating. She reminded Mary Helen of the centurion in the gospel who said to one man "Go" and he goeth and to another "Come" and he cometh. In Sister Thomasine's case, Mary Helen suspected it was women.

"So. We're mutually satisfied, I see," Sister Thomasine said when the two nuns' eyes finally met. Sister Mary Helen laughed aloud. Mother General Thomasine was indeed going to be good news.

Mary Helen walked quickly to keep pace with Sister Thomasine's long, decisive strides as the two nuns made their way up the hill toward a clearing in the wooded area behind the college. Mary Helen had suggested the spot: it was private, had a beautiful view of The City, especially on a clear day, plus it had a comfortable bench and was one of her favorite thinking places.

Sister Thomasine had been amenable and, fooled by the sun, refused a sweater. Mary Helen was glad she had traded her navy blue jacket for her heavy Aran knit. Even trying to keep up with Thomasine she felt the chill in the air despite the brilliance of the December sun. And by three o'clock it was brilliant. The morning fog had burned off early, leaving The City roofed in a crisp, crystal blue. Here and there, new-made clouds were piled like giant white mountains of whipped cream.

When the two reached the bench, Mary Helen sat silently for a moment, absorbing the sparkling city below them. The frosty wind etched the bay with a froth of small choppy whitecaps. Beyond it the campanile from the University of California stood out, sharp and clear against the

East Bay hills. Downtown she spotted a silver Christmas tree atop the long, projecting arm of a crane. Some construction worker had obviously caught the Christmas spirit.

Yet, out there somewhere was her caller. She closed her eyes, trying to blot out the thought, trying to savor the beauty of the moment.

Maybe this meeting would finally shed some light on Suzanne's identity and produce some good news, some healing on her murder. The possibility pleased her. She pulled in a long deep breath and tried to relax.

But Sister Thomasine wasn't into relaxing. "I'm glad you called," she said abruptly.

Mary Helen blinked her eyes open. Beside her, Thomasine was nervously twisting her long white scapular, anxious to continue the conversation. A nervous habit seemed out of place in a seeming pillar of strength. But even pillars have emotions, Mary Helen had to admit.

"I've been so worried about Sister Mary Bonaventure. She has always been very dear to me, very special. And now this."

It was Mary Helen's turn to interrupt. "Who exactly is Sister Mary Bonaventure?" she asked, wondering if her suspicions had been correct.

Thomasine stopped. She looked thrown off base for a moment.

"You don't know?" she asked.

"Not for sure," Mary Helen said, almost unable to contain herself.

Sister Thomasine's eyes searched Mary Helen's. "Suzanne and Sister Mary Bonaventure were one and the same person," she said slowly, painfully, then added, "may she rest in peace. . . ."

"Suzanne was Sister Mary Bonaventure," Mary Helen repeated, her thoughts tumbling down haphazardly, like wa-

ter over jagged rocks. Of course! Now it all seemed so simple, so logical; the mysterious past, privacy about her life,
trained to be a teacher, new location, quiet and efficient,
nun's watch, asking Mary Helen if she'd been happy. How
she wished now she'd been more patient, taken more time
with the girl. Why, even the letter opener dated August 8,
1973. The Feast of St. Dominic. Probably the date she'd
been received into the order.

Mary Helen should have trusted her instincts. She just
knew Suzanne had been a nun, and she was right. Suzanne
had been Sister Mary Bonaventure.

"But, the baby?" she asked aloud. "When did she have
the baby?"

"I don't know. I didn't even know she had one."
Thomasine twisted her scapular. "But I suppose I should
have guessed.

"Suzanne was a novice in our Order. She entered from
our college in Erie," she continued without Mary Helen's
even asking, like someone who had gone over the story hundreds of times in her own mind and was relieved to be able
to unburden it finally on someone else.

"The girl came from a blue-collar family. Her father
worked in a plastics factory, I think. She was a sweet girl, a
good girl, full of youth and idealism. You know the kind."
The blue-jay eyes focused on Mary Helen, who nodded
mutely.

"In our novitiate she got involved in all the social issues.
Soon she started writing to prisoners. She wasn't the only
one, of course, but with Suzanne—" Mary Thomasine stood
abruptly and gazed out at The City. "I should have stopped
it," she said.

"Why?" Mary Helen asked, afraid of the answer.

"Because she became involved. Very involved with one
young man. Emotionally involved. She started corresponding

with him regularly. Then the poor child thought she was in love. She'd never had much love at home from what I could figure." Thomasine stopped and fumbled in her pocket for a handkerchief to wipe her eyes. "She thought love could solve all problems."

"And she left the order to be with him?" Mary Helen asked after a moment, giving Thomasine time to compose herself.

"To marry him." Thomasine turned away. "And I've never really forgiven myself for not trying harder to stop her."

Mary Helen patted the empty bench next to her. Thomasine swished the back of her scapular aside and sat down. "You know that 'Love is a sickness full of woes, all remedies refusing,'" Mary Helen quoted. She wasn't sure who'd said that, but once again it rang true and she hoped its truth might help to console her visitor.

"I could have intervened. I should have. I should have put a stop to it sooner," Thomasine said, twisting the front piece of her scapular, "but, as Shakespeare put it, 'Those were my salad days, when I was green in judgment.' Very green indeed."

Thomasine smiled at a kindred spirit. Neither nun spoke for a few moments, each lost in recalling her own salad days.

Mary Helen searched for something profound or at least helpful, but nothing seemed to surface. "Hindsight is always twenty-twenty," she said, finally quoting the old cliché.

"Always," Thomasine agreed. Taking a deep breath, she continued. "Anyway, over the years, I've kept in contact with Suzanne. She never wrote back except for an occasional Christmas card with a short greeting. At least this kept me abreast of her address. . . . I'm curious, Sister. How did you happen to call me?"

"Through a *St. Jude's Messenger* that came for her. Sister Mary Bonaventure's name and address were crossed out, but it had your order's address."

Sister Thomasine laughed a halfhearted laugh. "Saint Jude! Patron of the Impossible. All these years, I've kept Suzanne's subscription up and made sure it was forwarded to her. I hoped somehow she'd find help, or inspiration—something from the articles. Silly, isn't it?"

"No, not really." Mary Helen felt a real pang of empathy for this pillar of strength. She cleared her throat. "Anyway, it led me to you."

"I couldn't believe it when I heard you'd called asking about Sister Mary Bonaventure. Then, when I came to this meeting in San Rafael and read about . . ." Thomasine stopped and fumbled again for her handkerchief and dabbed at her blue-jay eyes.

Mary Helen rose from the bench and made a pretext of stretching, hoping to give Sister Thomasine time to compose herself before settling back down. "This fellow—the prisoner she wrote to," she asked, suddenly remembering the sandy-haired boy in the snapshot. Could it be? "Do you know anything about him?"

"Only that he was in prison somewhere here in California. Vacaville, I believe."

Vacaville! Mary Helen couldn't believe her ears. Why, her old eighth-grade student, Ignatius Kelly, was the chaplain there. With a name like Ignatius, he had been expected by everyone to become a Jesuit. But Iggie had joined the Franciscans instead. As a Franciscan, he was chaplain to Vacaville Prison! She had been meaning to drop in on Iggie one of these days. What a break! Thomasine had, indeed, brought glad tidings. Impulsively she leaned forward and gave Mother General Mary Thomasine a big hug.

Thomasine blushed, straightened up, and checked her watch. "I really must be on my way," she said, silently blowing her long thin nose. "I've a plane to catch back to Erie. I hope I've been of some help, Sister. It would mean a lot to me."

"You've been very helpful," Mary Helen said with a surge of enthusiasm, feeling that at last something was beginning to fall into place. At least she knew who Suzanne was, where she had been, why she was there. There were still lots of blanks, but maybe, as with the computer program, she was beginning to get the right combination of facts. First, she must get that snapshot from Kate. Her prisoner was undoubtedly the fellow in the picture. She'd phone Kate tonight. Phone . . . The moment she thought of the telephone, her muscles cramped with tension. Was it possible that Suzanne's prisoner was out there somewhere? Was he the caller? Impossible! She tried to shake the thought from her mind but couldn't. If it was not impossible, at least it was improbable. The poor fellow was probably still in prison. Besides, how would he know she was helping the police look for Suzanne's murderer?

After she had the photo, she'd call Iggie and take it up to him. He wouldn't refuse to help his old eighth-grade teacher. Perhaps he'd even recognize the man.

Ridiculous, her common sense told her. Iggie must have seen hundreds, no, thousands, of slight, sandy-haired young men over the years. He might even have trouble recognizing her. Although they had kept up a casual correspondence, she hadn't seen him in years.

But, maybe, just maybe . . . It was a long shot, but at least it was a shot, which was one more than she'd had when the day began. This morning's theme had truly been an omen.

"And what do you suppose ever happened to the baby?" Sister Thomasine's question, asked more of herself than of Mary Helen, broke into her thoughts.

"I don't know." Mary Helen, plunged once again into reality, shook her head.

"You will let me know as soon as you find out anything?" Sister Thomasine rose to leave.

"Immediately," Mary Helen answered, knowing full well peace of mind would be the best Christmas present Mother General Thomasine could receive that year.

MONDAY—THIRD WEEK OF ADVENT

Dennis Gallagher was shuffling through the pile of paperwork on his large wooden-topped desk when Kate arrived at
the Homicide Detail.

She walked across the room to her desk. Resolutely, she
plunked a small tinsel Christmas tree in the crack where
their two desks faced each other.

"That's all we need around here, more crap!" He
pointed accusingly at the tiny tree.

"Bah humbug to you too." Kate hung up her coat and
put her purse in the bottom desk drawer. "Did you have a
nice weekend?"

"Weekend? Was there a weekend? I've been here fifteen minutes and I've forgotten I ever had a couple of days
off."

"Oh, oh." Kate sat down and folded her hands to listen.
"What happened?"

Before Gallagher could answer, his phone rang. "This is
what happened," he said, picking up the offending instrument.

"Yes, Chief, I know, Chief. We're working on it, Chief.
As soon as anything breaks, Chief. Same to you, Chief."
Denny replaced the receiver.

Kate checked her wristwatch. "Chief Gilligan's at his
office early this morning," she said.

"That wasn't Gilligan. He called ten minutes ago. That
was the fire chief. And the bastard had the nerve to wish me

a Merry Christmas. By the way, how come you got here so late?"

"Sister Mary Helen asked me to drop off a copy of that snapshot: you know—Suzanne and Lover Boy. So I stopped by Mount St. Francis on my way downtown. Besides, I'm only fifteen minutes late. What's going on here anyway?" Kate asked, anxious to change the subject before Gallagher realized Mary Helen was still very much on the case. It must have worked, since Gallagher went right on.

"Seems over the weekend that damn college had some kind of a Christmas party for their board of regents or alumnae or some damn thing. All those old bags got together, had a few pops, and decided the police weren't doing enough to solve the case. Then each one went home and bugged the old man. I must have gotten five phone calls this morning already. Everyone but the janitor at City Hall—and I would be surprised if—"

The ringing of the phone interrupted Denny's tirade.

Kate returned from the back room with two cups of steaming-hot coffee.

"Who was that?" She set a cup down in front of her partner and perched herself on the corner of his desk.

"Guy from the Water Department. Daughter's an alum." Loosening his tie, Gallagher took a sip. "This stuff'll burn the gizzard right out of you," he bellowed.

"Blow on it, Denny," Kate said, standing up and walking to her own side of the double desk.

"Did you have a chance to check on Reina Martinez Saturday?" she asked.

"Yeah, she lived in the Mission, whatever the hell that proves."

For once, Kate was glad to see him stick his cigar into the corner of his mouth and fumble for his matches. Maybe it would improve his mood.

Tilting back in his swivel chair, he lit the cigar.

"How was your weekend?" he asked, drawing in a long pull of smoke. Apparently it had.

"I had Sister Mary Helen and Sister Eileen to dinner." Kate took another sip of coffee. "It was interesting."

"How so?"

"Sister Mary Helen had made a list of possible suspects. The same ones we had, Denny, plus someone she called X."

Gallagher slammed forward in his chair. "X? We haven't got enough trouble? We need an X? Who the hell is X anyway?"

"The one you least suspect," Kate said with a smile.

"Jeez, Kate!" Gallagher stood up and started to pace. It had been a long time since Kate had seen him pace. "And what's this about the snapshot?" He pointed his finger at her. "Didn't I tell you to get that nun off the case? We've got enough trouble."

So he hadn't missed her comment. "I fully intended to. But . . . well . . . I just didn't have the heart."

"The guts, if you ask me." His tone was accusing.

Kate shrugged.

"Easy for you to say, big boy. I'm the one who has to tell her. Besides, she has some idea about the case that might help us."

"Idea! We don't need an idea. If she really wants to help, she can pray that the lab boys find Rosenberg's skin matches the skin under the victim's fingernails." Gallagher began to pace again. "What the hell idea has she got anyway?"

"She didn't say much and I didn't ask. I figured it was better that way."

Gallagher swung around to face her. "And if the old nun gets hurt? Do you know what will happen?" He pointed to the phone. "We'll be getting calls from everyone including the Pope!"

"Honest to God, Denny, you're getting to be a real morbid Irishman." Standing up, Kate patted her partner on the back. "What if she sheds some light on the case?"

"That we could use." Gallagher hitched his pants over his ample paunch. The back of his shirt was a mass of wrinkles. Mrs. G would have a fit, Kate thought, watching him walk to O'Connor's desk, then turn. "Got any ideas where we should go next?" Gallagher asked.

"Maybe back to Suzanne's apartment building to talk to the other tenants."

"We've done that at least twice."

"Maybe we missed something." Kate took her purse out of the bottom drawer and pulled her coat from the rack. "Maybe we'll get another idea of who this X might be."

Gallagher opened his mouth to say something, but Kate cut him off.

"Besides, the third time's a charm." Smiling, she headed for the door.

"The only charming thing I see about it"—Gallagher grabbed his jacket from the back of the chair and followed her—"is that it'll get me away from this goddamn phone."

Delia McGrath opened the front door of the apartment building as soon as Kate identified herself.

"Good morning, Officers." She greeted them cheerfully. "Can I get you a cup of tea? Some scones? I just took a batch of the Kerry scones out of the oven."

Kate could feel Gallagher weakening. "No," she said quickly, "we've come to talk to your tenants. Those who are home today."

"Not too many home this morning," Mrs. McGrath said. "Only three as far as I can tell."

She counted them off on the three middle fingers of her chubby left hand. "Pat Flaherty. He's always hanging around," she said with an air of disdain reserved for in-laws. "He'd be better with a little more to do.

"The boy doctor. Sleeping, I suspect. And that Adams woman."

Something in the way she said "that" made Kate realize that Iris Adams was not Mrs. McGrath's favorite tenant.

"Sure you won't have a bite before you go?" Mrs. McGrath asked again.

"We'll be back," Gallagher answered before Kate had the chance to refuse.

"Who first?" he asked as the two made their way up the narrow apartment house stairs to the second floor.

"Iris Adams. Obviously Mrs. McGrath doesn't care much for her. I'm curious to find out why."

"What's the Adams gal doing home on Monday morning?" Gallagher asked, opening the heavy door to the second floor and stepping back so Kate could go in first.

Stopping, Kate stared at him in amazement. "Hairdressers never work on Monday," she said. "Everyone knows that!"

"How the hell would I know?" Denny said.

Iris Adams opened the door a crack and peered at them over a short brass door chain. As soon as she recognized the pair, she closed the door, removed the chain, and let them in.

"You can't be too careful after what's happened around here," she said as she led them into her chrome and leather living room.

Kate and Gallagher followed Iris, who was wearing a

blue denim man's work shirt and, Kate figured, little else. The shirttails reached just above her knees.

Sitting down, Iris crisscrossed her long thin legs and lit a cigarette. "What can I do for you?" she asked.

Kate glanced over at Gallagher, who was sitting uneasily on the edge of the modern white leather sofa. His eyes were looking everywhere but at Iris.

Kate knew why. Denny was uncomfortable. The woman's honey-blond hair was precisely cut into the latest style. Long gold earrings dangled to her shoulders. Several heavy chains hung around her neck. Half of a large gold medallion was lost in the open neckline of her denim shirt. Everything about Iris Adams was sharp, angular—almost masculine— glamorous, and very, very sexy.

"We'd like to ask you a few more questions." Kate took a pad and pencil from her purse.

"I've told you everything I know, twice." With long red sculptured nails, Iris stamped out her cigarette. Kate noticed, with surprise, that the nail on her little finger was covered with gold and sparkled with a string of what looked like baby diamonds.

"The latest," Iris said when she realized Kate was staring at her pinkie. "From a friend."

Some friend, Kate thought. "Have you thought of anything since we last talked with you?" Kate asked. "Particularly about the night of Suzanne's murder. Any detail? Any feeling you might have had? Anything at all would be helpful."

Iris shook her head. Her hair swished this way and that, then fell back into perfect shape.

"We are particularly interested in whether or not you heard anything unusual that night," Gallagher said, studying the base of a chrome lamp set on the glass-topped table.

"To tell you the truth, I wasn't home the night in question." Iris lit another cigarette.

"Why didn't you mention that before?" Gallagher directed his accusing eyes to the woman's face.

Nervously the woman flicked ashes from the half-smoked cigarette. "Because I didn't think you'd keep asking," she said, swishing her hair to and fro, "and I was with someone. Someone I didn't want to incriminate."

"Who were you with, ma'am?" Gallagher moved up still farther on the leather couch. Kate was afraid, for a moment, he might slide off.

"Officer," Iris Adams shot back defiantly, "I was with my lover."

So that was it, Kate thought. She was afraid to drag someone else into it. Probably a married man. That's what Mrs. McGrath objected to. Iris Adams was someone's mistress.

"Could we have the gentleman's name, please?" Kate asked. "We'll be as discreet as possible. But we'd like to check out your alibi."

"Check out my alibi!" Iris exploded, stubbing out her cigarette with fast angry jabs. "What happened to Suzanne was done by a man. Surely you are aware of that." She sat back in her leather chair and pulled both bare legs up beside her. "Besides, Officers, I used to have men. Lots of them. But no more." She smiled at them with a catlike grin. "See what they do? I don't care for men anymore. My lover is not a gentleman. She's a gentlewoman."

"Whew, that's some broad," Gallagher said as the two made their way to Apartment 206 and the boy doctor.

"And definitely not a suspect," Kate answered, ringing

the bell. They could hear the door chimes echo inside, but no movements. Kate rang again. Still nothing.

The pair was about to leave when the door was opened by a groggy-looking Lee Slater clothed only in a towel.

This time, Kate averted her eyes while the doctor, clinging to his towel, retreated to a back room and emerged barefooted, pulling a faded robe tightly around him.

"What's up?" he asked, yawning and running his long fingers through his tousled blond hair.

"Not you." Gallagher laughed and sat down on the overstuffed couch. "Sorry we woke you, Doc."

"That's okay," Lee answered, and yawned again. His cold blue eyes, red-rimmed and bloodshot, stood out against his pale face. "I was on duty all last night." He rubbed his bare feet on the rug. "What time is it, anyway?" Nervously he smoothed his light blond beard into a point.

"About ten. Is Miss Heagerty home?"

"No, Mimi's not here, just me," he said.

"Isn't it early for her to be at work?" Kate asked.

"Would be if she were at work." Lee was beginning to fidget in his chair.

As Kate watched the young doctor wake up, she could almost see the energy pouring back into him. Everything about him—his snapping eyes, his near gauntness, his restlessness—said high-strung and intense to her.

"Isn't she working anymore?" Kate asked.

"Yeah, but what she isn't doing is living here anymore. At least for a few days."

"Oh?" Kate asked, hoping he'd go on.

"You know how women are." He drummed nervously on the arm of his chair.

Kate bristled.

"How are they?" Gallagher asked, a chuckle in his

voice. Kate shot her partner a withering glance, which he chose not to notice.

"Emotional, that's how. This murder business has really gotten to her. She talks about it day and night."

Gallagher nodded his head encouragingly.

"Then she wakes up screaming. It's getting to my nerves. So she's gone to her mother's for a few days to re-think our relationship." He gave Gallagher a knowing look.

"So you've no new insights into the crime?" Gallagher asked.

"Hell no! I'm too damn busy at the med center to even think about it."

"We are puzzled about one thing," Kate said, hoping her annoyance was not too evident. "How is it you happened to sleep through it all? Heard nothing. . . ."

"When I get into bed after twelve hours on my feet, I'm practically comatose." He yawned, almost ostentatiously, Kate thought.

"Thanks for your time, Doctor." Gallagher rose from the sofa. "By the way, what kind of a doctor are you interning to be?"

"A surgeon," Slater said, ushering them nervously toward the door.

"He at least would have the know-how to drive the letter opener into her heart," Kate said as the door of 206 closed behind them. "And, I might remark, the cold-bloodedness."

"You're hoping he did it, Katie-girl, just because of what he said about women. And the fact that he's a bit unfeeling. Right?" Gallagher gave her a friendly pat on the back.

"And, if I'm not mistaken, that was Mimi's apartment, not his." Kate glared at Gallagher.

"So you want him guilty 'cause she moved out and he had the good sense to stay?"

"How unprofessional do you think I am?" Kate squared her shoulders and straightened the strap on her shoulder bag.

"Make a hellava doctor, the kid will," Gallagher said. "Unemotional, objective, detached. Hellava surgeon."

"Definitely not the stuff Marcus Welby is made of." Kate shook her head. "Definitely not."

As a matter of fact, from where she stood, the fellow would just as soon kill you as cure you. Though she hesitated to mention this to Gallagher just yet.

"Bet he doesn't have a long Christmas card list either," she said instead, thinking of the half-done stack of cards Jack had been writing still on the dining room table.

Gallagher guffawed. "Bet you're right, Katie-girl," he said, giving her a fatherly pat on the back.

Patrick Flaherty must have heard them laughing in the hall. The door of his apartment opened and he walked right into them.

"Inspectors." He greeted them, doffing his tweed cap. "What brings you here on such a turrible day? And a turrible cold day it is too. Makes a body want to stay indoors by a fire, if you get my meaning."

Kate had hardly noticed the weather. But Flaherty was right. Downtown the sun was shining. The Avenues were still, cold, and cheerless. A screen of low-hanging fog wet the streets.

"Christmas weather," Kate said.

"Christmas," Flaherty said, as if he were surprised. "Now don't get me wrong, but with a murder so close to my own front door, I've scant thought of Christmas. Scares the bloody hell out of you to even go out in your own hallway." Flaherty's eyes roamed from one side of the corridor to the other. "Why, if a few of the lads weren't expecting me, I'd never leave my room."

Kate wondered for a moment whom he was trying to fool.

"We were hoping to get this thing solved before Christmas," she said, more optimistically than she felt.

"Then you better get a move on, young woman." Flaherty looked down at her. "Have you any idea the date?" he asked, amazingly aware, she thought, for a man who had scant thought of Christmas.

"Monday, December seventeenth," Kate answered. She knew the date well. One week until Christmas Eve. Her first real Christmas Eve with Jack. No one wanted this murder solved more than she did.

"Was there something I can do for you?" Flaherty asked, obviously impatient to get where he was going.

"We're just rechecking," Gallagher said. "Have you thought of anything? Anything at all you may have forgotten to tell us?"

"Not a thing. Now, don't get me wrong. It isn't that I haven't been racking my brain, such as it is. All I've got is a gut feeling."

"Gut feeling? About what?"

"About who did it. About who killed that lovely young girl."

"Oh? Whom do you suspect?" Kate asked, hoping the old man's feeling would shed more light on the case.

Flaherty said nothing, simply pointed his thick thumb toward Apartment 201: Arnold Shultz's front door.

Gallagher insisted they stop by Mrs. McGrath's apartment before leaving the building. "See what she has to say," he told Kate.

Kate knew it was more the aroma of fresh-baked scones than the quest for information that drew her partner to the landlady's apartment.

Delia McGrath was delighted to see them, ushered them right in to her kitchen table. She poured each a cup of steaming tea and placed a large scone, still warm from the oven, on plates before them. Butter oozed over the bread and ran onto the plates in little golden puddles. Gallagher bit into his, then licked his fingers appreciatively.

"How did it go?" Mrs. McGrath asked.

"So-so," Kate answered, her mouth full.

The door of the apartment building slammed. "There goes Patty again." Mrs. McGrath rolled her eyes heavenward and blessed herself.

"He said some men were waiting for him." Kate took a sip of tea.

Mrs. McGrath's chipmunk cheeks flushed. "Men waiting for him!" The cheeks quivered. "Nothing more than a few old coots up on Geary having a pint and gossiping. You'd think a grown man would have more to do." She shook her head. "Why, if he wasn't my Eddie's cousin—Eddie, that was my husband, God rest him—I'd throw the lad right out in the street."

Kate took another sip of tea to keep from laughing. Imagine anyone referring to Pat Flaherty as a lad! "He mentioned something about Arnold Shultz, Apartment 201."

"I know which apartment is Arnold's," Mrs. McGrath broke in. "And I know exactly what that old gossip must have said about him. If you're smart, you'll pay him no heed. Arnold is a nice young man, polite, helpful, a downright gentleman. Good with the girls too. If you ask me, all that's wrong with Patrick Flaherty is that he's got a touch of the green!"

Outside, the day was as damp and dreary as Pat Flaherty had predicted. It matched Kate's spirit. They should have been out running down the guy in the photo instead of back here rehashing. They had wasted the whole morning. Or had they? Something about the coldness in Lee Slater's blue eyes made her uneasy. And why had the old man singled out Arnold Shultz? Was it jealousy, as Mrs. McGrath suggested, or did he know something she didn't know? She was beginning to sound like Mary Helen, basing her suspicions on eyes and instincts.

Gallagher and Kate climbed into the car and started downtown toward the Hall of Justice. Even the bearded Santas they saw along the way ringing their bells looked paler and thinner than usual.

Gallagher must have picked up on her mood. "Cheer up, Kate," he said. "At least we got away from the damn phone. And with any luck at all, by the time we get back to the Hall, the lab report will be in. We'll be able to prove Rosenberg was the man the victim scratched. Then we can press him, and presto!" He stopped to let a woman loaded with shopping bags cross the street.

Kate sighed. It would be so easy. "I'm hoping you're right, Denny."

"You're hoping! I'm damn close to praying, I am," he said, "so we can wrap this whole business up before Christmas."

The pair rode the rest of the way in silence.

"Some of the girls are at the front door caroling," Sister Therese announced to the Sisters sitting in the Community Room.

Reluctantly Mary Helen pushed herself up from a soft chair. She hated to miss the Hallmark Christmas special. The program was helping pass the time until eight-thirty, which she considered a respectable hour to call Iggie Kelly at Vacaville—after his dinner and before his bedtime.

"Hurry, hurry!" Therese clapped her small bony hands nervously. "The girls are waiting. The girls are waiting. We can't keep the girls waiting. . . ."

Sister Cecilia rolled her eyes and filed out first. Such is the burden of leadership, Mary Helen thought, watching the tall college president leave the room.

"The girls are waiting," Therese repeated still again, in a high whine, then rushed toward the small convent kitchenette to make the traditional hot chocolate.

Which girls? Mary Helen wanted to ask, but Therese was moving too quickly to stop. With Therese, the girls could be the forty-year alumnae, the college freshmen, the neighborhood youngsters, or anywhere in between.

To Mary Helen's relief the group was Sister Anne's Campus Ministry Club. The singing would at least be well done and, she hoped, brief. She took a place toward the rear, just in case.

On the third verse of "Joy to the World," Mary Helen checked her watch. Eight-thirty on the dot. With all the nuns smiling appreciatively toward the front doorway, it was not difficult to slip down the hallway.

Father Ignatius Kelly's phone number had been easy to find once she located the proper section in the Catholic Directory. Finding the directory in the college library had been a bit more of a challenge, with Eileen following her suspiciously through the reference shelves, asking if she could help. Not that her visit to Iggie was going to be a secret from Eileen. She fully intended to ask her friend to go with her to Vacaville, but there was no sense stirring up opposition ahead of time. As the old saying goes, "Don't trouble trouble till trouble troubles you," Mary Helen told herself.

Mary Helen's stomach gave a quiver as soon as she heard the number begin to ring. Fear, apprehension, anticipation? She wasn't sure just what it was and she didn't have time to analyze the feeling. Iggie Kelly answered on the third ring.

"Father Kelly here," a deep full voice answered.

She hadn't remembered his voice was that low. But then again, the last time she had talked to him he was a seminarian. Probably a lot of things about Ignatius Kelly had changed in how many years? Resolutely, she refused to count them.

"Ignatius, this is Sister Mary Helen," she said. There was a long pause, which Mary Helen did not interrupt. It was only fair to give the man a chance to gather his wits.

"Sister Mary Helen? The Sister Mary Helen? I can't believe it!" the priest said.

"Believe it, it's true," she answered.

After they had established where she was and how she was, Mary Helen thought it only polite to tell him what she wanted, since he seemed too gentlemanly to ask.

"I'd like to see you as soon as possible. There's a photo of a prisoner I'd like you to identify."

"Gee whiz, Sister," he said boyishly, "do you know how many prisoners I see?"

"But, just maybe . . ." she said. "By some fluke . . ."

"I'll give it my best shot," Iggie conceded.

"Even angels can't do more than their very best," she assured him.

Tuesday was Father Kelly's day off. They set up an appointment at the prison for Wednesday afternoon at one P.M.

Sister Mary Helen hung up the phone, elated. On Wednesday she might know something about Suzanne's gentleman friend and her baby. Perhaps the information would lead Kate Murphy to the girl's killer. Suzanne might be laid to rest in peace by Christmas after all.

When she returned to the front door, the girls were just beginning "Hark! the Herald Angels Sing." Mary Helen joined in full-throated and, she suspected, a little louder than anyone else on the line "God and sinners reconciled"!

WEDNESDAY—THIRD WEEK OF ADVENT

About eleven-thirty, Sister Mary Helen found Sister Eileen in the Community Room, surrounded by rolls of Christmas paper, large boxes, spools of ribbon, and dozens of brightly colored bows.

Soft Christmas music played in the background. A welcoming fire roared in the fireplace. Several other nuns sat around the long table, each turning a cardboard box into a work of art. Sister Therese was directing the project. *Help wrap benefactors' Christmas gifts,* her terse note had read. *Community Room at 11:00 sharp.*

Fortunately Mary Helen hadn't seen it on the doorjamb until she entered the room. Eileen, however, made what Mary Helen considered a fetish of reading all notes and had been sucked right in.

"Want to take a ride with me to Vacaville?" Mary Helen whispered in her friend's ear.

"When?" Eileen whispered back.

"Right now."

Eileen untangled several loops of satinese ribbon from around her thumb and baby finger and placed on the table what looked, to Mary Helen, like a feeble attempt at a bow.

"You, old dear, have saved me from a fate worse than death," she said, following her friend quickly from the room.

"Why are we going to Vacaville?" Eileen finally asked when the two had crossed the Bay Bridge and were passing

Emeryville. The whole Bay Area was crisp and sparkling under a cloudless sky.

Mary Helen was surprised it had taken her so long.

"You've heard me talk of Ignatius Kelly?" she asked. "I taught him years ago in the eighth grade in Oxnard."

Eileen nodded with interest.

"Now he's a Franciscan priest, and of all places, he's at Vacaville prison, the chaplain there. I thought I'd drop by and say how-do."

Eileen's gray eyes narrowed suspiciously. "You've taught hundreds of boys in the eighth grade and at least a dozen of them are priests. I've never known you to get a bee in your bonnet and drive over an hour to say how-do to any of them."

"How many of them do I have an appointment with?" Mary Helen said weakly.

"Oh! Then he called and invited you to the prison?" Eileen asked, blinking her eyes innocently.

"To be perfectly frank, Eileen, I called him," Mary Helen admitted.

Eileen did not seem surprised. "And would this visit have anything at all to do with Suzanne's murder?"

"Everything, I hope."

As Mary Helen zipped along the straight, flat Highway 80, she told Eileen about her visit with Sister Mary Thomasine, getting the snapshot back from Kate, calling Iggie, her hope of solving the case, and even about the last obscene phone call. If Eileen was going to be her Watson, it was only fair to bring her up-to-date.

Eileen shuddered, but she said nothing, simply stared out the car window. Low flat farmland now bordered either side of the road. Brilliant yellow mustard grew wild in fields full of dark, barren fruit trees. Red-winged blackbirds skimmed along the tops. Winter-green hills, spotted with fawn-colored cows, gently rolled in the distance. Above it all stretched a vast sky of ice-blue.

"Penny for your thoughts," Mary Helen said after several miles.

"I was just thinking how impossible it seems that so much horror can live side by side with so much beauty." Eileen pointed to the countryside.

Mary Helen had to agree, yet she didn't want her optimism dampened. She was sure this visit would help solve the murder.

With her right hand she dug into her pocketbook and pulled out the snapshot.

"Take another look at that face." She handed it to Eileen. "Are you sure you don't recognize the boy?"

Eileen squinted, adjusted her glasses, held the photo in the light. "No," she said finally, "I wish I did. Do you?"

Mary Helen hesitated, then shook her head. "I can't tell, really. Maybe because I've looked at it for so long, I think I do."

Eileen gave her an inquiring look. "Oh?"

"Something is wiggling in the back of my mind," Mary Helen said slowly. "Are you quite sure he's not familiar?"

Eileen looked again. "He looks to me like a dozen other slight young fellows. But, honestly, I don't think I have ever seen this fellow before." She slipped the photo back into Mary Helen's purse. "Why didn't you tell me yesterday where we were going?"

Mary Helen didn't hear at first. She was still puzzling. "Oh, sorry," she said, "would it have made any difference?"

Eileen laughed. "Of course not, old dear. You know full well that I'd rather go anywhere, even to prison, than wrap benefactors' Christmas gifts."

Just south of Vacaville, Mary Helen turned right. The pair drove through a pleasant middle-class neighborhood. Christmas trees shone from several of the wide front windows where the curtains had been pulled open. Many of the low roofs were outlined with colored lights. Here and there lawns were decorated with elves and Santas and even an occasional Nativity scene.

"Are you sure we are on the right street?" Eileen asked in surprise.

Before Mary Helen could answer, a group of large concrete buildings surrounded by a high wall with several guard towers loomed on their right.

"This must be it," Mary Helen said. She turned into the spacious blacktop parking lot. They had no trouble finding a space. The dearth of cars in the visitors' section of the lot filled her with a sudden sadness.

Father Ignatius Kelly was in the front office, waiting, when the two nuns walked through the small, barren visitors' entrance. If he'd not been wearing his clerics, Sister Mary Helen was sure she would never have recognized him.

Iggie had grown into a lean, sinewy young man without, as the saying goes, an extra ounce of fat.

Wisps of gray had begun to sprout in his dark wavy hair, which looked to Mary Helen as if it badly needed a cutting, particularly in the back. It had begun to curl above his Roman collar.

His clean-shaven, ruddy face was no longer full, but almost craggy. Mentally, Mary Helen tried to calculate his age. To her utter amazement, she figured Iggie must be over forty. Impossible!

The moment he saw her, he removed the pipe from his mouth and smiled. The smile lit up his hazel eyes. Those eyes Mary Helen would recognize anywhere. Even as a youngster, Ignatius Kelly had had laughing eyes; eyes that sparked and danced and found fun and humor everywhere. Those hadn't changed. Mary Helen was glad.

"We'll go to my office," he said.

The armed guard ushered the two nuns through a metal detector much like those at airports, searched their purses, and gave them both visitor's passes.

They followed the priest down a path where the guard in the tower shifted his rifle so he could wave down at them.

Quickly, Iggie led them through the bleak visitors' room, past the armed guard at a steel door, and into the prison proper.

"Stay close to me," he said as they walked down the wide gray corridors. Dozens of men in blue jeans passed them. None spoke, but all looked. Some smiled, some looked sullen.

The passageway was littered with small bits of paper. Mary Helen couldn't believe it. Somehow she'd always thought a prison would be immaculately clean. Old movie images die hard! she told herself.

Father Kelly showed them through a door marked CATHOLIC CHAPLAIN. Inside a small outer office an inmate rose, smiled, and greeted them. "Nice to see you, Sisters," he said, shaking each one's hand. "No calls while you was gone, Father. I'll be out here if you need me."

The chaplain's office was a bit larger. Once inside, Ignatius Kelly turned, grabbed Sister Mary Helen in a big bear hug, and roared, "Gee whiz, Sister, is it good to see you!"

After he put her down, Mary Helen adjusted her skirt, jacket, and glasses and took a chair a safe distance from the chaplain's desk.

Iggie welcomed Sister Eileen a little less effusively, Mary Helen was glad to see, then filled two thick white mugs with coffee from a battered steel urn in the corner of his office. He set one down in front of each of the nuns, then pushed himself back in his swivel chair, smiled, and said nothing.

I guess I've changed quite a bit too, Mary Helen thought, watching his eyes study her intently. She blew on the hot coffee, then took a sip. Funny, she mused, inside she still felt thirty. Actually, she felt eighteen, but, please God, she had acquired a little more sense.

"Gee whiz, it's good to see you!" Iggie repeated, slamming his chair forward. "I've thought about you so many times. Every Christmas when I get your card, I promise myself I'm going to call you. Then, somehow, time flies . . ." He paused to strike a match and light his briar pipe.

Christmas cards! The thought hit Mary Helen like a thunderbolt. With all the goings on about Suzanne's murder, she hadn't even thought about buying cards, let alone writing them.

The aromatic smell of the priest's tobacco smoke filled the small office. They reminisced for a while about whom he remembered and whom she knew about. Mercifully, all his memories of his school days were happy.

"Well, you didn't come here to go over old times," he said, just as Mary Helen was beginning to get antsy.

"No. Not that it hasn't been pleasant," she added. "But what I really came about was a snapshot—this one." She plunked the Polaroid picture down in front of Iggie.

Then she sat back and watched him. The muscles of his jaw tensed.

"Gee whiz, Sister, you really picked a winner," he said, pushing the picture back to her with the tip of a forefinger.

"So—you know the fellow," Mary Helen said slowly.

"Well!" Iggie rose from his chair and poured himself a cup of coffee, almost as if he were buying time, Mary Helen thought.

She edged forward in her chair, waiting. The priest

combed the front of his wavy hair with his fingers. "The guy's a real sad case, Sister," he said, the laughter gone from his hazel eyes. "Came in here six or seven years ago. A real loner. Started hanging around the chapel. I felt sorry for him. Talked to his shrink—the psychiatrist—you know. I found out the guy was brutalized by his mother as a kid. Really a sad childhood. Turned him into a bucket of nuts."

Mary Helen studied the photo. "He looks so—so likable," she said. Again, the thought that she'd seen the man jostled and squirmed in the back of her mind.

"I've looked at this picture so often in the last few days, I feel that I know him," she said.

Iggie frowned and shook his head. "If you ever ran into him, Sister, believe me, you'd remember him." He gave her a knowing grin. "Anyway, as I said, I really felt for him. After a few months he started causing a lot of trouble. The other guys hated him.

"Funny," he continued, puffing at his pipe, "the guys have their own code. Most of them have their own miserable childhoods, so they don't give anyone a break."

"Is he still here?" Mary Helen asked.

"No. He was paroled again, maybe about a month ago." Iggie shook his head sadly. "Although if you ask me, he'll be back. He's a real loser."

About a month ago? Mary Helen wondered. Wasn't that when Sarah Farraday said Suzanne had changed? And when Suzanne had asked her if she was happy in the convent? How she wished they had been able to talk.

"If the fellow is mentally ill and a troublemaker, how on God's green earth did he get paroled?" Eileen burst out.

"That's the saddest part, Sister. Some poor dumb girl got interested in him. Started visiting him regularly. He wanted me to marry them. Actually begged me. Sorry as I felt for the poor bugger, I couldn't. But in my opinion, he wasn't capable of a commitment. When I refused, he went to another chaplain. One who was green. He accused me of being unchristian. Of not giving Kueneman a second chance. The whole ball of wax. The upshot is," he said, shrugging, "the guy married them. Our friend got the gal pregnant and finally convinced the parole board that, like the three bears, they'd all live happily ever after. That's how he got out the first time."

"How long ago was that?" Mary Helen asked.

"Mmm—two, two and a half years ago now. But he didn't stay out long. Back in before you knew it." Iggie tapped the bowl of his pipe on an ashtray. "Then the whole process started over. And as I say, he convinced the parole board that the poor dumb gal would want him back. To hear him tell it you'd think theirs was a marriage made in heaven."

"Do you suppose that poor dumb girl could possibly be our Suzanne?" Eileen said aloud what Mary Helen was thinking.

"Is the girl he married the same one as in the picture?" Mary Helen asked, her heart pounding so hard, she was sure Iggie could hear it.

The priest shook his head. "I never saw the girl," he said. "Is this someone you know, Sister?"

"She was my secretary." Mary Helen slipped the photo into her pocketbook. "You must have read about the case: Suzanne Barnes, a young woman who worked for Mount St. Francis?"

"Of course." Iggie hit his forehead with the butt of his hand. "Somehow I never connected that murder with you. Sometimes there's nobody home in the dome." His hazel eyes suddenly grew solemn. "I hope to God Kueneman didn't . . ." He didn't finish the sentence. "How in the heck did you connect up with Kueneman's ex?" he asked instead.

"It's a long story," Mary Helen answered, "and I know you're busy," she added, avoiding Eileen's stare. "Before we go, could I ask you another question?"

"Sure, Sister, anything." Iggie had regained his good humor.

"Do you by any chance know a Reina Martinez?" Mary Helen asked, suddenly realizing her fingers were crossed.

"You really can pick the winners." Iggie shook his head. "That poor gal is more to be pitied than censured, as the old song goes. Regular con doll! Belongs to one of the murderers in my congregation. The guy got her pregnant about the same time as Kueneman's wife. It didn't work out as well for him. Murderers are harder to parole, especially unmarried ones."

Mary Helen felt as though someone had punched her in the stomach. Punched her good and hard. So that was Reina's connection to Suzanne. She had come here wanting to find out about Suzanne and her young man, about her connection with Reina, but now that she had, she felt that she couldn't handle much more information. Enough already.

"Thank you so much for your time, Ignatius. You've been very helpful. One more thing," she said, scarcely able to believe she actually said it, "I'm curious. What crime was the Kueneman fellow convicted of?"

Father Kelly swallowed hard. "Rape, Sister," he said, "multiple rape. And the darndest part of it was, he felt like he was doing his victims a favor."

The ride home was long and, for the most part, silent. Mary Helen felt deflated. Yet she should have known that no news was going to be good news. Still, the thought of women like Reina and Suzanne—and she would have bet what was left of her life that the girl who married Kueneman was Suzanne—being so taken in, so victimized, made her both sad and angry. Why hadn't someone stopped them from taking such a foolish step? Even as she thought it, she knew that was a foolish question. No one, no amount of talking, could have stopped either woman. None so deaf as those who will not hear, she thought, improvising a bit on Jeremiah. The older she became, the more she saw the wisdom of those familiar sayings, even the ones she had to change a bit to fit her circumstances. Right at this moment, for instance, she was beginning to wonder why she hadn't just let sleeping dogs lie.

As they approached the Bay Bridge the winter sun began to set, streaking the slate sky with blood red. Downtown San Francisco stood out against it, a black silhouette with the Transamerica Pyramid and the Bank of America Building looming above the rest, and Coit Tower to their far right sticking out like a stubby thumb.

"Just as soon as we get home, Mary Helen, you call Kate." Eileen's brogue was a little thick.

"What's the matter?" Mary Helen asked.

"Glory be to God as if you didn't know! The man in your pocketbook's a rapist. Suzanne's dead. Now you are getting obscene phone calls from God knows who—probably him—and you ask me what's the matter?"

Eileen glared at her.

"Eileen, I do think you are overreacting just a smidgeon," Mary Helen said, more calmly than she felt.

"Would it be overreacting to say that I think you are in over your little gray head? And more than a smidgeon! Why, the next thing we know, we'll be investigating your murder!"

With that said, Eileen settled back in her seat, leaving Mary Helen with a mouth oddly dry and parched.

"I was going to call Kate Murphy just as soon as we get home," Mary Helen just managed to get her tongue around the words.

"That is the most sensible thing you've said all week." Eileen relaxed again and patted her friend's knee. "And I'm going right to the phone booth with you."

Kate Murphy could hear the phone ringing the moment she started up the front steps on 34th and Geary. The house was dark. Apparently she had beaten Jack home from work.

She fumbled with the dead bolt, but managed to catch the phone on the ninth ring. Anyone who lets the phone ring nine times really wants to get me, she thought, picking up the receiver.

Sister Mary Helen identified herself quickly, and without any fanfare launched straight into her trip to Vacaville, Father Kelly's revelation about Suzanne and Reina Martinez, and exactly what she thought Kate should do with the information.

Promising to call Kueneman's parole officer first thing in the morning, Kate hung up. I should feel elated, she thought.

Rosenberg's lawyer had agreed to let him take the skin test. Kate had the feeling that Muriel had insisted. Gallagher felt this would cinch their case. And, if the tests proved negative, Mary Helen had given them a second possible suspect, the most probable one to her way of thinking.

But for some reason she didn't feel elated. Much as she hated to admit it, she felt depressed. Depressed that a young woman could be so naive, so victimized, so just plain stupid, that a baby had been conceived by the union. But if she were really honest with herself, she would have to admit that she was especially depressed because this afternoon she had discovered she was not pregnant, merely a few weeks late. Probably due to the stress of the murder on Holy Hill.

Funny, Kate mused, hanging up her coat and holster in the front closet, I didn't want a baby, and now I'm sad because I'm not having one.

She switched on the kitchen light. The whole place seemed dark and cold and gloomy. Even the newly waxed linoleum looked tired. It was her turn to cook. She opened the refrigerator and peered in. It was nearly bare. It was also her turn to shop, she remembered. She moved the quart of milk. Behind it was a hunk of cheese, mildewing.

All at once, Kate began to cry.

"I am calling you, ooh, ooh, ooh" she heard as Jack turned his key and began the "Indian Love Call."

The neighbors must think we're a couple of nuts, she thought, wiping her eyes and blowing her nose. She was at the sink splashing water on her face when Jack came in.

"What's the matter, hon?" he asked, studying her seriously.

"Must be the onions," she said. Jack looked around the kitchen, but said nothing except "Oh."

Suddenly his arms were holding her tight and she was sobbing into his shoulder.

"What happened, Kate?" he asked gently.

"Oh, this murder, I guess." She hiccuped, then tried to catch her breath.

Jack led her into the sun room, sat her down, then returned with two glasses of wine.

She took a sip, then told him about Sister Mary Helen's discovery.

"And do you know who'll really suffer?" she asked. "That poor baby!" she said, answering her own question.

Jack twirled the stem of his wineglass between his fingers. "You're right," he said. "And you know what else? I've been thinking about what you said about our having a baby."

"Oh?" Kate felt a little shudder of dread run through her body.

"Yeah, and I think you're right on that score too. I don't think we should have a child until—" That was as far as he got.

Kate could feel the sob rise in her throat, then burst out. "How could you?" she sobbed.

"For chrissake, Kate, how could I what?" Jack looked at her, bewildered.

"How could you say that?" she asked.

"I'm only agreeing with you." Jack ran his fingers through his curly hair.

"But I've changed my mind." Kate hiccuped.

Jack's hazel eyes widened.

Before she knew it, Kate was telling him about the last few weeks, about thinking she might be pregnant; about her feelings of anticipation, dread, and finally her awful disappointment when she discovered it was a false alarm.

Jack took her in his arms and kissed her swollen eyes. "So what you're saying is you want to have a baby?" he asked.

"And now you've changed your mind." She sniffed. "Right?"

"Hey, remember me? I'm easy." Jack smiled. "The right glint in your eye and I could be persuaded to change my mind right back again."

Kate grinned, then gave her husband a hug. "Shall we try?" she asked.

"Hell yes!" he answered immediately. "The sooner the better."

Kate checked her watch. "You must be starved," she said. "It's my turn to make dinner and all there is in the fridge is some moldy cheese." She could feel the tears sting her eyes again.

"Don't tell me you're going to start to cry about a rotten piece of cheese."

"No." Kate started to get up from the couch. "It's not the rotten cheese. It's everything. I guess I'm a rotten housewife, rotten at getting pregnant, maybe even a rotten wife."

Jack grabbed her and pulled her down beside him. "You want the rotten husband's opinion?" he asked, planting a butterfly kiss on her cheek.

The winter dusk filled and darkened the small sunporch. I'm so lucky to have him, Kate thought, listening to a foghorn bleating in the distance. A yellow streetlight from the avenue shone across the backyard and through the large windows. It shot long, grotesque shadows along the wall.

"You must be starved," Kate said finally.

"What I am is madly in love with you and thrilled to death that we're going to start a family." Jack released her. Standing up, he took her by the hand. "And if you think for one moment that I'm going to let my about-to-be-pregnant wife cook . . . Get your coat, we're going to celebrate. There's a new little fish joint on Forty-second."

"But, Jack," Kate protested, following her husband into the front hall, "trying is not the same as being, you know."

"Kate, my love"—Jack helped her on with her coat, then wrapped his arms around her so tightly, she could feel his heart beat—"trying has got to be half the fun."

THURSDAY—THIRD WEEK OF ADVENT

Sister Mary Helen could feel the excitement the moment she walked into the Sisters' dining room. She joined Eileen and Cecilia, who were sitting together at a small table by the window.

"What's up?" she asked Eileen sleepily.

"Christmas." Eileen rolled her eyes toward Therese, who was muttering to herself and hurrying across the room carrying an armload of fat red candles. Several other nuns followed her with a procession of cardboard boxes, all labeled XMAS DECORATIONS—DINING ROOM.

"It's a week away." Mary Helen groaned, thinking of her unwritten Christmas cards.

"Only five days, not counting today," Eileen answered, sipping her coffee.

They watched silently as Therese stacked the decorations on the sideboard, then covered the lot with a dish towel so no one would notice.

"The people who walk in darkness shall see a great light," Therese muttered as she passed their table. "And soon."

"Therese is the last of the big 'anticipators,' " Cecilia said. "We could all profit from her good example."

"Wasn't it Mark Twain who said, 'Few things are harder to put up with than the annoyance of good example'?" Mary Helen asked, then glanced over at the college president. Deep black circles had formed under her eyes. Maybe they seemed blacker because Cecilia's face was so gray. Even her hair seemed whiter. The woman actually looked haggard.

"How are you doing?" Mary Helen asked, feeling a sudden sympathy for Cecilia.

"Better," Cecilia answered, her thin shoulders hunched forward. "We only made the fourth page, inside column, in this morning's *Chronicle.*"

Mary Helen bit into her toast and chewed slowly. If the information she'd given to Kate amounted to anything, they'd be right back on page one, she wanted to say, but one more look at Cecilia's bags told her this was not the moment for that piece of news. "Humph," she grunted, happy her mouth was full.

"How are you doing?" Cecilia asked back.

Before Mary Helen could answer, Therese tapped her on the shoulder. "While you were away yesterday, Mary Agnes Van Der Zee called," she announced loudly.

That blasted class list, Mary Helen thought.

"She's most eager to get in touch with you." Therese smiled sweetly, but the tone was accusing.

"I've had a few other things on my mind," Mary Helen growled.

"That's why it always pays to anticipate." Therese shot her stinger, then buzzed away, leaving Mary Helen seething.

"Touché!" Laughing, Cecilia rose and left the breakfast table.

"At least it gave her a laugh, poor dear," Eileen said brightly as she watched Cecilia cross the room. "Did you notice how bad she looked?"

Mary Helen grunted.

"What I'm dying to find out," Eileen continued, obviously oblivious to Mary Helen's mood, "is what Kate Murphy said last night."

"She said that she would look into it. They are working on a couple of leads. But not to get our hopes up."

"Oh." Eileen sounded disappointed.

"We'll talk later. Right now I have an important list to get together." Blast Mary Agnes Van der *Pest!*

The campus was empty and fog-filled as Mary Helen crossed it. Its bleakness fitted her mood. The inside of the college building was even worse: cold, desolate, dark.

Her footsteps echoed on the concrete floor as she made her way along the narrow corridor to her basement office. Not even Anne's light shone from under her door.

The metal key was cold in her hand. She fumbled for the lock, but it was unnecessary. Mary Helen could feel fear, like cold water, ripple down her spine. The heavy door was ajar.

Slowly she pushed it open. Her muscles cramped with tension. She felt along the wall for the light switch. The long rows of fluorescent lights blinked on and began to hum.

A light fragrance of perfume hit her nostrils and nausea rose inside her as she looked around. Suzanne's desk drawers were overturned. The contents looked as though someone in a great temper tantrum had kicked them all over the floor. The vase on her desk was shattered, the typewriter bludgeoned. File cabinet drawers hung open and empty. Manila folders were strewn every which way.

The pebbled glass in the door leading to Mary Helen's inner office was smashed. Sharp shards of glass still clung to the frame.

Inside, Mary Helen's desk chair was overturned, drawers dumped, floppy discs strewn across the floor, and the crucifix from the wall snapped in two.

A hole the size of a fist gaped precisely in the middle of the computer.

Mary Helen could feel a swirl of rage under her fear. The rage seemed to be getting the upper hand. "Whoever you are, I'd gladly wring your neck," she said aloud, rummaging through the debris and picking up the phone from under her desk. She listened. Thank God, there was a dial tone.

Still angry, she called Kate to report the damage to her office.

"Where are you now?" Kate asked when Mary Helen had finished her spiel.

"In my office of course," Mary Helen answered.

"Get the hell—excuse me, Sister—get the heck out of there right now!" Kate literally shouted. "Go to the convent and stay there. Inspector Gallagher and I will be right over."

"Whoever did this is, by now, surely long gone," Mary Helen said bravely, feeling her hands grow suddenly clammy.

"Whoever did it is a sicko." Kate's tone was icy cold. "And we have no idea where he, or she, for that matter, is. So get—"

"Get thee to a nunnery?" Mary Helen interjected, hoping to lighten the situation.

"And just as quickly as you can," Kate answered grimly. "We're on our way."

Replacing the phone on her desk, Mary Helen resisted the urge to tidy up. Tomorrow. She'd ask Eileen to help her tomorrow. When she was upset, Eileen was the original "tidy paws." This mess would be right up her alley.

Mary Helen picked her way across the littered floor and was just about to turn off the lights when the phone rang.

Mary Agnes Van Der Zee and that blasted list, she thought, retracing her steps. Will she ever believe this story? She lifted the receiver.

"Good morning," Mary Helen began as cheerfully as

she could manage, fully expecting to hear Mary Agnes's high nasal twang. But the line went dead.

Mary Helen slammed down the receiver.

"Jesus, Mary, and Joseph, protect me," she prayed, suddenly frightened. She bolted from the office. Her footsteps reverberated as she ran through the empty building.

By the time she reached the front steps of the college building her temples were throbbing and her chest felt as though it might burst. She leaned heavily against the stone lion guarding the entrance. The cool fog soothed her flushed face.

Hugging her own chest, she tried to catch her breath. "Dear Lord, get me out of this one and I'll never get myself into another mess," she prayed silently, knowing full well that the Lord protects fools, drunks, and old nuns, but seldom holds any of them to their rash promises.

Mary Helen had managed to calm herself down by the time Kate Murphy and Dennis Gallagher arrived at the convent. She watched the pair mount the front steps. Kate's arms were folded tightly across her chest. Gallagher followed, straightening up his loose tie. Both had worried looks on their faces.

Mary Helen opened the door before Kate could ring the bell. With a smile, she ushered them into a small front parlor and shut the heavy door.

God forbid that Therese should overhear even a shred of this conversation.

"Really shook you up, huh, Sister?" Gallagher asked once he'd settled into the brocade sofa. "You look white as a sheet."

"It's nasty business, walking into a ransacked room." Kate sat next to him. Mary Helen knew she was trying to be reassuring.

"It's not so much the office, although that's bad enough. It's what happened after."

"After?" Kate's lips were tight. "Sister, I thought I told you to leave there immediately."

"The phone rang. Naturally I picked it up. As soon as I did, the person on the other end hung up."

"First time that happened?" Gallagher asked, leaning forward in the soft sofa. He loosened his tie.

Mary Helen was too exhausted to fudge. It's the first time *that* happened, but . . ." She told the two inspectors about her other calls.

"Why didn't you mention these calls before?" Kate's blue eyes narrowed.

"They seemed to have no bearing on the case." Mary Helen averted her eyes from Kate's stare.

"Jeez, Sister." Gallagher ran his hand over his bald head.

"Why don't you let us be the judges of what has bearing on this case?" Kate suggested coldly. "And now, Sister, for the duration of this case I insist you stay inside this convent. Probably the smartest thing for us to do would be to set up a police guard. . . ." She looked at Gallagher, who merely shook his head in exasperation.

The thought of telling Cecilia, not to mention Therese, about the break-in was going to be bad enough. Having to explain a policeman on duty outside the front door of the convent was more than Sister Mary Helen cared to handle.

"That would be a perfect waste of the taxpayers' money," she said, adjusting her glasses for emphasis. "I was just going to my room. I could use a little nap, unless, of course, you want me to go with you to my office."

Kate's flashing blue eyes were all the answer Mary Helen needed. Meekly she handed over her keys and padded upstairs to her bedroom.

Kate and Gallagher inspected the overturned office in silence.

"I'll call the guys in to fingerprint," Gallagher said, dialing. "Although I don't think they'll find anything much. Looks like this guy was a pro."

"A sick pro," Kate said. She moved her toe through the debris on the floor. "Nothing valuable seems to be gone, just wantonly destroyed." She twisted one strand of her thick red hair around her index finger, then pushed it into a curl.

"What's on your mind?" Gallagher asked when he'd hung up the phone.

"Maybe you're wrong about Rosenberg. Maybe the guy who tore up this office is the guy who killed Suzanne. And maybe that guy is "Lover Boy" Kueneman, of photo fame."

"Jeez, Kate. That's all we need. The old nun setting herself up to get murdered. I told you to get rid of her. Besides, I'm putting my money on Rosenberg. Remember what he did to the kid's apartment."

"I think you better start thinking about Kueneman. I called probation this morning. Hal Garden's his parole officer. But Garden was out of the office today. Be back tomorrow. I never had the chance to talk to him."

"So how could it be Kueneman?" Gallagher was reluctant to give up Rosenberg. The guy wouldn't even know the nun was on to him."

Kate didn't answer right away, she just stood there twisting her hair.

"That's an annoying habit," Gallagher finally said in exasperation.

Kate stopped and glared at her partner. "Easy for a cigar smoker to say," she answered.

"For crissake, Kate, what are you thinking?"

"That maybe Kueneman is our man and maybe someone else in this case talked to him," Kate said slowly. "Martinez, for example."

"I'll tell you what." Gallagher fished through his jacket pockets for his cigar stub. "Whoever our killer is," he said, pointing a finger at Kate, "I want that old nun off the case before she gets herself hurt."

Gallagher went on after a moment's pause. "Not that we got a snowball's chance in hell of getting one, but . . . you think that crap about a police guard might stop her?"

"Not after she thinks about it." Kate smiled. "But it may slow the old girl down for a day or two."

SATURDAY—THIRD WEEK OF ADVENT

Sister Mary Helen was beginning to get cabin fever. She had not left the convent since Thursday, except, of course, for prayers and meals. But then she had been in the company of dozens.

She had cleaned, washed clothes, decorated, written Christmas cards kindly purchased by Cecilia, puttered, and then started to clean again. She had been sorely tempted to slip over to her office with Eileen to start to straighten things. The thought of running into Kate, however, had stopped her cold.

At one point she was so utterly bored that she even considered reneging on her Advent resolution and finishing her mystery.

She was thrilled and relieved, therefore, when Anne knocked on her bedroom door and asked her out.

"Mimi just called," the young nun said. "Mr. Rosenberg, her boss, is closing the Sea Wench Saturday night for a staff Christmas party. Seems it's an old Rosenberg tradition. His wife comes, all the help and their significant others, and, because of what happened to Suzanne, he's asking Eileen, you, and me."

Mary Helen hesitated, but only for a moment. Kate had expressly told her to stay home. What she really meant was not to be alone in a dangerous place. What could be safer than a crowded party at the Sea Wench right in the middle of a tourist-packed Ghirardelli Square? It was surely the last conceivable place her caller would think to look.

Mary Helen had a little twinge of conscience, but only a little. Although going out tonight might not be keeping to the letter of Kate's law, it was most assuredly keeping to the spirit. Even Kate couldn't miss the logic of her conclusion.

"I'd love to," she said. "What time?"

"We'll leave at six-thirty," Anne whispered. "And this time I'll drive."

Without a word, Gallagher shoved the lab report across his desk and onto Kate's.

From the look on her partner's face she could tell it was bad news. "Skin test was negative?" she asked, not even bothering to pick up the sheet of paper.

Gallagher nodded. "Damn it!" he said, then stared out the window.

"What do we do now?" Kate asked.

Gallagher stood up and hitched his pants over his paunch. "Let's get the hell out of here, Katie-girl. It's Saturday. Decent people should be home mowing the lawn."

"What about tomorrow?"

"Hell, there's not much we can do on Sunday. We'll follow that Kueneman lead on Monday. Things will look better by then," he said.

She nodded in agreement, although she was disappointed. She desperately wanted to solve this case before Christmas.

"Couldn't look worse," Gallagher added, taking his jacket off the back of the chair and straightening his tie.

Grabbing her own coat, Kate waved to O'Connor, who was on the phone, and followed her partner out of the detail.

When the three nuns arrived at the Sea Wench, the party was already in full swing. Christmas wreaths, bright poinsettias, and tinsel garlands had been added to the nautical decor.

"The place looks for all the world like Christmas aboard a pirate ship," Eileen whispered. Mary Helen nodded in agreement. "And here comes Captain Hook now," she said, cocking her head toward their approaching host.

"Welcome, Sisters." Mr. Francis Xavier "Punch" Rosenberg extended his hairy hand, but that was as far as he got before a petite middle-aged woman with large hazel eyes and frosted hair stepped out from behind him.

"Are these the Sisters, Francis?" she asked.

Rosenberg nodded.

"Let me present my wife, Mrs. Rosenberg," he said meekly.

"Muriel to my friends," Mrs. Punch began. Her voice was soft, gentle, and low. What had Shakespeare said? "An excellent thing in woman." Yet Mary Helen could tell from the spark in those bright eyes that Muriel Rosenberg did not miss a trick.

"I'm so glad you could come," she said. "Francis told me about you."

Chatting cozily to Eileen, Muriel Rosenberg ushered the three nuns away from her husband before they had a chance to find out exactly what he had told her.

The four women headed toward the refreshment table. On her way over, Mary Helen surveyed the room. Young men and women stood in groups, laughing, talking, eating. Some gyrated on a small raised wooden floor to the beat of a three-piece combo. If her memory served her correctly, during working hours this was where the staff performed. In her mind's eye she could see a very alive Suzanne performing in a darkened room. The suddenness of the vision gave her a start and something else loomed on the edge of her consciousness, yet hard as she tried, she couldn't quite grasp what it was. Never mind, she thought, feeling oddly frustrated, tonight the wooden platform made a perfect dance floor.

Before they reached the refreshments a tall, pleasant-looking fellow with a blond Afro asked Anne to dance.

Anne hesitated for a moment, then accepted. Mary Helen watched the young nun follow her partner, glad that Therese was safely back at Mount St. Francis, especially when Anne began to twirl and spin and wiggle with the best of them.

Scandalous! she could almost hear Therese hiss, in that outraged tone of hers.

From what Mary Helen could see, the partners rarely touched. As a matter of fact, it was difficult to tell who was dancing with whom. A person would have to go to some lengths to create a scandal, she mused, determined that if the band played a Charleston, she might lay a few steps on them herself.

Mary Helen was so busy watching that she didn't notice Mimi until the young woman was standing right beside her. But then it was hard not to. Mimi was wearing, or almost wearing, a low-cut tunic that slid off her left shoulder over skintight trousers. The trouser legs were tucked into high leather boots and the whole outfit was fastened with a wide gold chain link belt.

"Hi, Sister," Mimi said in her bright, perky voice. Her blond curls bounced as she leaned forward and planted a loud kiss on Mary Helen's cheek.

"So glad you could come," Mimi continued. "You remember my boyfriend, Lee?"

Indeed Mary Helen did. He stood gaunt and bearded behind Mimi, his cold, restless eyes wandering the room. His whole demeanor reminded Mary Helen of a coiled spring waiting for release.

Vaguely, Lee nodded toward her. "I'll get us some champagne," he said. Before either woman could answer, he headed toward the refreshment table.

Mary Helen was glad. It gave her an opportunity to talk to Mimi.

"How have you been?" Mary Helen asked.

"Fine, and not so fine," Mimi said, her eyes, one brown and one blue, staring earnestly at Mary Helen.

"Oh?" Mary Helen wondered why.

"A day doesn't go by that I don't think of Suzanne," Mimi continued, blinking. "I really miss her."

Mary Helen simply nodded, feeling sure Mimi needed little prodding to go on.

"I wish we could find her killer." Mimi wrinkled her pug nose and brushed a tear from her blue eye. "It seems so wrong that a nice girl like that . . ." She stopped, attempting to control her voice, which had begun to quiver. "And when you three walked in here tonight, it brought back everything. Poor Suzanne."

Mary Helen waited a moment for Mimi to compose herself. "Yes, our poor Suzanne. She didn't have a very happy life, did she?" Mary Helen was wondering just how much of it she should divulge to Mimi.

"No, she really didn't. Her aura was awful."

Auras again! Mary Helen had almost forgotten about Mimi's ability to read them. She adjusted her bifocals, feeling a little uneasy for a moment, sincerely hoping that her aura wasn't a hazy gray for disbelief.

Before Mimi could continue, Lee returned with the champagne, the band paused between numbers, and Anne returned to the group.

Drat! Sister Mary Helen had hoped to probe Mimi for

a few of the facts she might have learned about Suzanne's life. Especially her life with Kueneman.

Before she could figure out a way to get Mimi alone again, Muriel Rosenberg came over with Eileen. In her soft, gentle way she insisted that the nuns follow her around so she could introduce them.

When Mary Helen finally checked her watch, it was ten o'clock. Her feet were killing her. She wished she'd worn her sensible flats. Anne was dancing yet another dance, and Eileen, who never met a stranger, was entertaining a group in the far corner. Punch Rosenberg was mingling with his guests, but, Mary Helen noticed, he was definitely keeping his hands to himself. Must be Mrs. Punch's influence. Obviously her husband knew from experience that she didn't miss a trick.

As soon as she saw her chance, Mary Helen escaped to a vacant table. She needed to catch her breath and relieve her feet. When she settled down and slipped off her pumps, she realized that she had chosen the very table where she had sat the night of Suzanne's murder. Involuntarily, she shivered. Something—what?—kept bothering her. Something she should remember. The thought, like an itch on the edge of her mind, kept annoying her. Closing her eyes, she tried to reach it, pull it back, but she couldn't. Hard as she tried, whatever was there kept eluding her. Mary Helen shook her head. Getting old was frustrating. Sometimes you just couldn't remember. When she finally opened her eyes, she realized Mimi had joined her.

"Have you any leads to Suzanne's murderer?" Mimi asked without any preliminaries.

Mary Helen blinked and brought her mind back to the present. She liked the girl's style: direct and uncomplicated.

"Yes, as a matter of fact, I may have," she answered just as directly. "I think I have discovered Suzanne's former husband." She fumbled in her pocketbook and took out the picture of Suzanne and Kueneman.

"You may have seen him around Suzanne's apartment," she said hopefully, handing Mimi the snapshot.

Mimi held it next to the candle in the middle of the table. She examined it for a few seconds, then shuddered.

"I remember him all right. Horrible aura. Passion, violence, cruelty, all around him."

Mary Helen's heart began to beat faster. She held her breath. "At Suzanne's apartment?" she asked. That fact might clinch the case. If Kueneman knew where she lived, came to see her . . .

"No," Mimi said. Mary Helen felt as if someone had punched her. She was so disappointed, she hardly realized Mimi had continued.

"Not there. Here. The night Suzanne was killed. I'll never forget that guy. He sat right there." Blinking her eyes, she pointed toward a table.

Of course, that was it, the scene that had been fluttering on the edge of Mary Helen's mind. The night came rushing back upon her. If there was ever an example of déjà vu, this was it! So that was where she had seen the face in the photo! That's why the face had looked so familiar. It wasn't a delivery man or the UPS driver. The face was the young man she had noticed when Suzanne was singing, the one who had sat up so straight to watch. The sandy-haired fellow! The one she'd hoped might be smitten with Suzanne.

Mary Helen shivered. Little had she realized. And when Mr. Rosenberg asked him to leave? What had his girl friend called him? Cooey or Cluey? Mary Helen hadn't been sure. Of course! That was it! *K*, not *C*. Kooey! A nickname for Kueneman! He had been right there watching Suzanne. No wonder she had stiffened and turned away.

Mary Helen was elated. This could be just what Kate Murphy needed to solve the case. Opportunity, although she still wasn't sure how he entered the apartment building. And motive? Mary Helen shuddered when she thought what his motive might be. Still, Kueneman must be the X on their suspect list, the person they'd never thought of because they didn't know. Impulsively she reached over and gave Mimi an expansive hug. Cheerfully she accepted a refill glass of the champagne Lee had brought them at the table. Maybe he wasn't so bad after all.

"Merry Christmas!" Lee, looking surprised, held his glass high for a toast.

"To all," Mimi added, clicking her glass.

"And to all a good night!" Mary Helen chimed in, knowing that this had, indeed, been a very good night. She could hardly wait for morning to call Kate Murphy.

SUNDAY—FOURTH WEEK OF ADVENT

Sister Mary Helen woke very early on Sunday morning. She was up, dressed, and down to the early Mass at St. Ignatius almost before the sun rose.

And the sun did rise. "Splendid silent sun with all his beams full-dazzling." Mary Helen couldn't help quoting Walt Whitman, glad that San Francisco was having another of its clear, crisp December days.

"Go, do whatever you have in mind for the Lord is with you," David had said to Nathan in the first reading of this morning's Mass, and as far as she was concerned, to her too.

And what she wanted to do was call Kate Murphy as soon as possible to tell her about last night.

In the Sisters' dining room she settled down next to Eileen.

"Why are you so jumpy this morning, old girl?" Eileen asked when Mary Helen had checked her wristwatch for the sixth time.

"I didn't want to say anything on our way home last night, alarm anyone," Mary Helen began, then she repeated her whole conversation with Mimi to Eileen. Her old friend's bushy eyebrows shot up and her eyes seemed to become larger and larger as Mary Helen spoke.

"So what do you think?" Mary Helen asked when she finally finished.

"What I think, Mary Helen," Eileen said with a noticeably thick brogue, "is that if you remember the young lad, he most assuredly remembers you. So the faster you get on the horn to Kate Murphy, the better off we are all going to be."

That was all the encouragement Mary Helen needed.

Kate Murphy and Jack Bassetti were still asleep when the phone rang. Jack fumbled for the receiver, listened, then handed it over to his wife.

"Sister for you, hon," he said, then rolled over on his side.

"Hello," Kate answered, her voice hoarse with sleep.

She didn't even have to ask "What's up?" Sister Mary Helen launched right into the tale.

"I thought I told you to stay home," Kate interjected once, but only halfheartedly.

"Anything wrong, hon?" Jack asked when she hung up. He didn't even roll over, just yanked the covers up around his bare shoulders.

"Everything's right!" Kate said, quickly gathering her clothes. "I think we may have a breakthrough in this damn case."

Hastily she brushed her teeth, splashed water on her face, and pulled a comb through her thick hair.

"See you later, pal." She leaned over the bed and kissed her husband on his forehead.

"That was fast." Jack opened his eyes.

"I'll bet I look terrible," Kate said, remembering that she had put on no makeup. She glanced in the vanity mirror.

"Angie Dickinson should look so good!" Jack replied, yawning.

Turning, Kate smiled and blew him a kiss. "Be back as quick as I can," she said. "I love you."

"If you really love me, you won't leave me alone with

my mother," he said. "Remember, she'll be here around three."

Of course Kate had remembered. An impending visit by Mama Bassetti was something not easily forgotten.

By the time Gallagher arrived at the Homicide Detail, Kate had already contacted Hal Garden at Probation.

"Why the hell can't a breakthrough come Monday through Friday," Gallagher growled the moment he saw Kate. "Did you get hold of Garden?"

"I did, boss," she said, "as soon as I came in."

"I'll bet he was about as glad to hear from you as I was."

"That's what he gets for not calling back on Friday." Kate wasn't giving one inch. She'd be so happy to have this case wind down before Christmas, she'd work till midnight, if need be.

"What did he say?" Gallagher poured himself a mug of coffee.

"Gave me Kueneman's known address. Lafayette Street. I checked it. It's a little alley off Eleventh. Between Howard and Mission." Kate pointed to the spot on the detailed map of The City. "But it's what he didn't say that's important."

"Then what didn't he say?" Gallagher leaned over to pull up his socks. He must have still been in bed, too, Kate thought, watching him stand and shake down his pant legs.

"He didn't say 'poor guy's innocent. Couldn't happen.' Nothing like that. All he said was 'Oh, oh' and 'Didn't get your message until late Friday.' "

"Sounds like he may have his doubts about our friend Kueneman," Gallagher said, and hitched his trousers up over his paunch.

Kate nodded.

"Well, don't just stand there, Katie-girl. Let's go." Gallagher slammed his half-empty mug on his desk. "Be sure your gun is loaded. I'll alert a black-and-white to back us up."

The car tires on the department's Ford screeched as Gallagher pulled out of the Hall of Justice parking lot onto Harrison and passed the empty playground of the Bessie Carmichael School. The wide one-way street was deserted. In fact, at this hour on a Sunday morning the whole downtown area looked like a brick and galvanized ghost town. Not even the street people were moving around. The sun was beginning to creep down the flat faces of the buildings.

"Take it easy, Denny." Despite her seat belt, Kate held on to the door handle when Gallagher swung right onto Eleventh. The clock on the Coca-Cola Building pointed to just before nine o'clock. They turned into Natoma.

"I want to catch the bastard in bed," Gallagher said.

Small wooden houses, peeling blue, faded yellow and white paint lined either side of the cramped alleyway. Thick clumps of grass grew up through the cracks in the narrow sidewalks. Rusty cars, parked half on the curb, left just enough room for Gallagher to maneuver down the short alley to Lafayette. The two streets formed a sort of stunted, hidden cross between Howard and Mission.

Here and there Kate saw a curtain move or a shadowy figure standing well back from a dirt-encrusted window. She was sure she even saw a pair of scared-child eyes peer out from behind a small Christmas tree.

"Obviously the neighbors have noticed a strange car," she said when Gallagher parked in front of the San Francisco Gear Company. The square letters painted on the metal door clearly said NO PARKING.

"I'll bet that's the place." Quietly closing the door, Gallagher pointed to a two-story wooden house on the corner. Red geraniums clung tenaciously to the chipped wooden windowboxes below the square bay windows. Dozens of green plants packed tightly against the windows filled what little glass there was left with moisture.

The pair quickly crossed the street. "Get a load of that!" Gallagher nodded his head toward the lower half of a window on the first floor. "Bet that's our guy's room."

Kate stared in amazement at the word LOVE printed on the glass in large wobbly letters of gold leaf.

The door to Kueneman's small first-floor room was ajar. Gallagher knocked loudly. "Police. Open up," he shouted into the room.

No answer. Cautiously, gun poised, Gallagher hugged the wall and with one karate-like kick shot open the door. "Police!" he shouted again.

Both officers waited tense, guns pulled. Nothing. No one spoke. Nothing moved. Slowly, carefully they entered the small room. The rumpled bed in the middle was empty. The sparcely furnished room deserted. Beer cans, dirty dishes, and garbage cluttered in one corner near a hot plate mingled smells with the heavy odor of men's cologne that hung on the stale air.

With her free hand Kate yanked back a faded curtain covering a cubbyhole that served as a closet. Nothing but a few shirts, old jeans, and a battered suitcase.

"I'll check the john." Gallagher started toward the hall.

"No one's in here but me, damn it," a woman's shrill voice shouted over a flush. Clutching her bathrobe to her throat, a dumpy middle-aged woman cracked open the door, her henna hair still in curlers. The washroom looked barely large enough to hold her. "The guy you're looking for just beat it the hell out of here."

"Sorry, ma'am," Gallagher apologized, and moved his gun back in his holster.

"Guess we missed the bastard." He ran his hand over his bald head. "Where the hell do you think—?" Gallagher stopped.

Kate's whole body tensed. "You don't suppose he's—?" She didn't say another word.

Sirens shrieking, they tore down Howard and turned right onto 12th. Even the break dancers on the corner stopped to gawk.

By the time they crossed Mission, Kate had radioed the black-and-white to head for Mount St. Francis.

"You don't suppose he's crazy enough to hurt her?" she asked, holding on while Gallagher zigzagged on Market past the old Roosevelt Bar and out Franklin.

"If you ask me, he's crazy enough for anything. You do remember what the bastard did to Suzanne and how the Sister's office looked, don't you?"

Kate didn't say anything, just swallowed hard. Gallagher swung left on Turk, past James P. Lang Field and went by the projects.

"Let's hope we're wrong," she said as the car roared up the hill at Turk and Broderick.

"If you're the praying kind, now's the time to do it." Gallagher's knuckles were white on the steering wheel. The screech of the siren blotted out any answer Kate could give as Gallagher raced past Irwin Memorial Blood Bank on his way to Mount St. Francis College.

All the nuns were busy with Christmas preparations. Mary Helen was too nervous to concentrate on anything.

Besides, in her two-day confinement she had just about done all the preparing she was going to do. Her office was still in shambles, but she couldn't bring herself to go there. Furthermore, Kate had not yet given her the okay to go back.

Grabbing her Aran knit sweater, she walked briskly up the hill to her favorite thinking place.

The December sun flooded the spot. Sitting, arms folded, eyes closed, she let it warm her outstretched feet and calm her nerves. Her mind began to wander. Somewhere below her in The City, Kate Murphy and Dennis Gallagher were probably at this moment apprehending Kueneman. She pondered briefly on what twist of free will made one man choose to be a rapist, another a priest. What caused a fine, sharp-looking young man like Kueneman to do such ragged, ugly things? And why to Suzanne? Mary Helen was sure it was he who had raped and killed Suzanne.

How would she tell Sister Thomasine? She knew she'd have to. Right after Christmas, she'd call. She owed it to the woman. But what could she say?

So many questions were yet unanswered. Had Kueneman followed the girl home? How had he gotten in? Where was the baby? How did Reina Martinez figure in all of this?

Mary Helen sighed, unfolded her arms, and felt the sun ease the chill from her fingertips. Somehow, she and Kate had come up with the right combination of person, motive, and opportunity. Just like that silly computer. That was another thing, another two things really, she must face after Christmas. The computer and Mary Agnes Van Der Zee! She had tried "Class of 1940" and "Class of 40" and even "Class of '40"—what would efficient, exact Suzanne have done? Mary Helen's eyes shot open. Of course! Put a period at the end! "Class of 1940."

She rose from the bench and started down the hill. What harm could it do to slip into her office and grab the floppy disc? She was sure Eileen's library must have a compatible computer. Why not? It was worth the try.

Mary Helen was midway down the rocky path when she heard it. Below her, a car engine rounded the driveway and stopped abruptly. She heard the car door bang.

It's most likely a florist with a poinsettia or UPS with a special-delivery Christmas present for one of the Sisters, she thought, happily humming a few bars of "Santa Claus Is Coming to Town." She stopped to admire the morning sun dancing on the fresh new needles of the evergreen. Closing her eyes, she drew in a deep breath.

She smelled it before she heard anything. The heavy spicy odor of men's cologne mixed with dusty sweat.

She heard a rustling; then suddenly, like an animal emerging from the wooded underbrush, the dark form leapt out toward her. Face twisted, eyes blazing, brandishing a long, thin butcher knife in his right hand, the young man in the snapshot, Kueneman, stood blocking the path.

Stunned, Mary Helen staggered backward. The young man lunged toward her, grabbing wildly at her arm, catching the end of her sweater. Dazed, Mary Helen spun around, her reflexes taking over, charging her with unexpected strength.

Twisting, slamming, bolting, she felt the pocket rip as she tore her sweater from his strong, hard grasp.

She scrambled back up the path, legs cramping against the hill, not daring to look back. Running as fast as she could. Stumbling, pulling, tripping.

Behind her she could hear him crashing closer. Her lungs throbbed. She was trembling all over. Shrieking, she stumbled over the side of the path, running blindly down into the wooded underbrush. Branches stabbed at her, tearing her nylons, catching her skirt, yanking at her hair, knocking her glasses askew. Above her she could hear the heavy footsteps thudding closer, gaining.

She rattled down the steep hill, slipping, sliding on the shale, rocks digging into her feet, scraping against tree trunks, falling deeper into the cold wetness of underbrush.

Her side aching, she threw a wild glance behind her. Thumping, crashing, the dark form hurled forward and, throwing himself against her, locked his wide fingers around her upper arm.

Punching, clawing, screaming, she struggled to pull away from him. But his fingers dug into her arm, ripping into her flesh. With his hairy forearm he knocked her, forcing her to the ground, straddled her writhing body. She could feel the weight of his body and the cold sharp edge of the butcher knife under her chin.

Panting, sweating, nose running, Kueneman stared down at her.

"Why didn't you leave me alone? I warned you!" he screeched, his hot breath pulsing on her face. "I loved her. I loved them both. All I wanted was my baby. But she had been with someone else. She said she wasn't, but I could tell. She wouldn't tell me who, or where my baby is. I had to kill her. Don't you see? I had to. Now I've got to kill you, too . . ."

Mary Helen saw the muscles on his arm tighten; slowly, deliberately he raised his arm, poised the knife above her heart.

"God forgive you, you poor kid," she said, then closed her eyes and, strangely calm, wondered what God's first words to her would be.

The sharp crack of a shot rang through the hillside. She could feel Kueneman's body slump over to her side.

"Thank God we made it," she heard Kate Murphy say just before she blacked out.

The moment Kate opened the front door on 34th Avenue, she could feel the tension. The old clock on the mantel struck four.

"Hi," she said brightly, hanging her coat in the entryway closet and putting her gun on the top shelf. "Sorry I'm late."

Jack just grunted. Mrs. Bassetti sat on the edge of the sofa, her soft, chubby cheeks flushed.

"Smells good in here," Kate said, and it did. Mama Bassetti had most likely come bearing gifts and one of them was no doubt currently in the oven! The delicious aroma of roasting beef filled the house.

"Sorry I'm late," Kate repeated. She kissed her mother-in-law on the cheek.

A cozy fire roared in the fireplace and a stack of carefully wrapped gifts had been added under the Christmas tree.

"How'd it go, hon?" Jack asked.

"I need a drink," Kate said, sinking with a sigh into the couch beside Jack's mother.

"Of course she does, Jackie," Mama Bassetti began. "The poor girl is exhausted. Look at her. What kind of a man lets his wife go out to work on a Sunday, a day of rest, a family day, a day when a family should go together to Mass."

"We went last night," Jack interrupted, then left the room to fix Kate's drink.

"That's the trouble with the Church today," his mother shouted after him. "Nothing's the same. That's not the way we raised you, Papa and me. We raised you to be a good husband, take care of your wife, be a good provider and go to Mass on Sunday."

Mrs. Bassetti shook her head in disgust, blessed herself, and took a sip of her old-fashioned.

Kate took advantage of the pause in the tirade. "My

working is not Jack's idea, Mama Bassetti," she said, "it's mine."

The older woman's brown eyes opened wide in horror and disbelief. "Kate, you're a good girl," she said, patting her daughter-in-law's hand. "A good girl," she repeated. "Come from a good family. Irish, but good! I know your Mama, Lord have mercy on her, would not want you out with criminals. No. It's my Jackie's fault, his business as a husband to tell you, 'No, you stay home, I will make the living, you stay home, have babies when God sends them.'"

Kate could feel her temper start to rise. "Mama Bassetti, Jack doesn't tell me anything. And whether he and I decide to have a family . . ."

Fortunately, the phone in the hallway rang before she said another word. It was Sister Mary Helen.

"How are you feeling?" Kate asked.

"Pretty good," Mary Helen said. "A little stiff and bruised. And very, very tired. I haven't run like that in years. Maybe ever." The old nun chuckled. "And you? How are you?"

"I'm very grateful we arrived in time," Kate said, feeling suddenly weak at the thought of what might have happened. "Sister, when you're feeling better, we've got to talk about your getting involved—"

"Eileen tells me Kueneman was just wounded," Mary Helen interrupted, as though Kate weren't speaking. "Is he conscious? Did you find out anything from him yet?"

"Sister, did you hear me about getting in—"

"I'm sorry, Kate, we must have a bad connection. These blasted phones haven't been right since the phone company split up. What did you say about Kueneman? Speak up, will you, dear?"

After today, Kate didn't have the energy to argue, even

if she thought it would have done any good. "Kueneman was conscious when Denny and I left the hospital," she said.

"He claims he only wanted to love Suzanne and find his baby. Apparently, after he had dropped his date, he came into the apartment building around eleven-thirty. When he realized Suzanne wasn't home yet, he hid on the stairwell until he heard her come in. He saw Rosenberg go into the apartment with her. The guy became enraged. When Rosenberg left, he forced his way in and saw the bedroom in a mess. Suzanne was on the bed sobbing. The creep thought she was making time with Rosenberg. Apparently that was how he treated her when they were making love. What's worse, she refused him. Between his jealousy and his rage at being refused and his frustration over not being able to locate the baby, he finished tearing up the bedroom, then killed her.

"He threatened the Martinez woman too. But she wouldn't tell him where the baby was either. Apparently she did tell him about you asking questions."

"Do you think he was my caller?"

"I'm sure he was," Kate said. "But he was heavily sedated, so we'll clean up the loose ends when he's more able to answer questions. Actually, Sister, his biggest mistake was running into you," she continued. "He must have sent Suzanne that snapshot to rekindle old memories, but he sent it to her at work. I guess she shoved it under the blotter, where you found it and—"

"What about the baby?" Mary Helen asked, as though she hadn't heard.

Kate smiled. The old nun's act was good, darn good.

"As I say, Sister, there are some loose ends. Like how Kueneman got in and what actually did happen to the baby. We'll talk to Reina Martinez again. The whole thing should be cleared up in the next few days."

"I'm sure it will," Mary Helen said. "It sounds good, she continued, "yet I can't get that baby off my mind. Christmas and all, I guess." She paused. "So often it's the child who is the victim. And there are so many people, you know, who'd do anything to have God send them a child and then . . ." She didn't go on, she didn't need to. "I hope you weren't busy," Mary Helen said.

"Not really," Kate answered. "My mother-in-law is here with us. She brought us dinner."

"Aren't you lucky, Kate! To have such a wonderful husband, a loving family. When you think of poor Suzanne. But I'm sure you appreciate it."

Kate looked from the hall into the living room. Mama Bassetti sat quietly on the couch, staring into the fireplace. Jack sat across from her sipping his drink. Roaring flames licked and jumped and cast their light against the Christmas gifts and against the older woman's face. How vulnerable she looked, Kate thought suddenly.

All at once Kate felt ashamed of herself. She was lucky to have such a loving family and she should appreciate it— even Mama. Mama, she supposed, was just like Mrs. G— what had Denny said? "So used to giving that stopping would kill her." It was a mother's disease. Someday she might even contract it.

She was lucky to be able to have a child whenever God sent it and to be able to bring that child into the world amid people who wanted it: people who would welcome it with as much love as the Christ Child Himself might receive. Especially Mama Bassetti. Poor "giving" Mama.

Jack and she had already decided to have a child, God willing. How could she be so small as to deny the woman a share in their secret, a share of their happiness? Why couldn't Mama know? She would be ecstatic!

"I'll let you get back to them now," Mary Helen said. "You will keep me posted, won't you, Kate?"

"Better than that, Sister. Tomorrow night Jack and I are having a little Christmas Eve party."

Overhearing, Jack stirred in his chair. I thought you wanted to be alone, his look said.

"We are so lucky," Kate continued, feeling a warm glow. "We'd love to share our happiness and our home with a few people we care about. So please, if you're feeling up to it, you, Sister Eileen, Sister Anne, do come over. We're inviting a few special people. My mother-in-law, of course."

Mama Bassetti pushed forward in her seat and beamed at Kate. "Jack's sisters, his cousin Enid." Mama looked like she might burst. "The Gallaghers. About six o'clock, then?" Kate hung up.

Jack came into the hallway. "A party? Has the cheese slipped off the cracker, hon? I thought you wanted to be alone on our first Christmas Eve."

"I'll explain later, pal," Kate said, passing him by. "Mama," she addressed her mother-in-law, knowing she was about to give the woman the best present she could receive. "There is something Jack and I been wanting to tell you."

CHRISTMAS EVE

Several of the Sisters were already beginning to decorate for midnight Mass when the community assembled in the chapel for a special Christmas Eve morning office.

Tall full spruce trees filled the sanctuary, their tangy aroma hanging in the chapel like incense.

Mr. Sartori from the Flower Mart came through the side door of the sanctuary toting still another tree. Putting it in place, the man pulled a clean handkerchief from his back pocket and mopped the sweat from his wrinkled forehead. He made a semigenuflection toward the tabernacle.

"Poor devil," Eileen whispered to Mary Helen, watching him straighten up. "He's been bringing those trees since his daughter went here. And Emma Sartori is old enough to be a grandmother herself."

"Why does he still do it?" Mary Helen whispered back.

"He's a friend of Therese's. The only respectable way out is death," Eileen answered. "And the poor man doesn't look ready."

Mary Helen stifled a laugh as Anne intoned the Opening Antiphon. "Today you will know the Lord is coming . . ." she chanted.

"And in the morning you will see his glory," the rest sang back.

Mary Helen and Eileen had just settled down at the breakfast table when Anne came over to join them.

"How are you feeling?" Anne asked.

"A little stiff and sore," Mary Helen said, "but, all in all, not too bad for an old lady."

"You must be feeling worse than I thought, old dear. Perhaps even a tad light-headed," Eileen said.

Mary Helen raised her eyebrows quizzically.

"This is the first time I've ever heard you admit to being an old lady."

Mary Helen winked at her friend. "It was just a figure of speech," she said. "But, speaking of old ladies, take a look at Cecilia."

The trio glanced over at the college president. She looked terrible.

"She was looking better until you appeared on the front page of this morning's *Chronicle*, right next to the human-interest story of Santa visiting a sick child," Eileen said.

"Think how much better she'll look now that it's all solved and she won't have to worry what the *Chronicle* says." Mary Helen hoped she didn't sound too much like Pollyanna. Before either nun could comment, she continued, "I talked to Kate Murphy last night. She mentioned that Jack and she are having a little party tonight. They want us to come. About six?" She looked questioningly at her two companions.

"Are you feeling up to it?" Eileen asked.

"Of course," Mary Helen said, moving her shoulder stiffly.

"Well, I talked to Sarah Farraday too," her friend continued, "or rather listened. This afternoon is her annual Christmas party. She's invited us. It is from three to six. Shall we stop by on our way to Kate's?"

Mary Helen nodded. "For a few minutes."

Anne rose. "I'll sign a car out," she said. "Then, I've

got a few things to do between now and then for midnight Mass. I'll meet you girls about four-thirty?"

Eileen and Mary Helen nodded.

"You know what?" Anne asked, gathering up her dishes from the table.

"What?" her companions asked in unison, then linked baby fingers.

"I think I'm getting a little old to keep up with you two. You'd both make me feel better if you took a nap."

Mary Helen didn't have to be asked twice.

When the nuns finally managed to find a parking place on California, and arrived at Sarah Farraday's, her small apartment was already full. Christmas carols from an old Andy Williams record played above the noise of conversation. Sarah in her bright poinsettia-print mumu squeezed around the room, between people and decorations, passing out tiny rich-looking hors d'oeuvres.

"Oh, oh, oh. Look, look, look," she said in her cheeriest primary teacher voice when she spotted the nuns.

"Run, run, run," Eileen whispered to Mary Helen, who had just spotted Pat Flaherty standing under one of Sarah's hanging plants. The top of his head came so close to the pot that, at first glance, it seemed as though the delicate spider plant was growing right out of it.

"Merry Christmas, Mr. Flaherty," Mary Helen greeted him, feeling a twinge of guilt that she could have ever suspected poor Pat of murder.

Automatically he reached up to tip his hat, which was already off. Instead he simply bobbed forward. "To you, too, 'Ster," he said politely. "Turrible business. I read in the *Chronicle*. Turrible thing! Imagine a crazy fellow right here in our own building. Not a one of us realized it! Time was you could buzz a neighbor in and not worry." He shook his head sadly.

Mary Helen stared in astonishment. "You buzzed him in?" she asked.

"Didn't say I did. Could have, if you get my meaning. I buzzed someone in that night. About eleven-thirty."

"Eleven-thirty! Who?"

"Don't know. Thought it was the doctor." He pointed toward Lee. "Guy is always forgetting his key. I ask you, 'Ster, what's going to happen if he forgets a scalpel when he's operating?"

"But, Mimi?" Mary Helen was nearly speechless.

"I thought maybe she wasn't home yet from the café. Or maybe sound asleep. Must have been him too. Heard the footsteps. Stopped right by that door."

"Why didn't you tell the police?"

"They asked me if anything unusual happened. Don't get me wrong, 'Ster, but the doc forgetting his key ain't unusual."

"But I asked you," Mary Helen started to say, then remembered with crystal clarity that she had been just about to when Mrs. McGrath had interrupted. All this time, Patrick Flaherty had held an important key to the mystery and didn't even know it! She could hardly wait to tell Kate!

"Turrible world we live in," Flaherty went on, taking a large swallow of the brown liquid in his glass.

That was as far as he had got when Delia McGrath came up holding a tray of freshly baked buttermilk scones. "Pay him no heed, Sister. The old coot likes to hear himself blather," she said. "We're all glad they caught Suzanne's killer."

"Alleged killer," Arnold Shultz broke in. "Give the poor bugger his constitutional rights anyway," he said in his deep voice. "Maybe he couldn't help himself . . . full of toxins from too much sugar." Arnold sipped a vivid orange combination that looked to Mary Helen suspiciously like carrot juice.

You were on the alleged list yourself, Mr. Healthy Body, with your weapons and your how-to books, Mary Helen thought.

"You're right, Arnold," she agreed. "A man is innocent until proven guilty."

"Not this man, honey." Iris Adams slinked up to the group. "This man is an animal just like the rest. Thinks any woman is his property." Iris tossed her honey-blond hair angrily, then stared at Arnold.

"I resent that," he said.

"Yum, yum, yum." Sarah pushed a plate of hot cheese crackers between the warring parties.

Mary Helen took the opportunity to move across the room to where Mimi and her young doctor were talking to Anne. She could hardly wait to slip away from Farraday's and tell Kate Murphy the latest piece of news.

"Hi, Sister." Mimi gave her a big smile and then a warm hug. "I guess you did it."

"Did what?" she asked, wondering for a moment if her latest discovery showed in her aura.

"Found the killer. I read about you in this morning's *Chronicle*," Mimi said.

"But the police could have found him much sooner if his aura could be seen." Mimi's blue-brown eyes opened wide with earnestness.

"What the police need to convict the man, Mimi, is motive and opportunity," Lee Slater interjected logically.

And for a short while I thought you might have both, Mary Helen mused, studying the intense young surgeon, dying to ask how he had known Suzanne had a baby. She didn't need to ask.

"I've wondered who the father of her child was ever since Lee examined her the night she was so sick and we found out she had a child." Mimi blinked at Mary Helen. "Lee does a lot of charity work, Sister," she explained. "Although he doesn't like people to know. It hurts him to see anyone suffer. Suzanne was so ill and so broke . . ."

Once again Mary Helen realized you can never tell the book by its cover. No wonder those blue eyes looked so steely and he talked so coldly. He was forcing himself to be objective so he could survive.

"I wonder what ever happened to that baby," Anne said, interrupting her thought.

"Maybe Kate Murphy will be able to tell us," Mary Helen said, checking her watch and taking advantage of a perfect exit line. "Speaking of whom, we'd better excuse ourselves."

Eileen was more than happy to have her ear extracted from Sarah Farraday and the three nuns wiggled their way out of her crowded apartment.

The trio drove out Geary Street to Kate's house. By six o'clock the winter sky was a deep inky black, yet the boulevard was alive with color.

Christmas-tree lights shone from nearly every front window along the way. A few of the more creative homeowners had bordered their windowsills or front doors with small colorful bulbs. Some even outlined their peaked roofs with strings of red and green and gold.

A few cold-looking stars were beginning to appear when Anne finally parked. "Look," she said, pointing at an especially bright white light in the sky. "Maybe that's the very star that shone in Bethlehem."

Mary Helen and Eileen exchanged glances. Neither one of us has the heart to tell her she's pointing at a jet, Mary Helen thought, hoping the darn thing wouldn't blink.

Kate answered the front door before they even rang. Mary Helen sucked in her breath. The young woman looked radiant. The bright shades in her full-length, flowing hostess gown brought out the color in her cheeks and made her blue eyes flash and sparkle. Or was it just the gown? Mary Helen wondered, following Kate into the crowded room.

"You must be the Sisters!" A short plump woman greeted them before Kate could begin the introductions. "I'm Jackie's mother," she said. "Come, come." She herded the three toward a buffet table in the dining room. *"Mangia, mangia,"* she commanded, pointing to a large platter overflowing with sliced turkey, ham, salad, cheese, roast beef, and mortadella. "Jackie," she ordered, "get these good Sisters a drink. I raised him better than that," she confided to Mary Helen. Then, beaming, she continued, "Let me introduce you to the family."

"May I see you a minute?" Kate whispered, rescuing Mary Helen from the conversational clutches of Cousin Enid. Mary Helen, her mouth full of potato salad, nodded gratefully, and following behind Kate, wound her way through the crowd into the small empty sunporch off the kitchen. Gallagher joined them.

"We talked to the Martinez gal today," he said. "She's something else!" Gallagher shook his head. "Scared to death of Kueneman. So scared, she nearly killed you to stop you from asking more questions."

Mary Helen remembered how her skin had prickled when Reina's hand had touched her neck in Calistoga.

"Lucky for you she couldn't bring herself to kill a nun. And she loved Suzanne.

"The two of them had boyfriends in Vacaville about the same time, were pregnant about the same time, both moved to the Mission. Apparently that's where Kueneman was paroled the first time and then was picked up again for more of the same. That's where Suzanne got smart and wanted out."

"And when he was paroled a month or so ago, he went looking for her again?" Mary Helen asked.

"That's about it."

"Why did he kill her?"

"He wanted her and the baby." Gallagher shook his head. "To hear him tell it, he's the father of the year. What really pushed him over the edge was Rosenberg's little stunt."

"Poor Rosenberg! He must feel terrible," Mary Helen said.

"Muriel, I'm sure, will see to that." Gallagher shrugged his shoulders. "Our one missing link is how he got in."

"I know." Mary Helen reddened as the two inspectors stared at her in disbelief.

"Why the hell didn't you—?" Gallagher began.

Mary Helen cut him off. "I just found out tonight. Mr. Flaherty buzzed him in thinking he was young Dr. Slater. Poor devil, he didn't realize it was significant," she added the moment she noticed Kate's eyes flash.

"So everything is solved?" she asked, hoping to distract them from Flaherty's faux pas.

"When we left the guy he was crying like a baby," Gallagher said, "cursing, swearing, claiming he's no rapo; that he didn't want to hurt her, only love her. If you ask me, he's a card-carrying crazy.

"And so we came home. There was nothing more we could do today. It can all wait until December twenty-sixth. We got him dead to rights."

"Thank God," Mary Helen said. "And there's no reason I can't go back to my office?"

Gallagher nodded his head. "Yeah, Kueneman admitted

he was the one who had been calling you and wrecked your office."

"By the way, Sister." The older man shuffled uncomfortably. "Before this case becomes history, we just want you to know we appreciate your part in it." He coughed self-consciously. "Thanks," he said, "you're a great gal."

Mary Helen blushed, almost at a loss for words, but not quite.

"Don't underestimate yourselves," she said generously, wanting to share that warm, happy glow of being appreciated.

The three smiled at one another in mutual admiration.

"Here you two are." Jack entered the small room. "My mother's looking for you, Kate." He pointed to Gallagher. "Mrs. G is about to file a missing person's, Denny."

Kate snuggled up to her husband. "You'll never guess what Kueneman's first name is. Jack. Jack Kueneman. So different from my Jack."

"Thank God," Mary Helen said, pondering for a moment why one young woman she was fond of would choose a winner, while the other one she was fond of would shackle herself to a loser.

Gallagher hitched up his pants and broke into her thoughts. "Guess I better get back in there and calm down the little woman." He smiled. "Thanks again, Sister."

"One more question before we go back in." Mary Helen caught Kate's arm. "The baby. What happened to the baby?"

"According to Martinez, Suzanne had a very difficult time. But she finally gave birth to a healthy little boy. Called him Jude. Knew she couldn't keep him. Gave him up to Catholic Charities. From what the Martinez woman says, they placed him in a good home with a childless couple who had been waiting years for a baby."

"Thank God for that too," Mary Helen said, forced to agree with Eileen that it's an ill wind that turns none to good.

"And speaking of babies." Kate giggled. "Jack and I have decided to have one of our own," she said, beaming at Jack. "We're going to use that natural childbirth business; the whole bit."

So that explains the radiant look, Mary Helen realized. Kate squeezed her husband, who squeezed her back. Watching them, Mary Helen wished she could squeeze right out of the room and leave them alone.

The college chapel was aglow with candles and lights. Fresh spruce trees and banks of poinsettias crowded the sanctuary. A delicately embroidered linen cloth covered the main altar. Huge bouquets of anthuriums in tall gold vases flanked the tabernacle. Excitement crackled the air as the Sisters waited for midnight Mass.

Mary Helen felt tired and sore. So tired and sore, she had turned down her bed before coming to chapel. Maybe she'd have to stick to reading mysteries rather than solving them. She had set out the mystery she had been reading, the one she had given up before this whole mess began. She could hardly wait to read a few chapters before falling off to sleep. It had been a long, dry Advent.

To the right of the main altar large plaster statues of Mary and Joseph knelt in a wooden stable. In humble adoration the couple stared patiently at an empty manger. Behind them plaster shepherds watching plaster sheep gathered to worship. Over it all a long-haired angel hovered, gown flowing, wings spread wide, unfurling a banner of peace.

At five to twelve, Sister Therese's nervous footsteps scurried up the side aisle carrying the small plaster Jesus with arms outstretched as if to embrace the whole world. Reverently she placed him in his manger bed.

The organ swelled and Sister Anne's choir began. "A child is born this day," they sang, "rejoice, rejoice!"

Flanked by nuns carrying the crucifix, the Mass candles and book, Father Adams processed up the middle aisle, magnificently robed in a chasuble of gold lamé.

Mary Helen could feel some of the weariness slip from her body as she rose to begin the Mass.

A sense of calm flooded her. Christ was born again. Once again he had come bearing tidings of great joy. Once again he had come giving glory to God in the highest and on earth peace to all those of goodwill.

Closing her eyes, she prayed fervently that this peace would descend on her family, her friends, her community, all those lovely people she had met on this case. On Gallagher, God love him, and on poor Reina, on the little baby boy out there somewhere, on dear Suzanne and her murderer, on Kate and Jack and the baby they so wanted.

Mary Helen's eyes shot open. What was it Jack had said to her tonight? Just before they left? "I know we can count on you if I get stuck at work." A joke surely.

"And, Lord, you better give me an extra dose of that peace," she prayed just in case, "not to mention a strong shot of moxie. Especially if Jack wasn't kidding and you're going to call on me, Lord, to be the one and only nun at Lamaze."